EMERGENT

EMERGENT

ALISON RISING

ANGIE GALLION

Beech House Books

First edition 2016 (Published by Beech House Books)
Second Edition 2018
Published in the USA by thewordverve inc.
Third Edition 2021
Published in the USA by Beech House Books

eBook ISBN: 978-1-954309-07-4
Paperback ISBN: 978-1-954309-06-7
Library of Congress Control Number: 2018963484

Emergent
Alison Rising
Cover Design, Interior Design, and eBook Formatting
by A.L. Lovell
www.angiegallion.com
Cover are created by Alexandra Haynak

Dedication

For my sister, Sandy.
For braiding my hair so
I could be Garfield in the school play, for
giving me guidence when I was floundering,
for believing that I had something special
inside of me, long before I did.

Special Thanks To

Alexandra Haynak, from St. Petersburg, Russia, for the use of her beautiful artwork on the cover of this book. Ms. Haynak's work was made available to me through her participation at Pixabay.com, a photo/art sharing site. Pixabay has amazing collections from very talented people all around the world.

DeAnne McNeil, who spent several days working with me on fine tuning the medical details at the beginning of the book and finally gave me permission to not be 100% accurate. Trust me, we think it is better this way.

Kali Bhargave. Without her encouragement and near insistence, these words would have stayed in my computer, a series of never-ending project pieces.

Janet Fix, my first editor, and champion not only of my writing but of all my creative potential.

Prologue

When I was young and my life was full of chaos, before my mother died, before my life began, I loved a boy. I've tried to relegate what I felt for him to "first crush," but all the days since the last time we met, my heart has longed for him. In my soul, I believe that he loved me once, but we could never seem to wait for each other. We left on bad terms the last time I saw him, and we've never found our way back. Dylan, the boy, is a married man now, with a son, and I am too broken to even consider going on a date. My best friend Charley thinks I should warm up to dating by going out with a woman, which might be less threatening. I'm barely capable of making friends—lovers seems a stretch.

Once, during that last horrible year, he came for me after my mother had been in a car wreck and brought me back to his family home. It was a frozen night with ice coating the road and the winds growling like some wild, rabid beast, I remember it like it was yesterday. I remember the spillage of his headlamps into the inky blackness and the cautious slippage that passed for driving on this night. When we had arrived at his home, his parents met us in the living room, lit only by the glow of the fireplace. Powerlines had given way under the weight of the ice, and we sat together, almost like a family. "What do you want to be when you grow up?" Dylan's father, Jake, had asked, because that was the kind of man he was. How was I planning to support myself? How was I going to grow up and not be a burden on society? How was I going to grow up and not be my mother?

I've been trying to answer that question ever since the moment he asked it. At the time I gave the simple answer, "I want to be an artist." I can almost hear the sound of my younger self saying the words. It was like whispering a dream or speaking a magic spell. I didn't know the proper sounds, the right herbs to put in the boiling cauldron to make it a reality. There was no rhythm to my incantation. I had no concept of how I moved from that dirty little spot in my life to anything else. Nobody ever asked about *who I wanted to be* when I grew up. Who I wanted to be was a different answer, a more real answer. Who I wanted to be was someone who wasn't hungry all the time, someone who didn't eat peanut butter, ever. I wanted to be a person surrounded by peace and calm and quiet. I wanted to be able to sit from one day to the next and watch the light shift without any chaos. I wanted my life to be smooth and comfortable. I didn't know then that peace and calm would turn out to be so lonely.

I still believed I could grow up to be normal.

I wanted to be anybody but myself, anybody but Alice Hayes's daughter.

I'm in my art room, putting paint to canvas. The echo of Jake's voice, the precise formation of words, rebounds again in my mind. There is something wrong in the memory, something missing, but I can't figure out what I've lost, what I've misremembered. I messed up something in the spell, but what?

Remembering the girl I used to be is like picking at a dry scab, which never peels free. I thought that if I ever got free of my mother that I would never think of her again. Instead, I think of her always and try to understand, now that I'm an adult, what made her the way she was. It runs in the blood, maybe. Her dad was an alcoholic, too, and my grandparents have told me what they could about my mom. She was a victim of abuse, like I was. But she suffered from Stockholm syndrome, the victim who loved her abuser, and back then, nobody talked about what had happened. They just expected her to be okay once her dad was gone. She wasn't. We never are. Abused children can grow up to function, to seem okay, but inside there is always some shattered place that we can never entirely rebuild. I finally understand that she was using the alcohol to be numb, to not have to look at all her parts. My mother was always the child she was. She never matured; she never grew up. She was stuck emotionally at her most traumatic point—when he left. It's a real thing, arrested emotional development; I looked it up on the Internet, and when I found that information, it felt like the biggest piece of the puzzle clicked into place. It explained so much about the woman I remember. She was always an adolescent. It doesn't make it better, understanding that. It makes it more tragic, because she never knew that what had happened wasn't her fault, that she didn't have to own it, and if she had been willing to work through some of her issues, maybe she could have grown up. Perhaps she would still be here, and we'd know each other in some real way.

I've analyzed my life and think I've got it all figured out; I understand why I am the way I am. Most of my adult choices have been fueled by doing the opposite of what my mother would have done. I didn't want anybody ever to say that I repeated my mother's mistakes. I didn't want anybody ever to say that I was like her. I refused to be stuck, the way she was. The reality, I know, is that I've just painted myself into a different corner, and I'm every bit as stuck.

The only sounds in my apartment are from the open window, voices from the alley, cars moving down the street on either end of the block. It's early afternoon, and the light cuts a stark elongated rectangle into the room, splashing across the canvas.

Haven't I done just what I said I wanted to do? Didn't it work? I must have said the right combination of words, the right incantation, all those years ago when Jake asked me those questions—because I am all of those things. I am an artist. I am not a burden on society. I can afford my bills and have some to put aside in the bank. I work as a nurse at the hospital, I am giving something back to society. On my days off, I paint. I do the circuit of summer festivals every year, and sometimes I get a commission to paint a family or a beloved pet. Two years ago, the hotel on Lincoln commissioned a piece for their lobby, and I'm in the running to do a series of line art for the Charleston Historical Society annual holiday cards and calendar. I'm still waiting to hear about that. I've already started work on them, sketches of the historic houses lining 7th Street and Old Main at the university.

I never eat peanut butter. My life is quiet. I have no chaos.

I am insanely bored.

A low hollow pit sits in my stomach, and I feel that something is wrong. Something is missing. It's been riding there for days like an omen and feels like the beginning slide of depression. Since I started working on the town sketches, I've been dropping into the past more often, remembering the town as it used to be, thinking of the houses as they once were, remembering who lived where. It has made me ache for the past. It's like picking that scab.

I miss my mother.

I am nobody's daughter.

I will be older than she ever was on my next birthday, and I am nothing like her. She was passionate and always looking for love or her next fight. She was never bored. She is heavy on my mind, filling the edges of my thoughts. My mother. She has been gone as long as she was with me. I don't know how to live the rest of my life without her as a barometer. She haunts me.

My brush touches the canvas, filling in the highlight for a rail on a sailboat, overlooking a vast and stormy sea. There is still space, left white, with only the shape of bodies yet to be painted. All the painting I do for me is from my memory and captures my regrets, in vivid color. I hope that I have left nobody worse for knowing me, but I know I have. I've hurt people along the way, I've lost people, and like an alcoholic, I'm stuck on the ninth step, making amends.

Along the walls, leaning, are paintings already mounted and ready to hang. They are finished, but they'll never hang anywhere. They are just paintings I had to complete as part of my private therapy. There is Jenny, a little girl I knew when I was in California, with her wide-set eyes and wispy blond hair, sitting on the swing at her family's Del Mar home. A book is open in her lap. She is smiling, happy.

There is my mother, standing on the back step of the trailer, her shirttail blowing in the breeze, laughing back at me. I had been so humiliated that day when she tottered across the yard offering lemonade to Dylan and me. The image sticks in my mind, like a photograph. She was trying to do the right thing, to be a mother. If I were to meet her now, I think I could help her. I understand so much more about what drives people now. But I was just a child, angry and hormonal, with my private side of issues.

Another painting is of Dylan, riding Pride in front of me, his face turning, caught in profile. Another is of Trey, his hair tousled and blowing, looking out toward the incoming wave from the top of his surfboard.

There is Cici, who I followed to California, pregnant, sitting on the sofa in the common room at Life House, smiling that radiant, intoxicating smile. There is another of her with black wings erupting from her shoulder blades. Cici was two different people.

There is Warren, smiling, the silver glint of his pierced eyebrow catching the light.

There are the girls from the Mexico modeling shoot, tall and lean and beautiful, hollowed out with chosen hunger.

There are Vicki and the twins, and Ina, with all the deep crags of her face. Ina gifted me an understanding of the life I could make; she made me see that it was my choice how I would live, as a river or a canyon.

There are several of the bird Cotton, who gave the most beautiful hugs. He was almost human, better than human. Sometimes I think what I need is a bird, a Cotton, to talk to me when I am home, but I work long hours and am gone more than I am here. No other bird would be Cotton.

There is my daughter, as I remember her, held in my arms that first and last day before I handed her over to another mother.

None of these will ever be displayed. These are therapy sessions, my regrets, my memories, the ones I can't seem to let go. These are the people that are forever stuck with me in the ninth step, as I wait to make amends.

The rest, the festival pieces, are of scenery, animals, and children that I've compiled from my imagination; pictures people could put behind a sofa or in a hall or above a toilet. They are marketable. My memories are not.

The paint has dried, and I am still standing, staring at, but not seeing, the space where the people will be. I drop the brush into the water and step away. I'm not ready to finish it yet, and now I want to be away from all the memories. I have holes in the exhibit collection that I should be working on, but the mood to paint has passed. I clean my brushes and my palette, stacking everything to dry. I close the window, and the room gets quieter, tuning out the traffic, the wafting voices. I latch the door behind me.

The walls of my apartment are bare. There are no paintings, no images, not even a calendar hanging. On the refrigerator is a single sheet of paper with my schedule for the month, printed from work. As each day passes, I mark the date, another day down, another day put in the bottle and tossed to sea. I glance down at my watch; it's just after three. My restless blood stirs.

Time moves at a snail's pace when you are all alone.

The fridge is empty, and I let it fall shut, the condiments rattling in the door racks. I'm not hungry. I'm bored, or restless. "Antsy" is the word my mother would have used. I'm antsy. I feel expectant, like something is coming, something is going to happen, I am on the edge of something. My mother would have made herself a drink and forced the feeling to pass.

Part One: Spring

1

The little dark-haired girl is vomiting when I open the door, and her father looks up at me with pleading eyes. He doesn't say anything, but I read his thoughts clear enough: *Make my ∙aughter well.* I pass behind him and place a damp towel on the back of the child's neck, up beneath the thick mane of her hair. She is sweating, her bony arms encased in a sheen. The heaves subside, and the mother wipes a different towel across the child's mouth.

"Darling? How is your head?" I ask the sweating girl, and her lower lip trembles as she opens her eyes to look at me. She immediately drops them closed again, and that tells me plenty. "Okay." I explain to the parents about the medicines I have for her: an anti-nausea and one for pain. We've already been through known allergies and a brief history. She fell from the top of the slide, and they think she hit the base of her skull on an exposed root, which explains the double vision she is experiencing. "Dr. Kuhn wants to do an MRI, just to make sure what we are dealing with."

"They said it's a concussion," the father says, not remembering that it was me who said that to him.

"Yes, sir," I say with a nod. "We need to understand the severity. We want to make sure there isn't a bleed."

The mother gasps, her hand coming to cover her mouth, and she melts around her daughter as if she can shield her baby with her own body. The father pats the child's thin arm.

When I was seven, I tripped off the landing at the top of a slide, pushed backward by the boy in front of me who was swinging in preparation for his plunge forward. I should have seen it coming. We all did that, but I was unprepared, daydreaming, and when his rear pushed against me, I jerked back and careened to the ground. I landed with my arm outstretched, trying to break the fall. I got up from the dirt and brushed myself off and walked stoically away as if nothing had happened. I made it through the day, my forearm throbbing and aching, without giving myself away.

When I got home, I told Eddie, my mother's then-boyfriend, I had fallen and hurt my arm. He grabbed my wrist. "Shake it off," he said. I fainted, overwhelmed by the sudden, excruciating pain from his pull.

When I woke from the shock, Eddie was on one side of me, my mother on the other, patting my arm like it was a pet. "Alice, get me one of your wooden spoons." My mother did as she was told. "And something to wrap it," he added. She came back with a spoon and a pillowcase, and he set to work aligning the bone of my forearm, calling out again for duct tape, which my mother supplied. He wrapped it in a thick layer around the pillowcase covering my arm. He then fashioned me a sling while my mother sat and watched. I'm pretty sure it was broken, but we had no money to spend on a doctor. I stayed home from school for two days, and Mom gave me adult doses of ibuprofen. When I finally went to school again, I wore a jacket with my arm tucked inside, not wanting anybody to see my homemade cast.

I was embarrassed by her even then. Yes, my arm healed, but I was so humiliated that we couldn't afford to go to a doctor for a proper sling. Cori Radcliffe had a broken leg at the same time, and everybody in class signed her purple cast. I just wanted a regular cast, like everybody else. But even then, I was different; I was standing outside the room looking in through the window. By the time Eddie cut the grimy tape and pillowcase from my arm, the muscle was withered and atrophied, but the bone had set and healed. It wasn't maybe the best thing to have done, but he'd fixed it.

Beth and Cheryl, techs from the MRI lab, are at the door, and I turn my young patient over to them.

"I want to go with her," the mother says to the new team, and I step through the door and out into the hallway, leaving Cheryl and Beth to work it out.

Chaos has erupted at the end of the hall, and I race to meet the incoming paramedics. They are wheeling the stretcher through the door, one of them counting compressions and the other squeezing the AMBU bag. Dr. Jerry Kuhn is already at the entrance, ready with the crash cart. He had received the call from the medics en route.

Cardiac arrests that happen outside the hospital are nearly always fatal. Very few survive. Of those saved, there is often some level of neurological dysfunction after the fact; the brain has gone too long without oxygen. The screen of the mobile monitor shows an irregular rhythm, a fluttering of the heart muscles. Without an organized beat, no blood flows.

I join the team at the stretcher, relieving the medic of the AMBU bag, taking up his count to keep the same rhythm. Lisa takes over compressions. I place two fingers on the flesh of the patient's thin neck, feeling for movement in the black ink of a tattoo, although the screen tells the story. He is mid-forties, thin, gaunt—maybe older. Lisa's eyes connect with mine, pausing her compressions. Her fingers lace together, and her forearms are ridged, waiting for the next count.

The crash cart hums.

"I've got no rhythm," I say, answering her unspoken question.

Jerry steps closer, wielding the paddles, and Lisa steps back, giving him room for this last-ditch effort to reignite the electric impulses in the man's heart to establish a pulse.

The man's shirt is already tattered, exposing pale skin with a bright red area where Lisa, and before her, the medic, have pressed, forcing blood from the man's heart through his body again and again.

His arms are thin; recent tracks of needles step over enlarged veins.

He's a junkie. The whole of the Midwest is full of junkies. As the factories have closed and moved production overseas, the Midwestern middle class has devolved into the upper lower class. People who work at the university or the hospital make a decent wage, but beyond that, it's minimum wage in retail shops and fast food. I would never have dreamed that Charleston could become more depressed than it was. We used to have family farms that ringed the edges of all the small towns outside of Charleston, but the farm crisis in the eighties destroyed them. Farmers sold out because the big guys could do it cheaper, and land that had been in the same family for generations was sold off for a winter's worth of comfort. Kids growing up here used to have hope that they could stay in town and make a living wage, but now they don't. If they have ambition, they pack up and leave. Those who lack purpose or direction stick around and stew in the soup of poverty and addiction.

Meth is an epidemic. It is cheap and made with everyday chemicals: battery acid, drain cleaner, acetone combined with a variety of different cold medicines. It's a horrible drug. Once a month or so, some makeshift lab explodes, and another of the daughters or sons of the town goes to hell. You can see them, walking down the street with holes dug into their flesh, their teeth rotting from their skulls. Meth is so addicting, worse than any other street drug out there. Even if they get clean from it, they're never the same. The detox alone is sixty to ninety days, and most people relapse. Meth gets into your body at a cellular level and destroys the dopamine receptors in your brain. Methheads are the walking dead, their jaws ratcheting, the skin melting from their faces.

This man is probably one of those, I think, taking a look at the tracks on his arms, where his veins had given out and he'd searched for another place to insert the needle. I'm sure his legs look the same. I don't lift his lips to see his teeth, which would tell the whole story. I hope heroin was his mistress, which is almost as addicting but less toxic inside the body. I shake my head. It's too late to matter for him, anyway. It's all dangerous, heroin or meth or copious amounts of alcohol; it's all suicide by different names.

"Clear!" Jerry yells. The paddles touch the man's narrow rib cage, and his body arcs. I place my finger again on the inky neck, pressing, feeling the artery, like a snake beneath the skin. I press the bulb with my other hand, keeping the rhythm, keeping air moving in and out of his chest. "I've got no pulse," I repeat.

The crash cart hums, regenerating, and Jerry readies the paddles.

Two more times the body arcs, two more times it settles, silent and pulseless. I look at Lisa, my fingers on the non-throbbing carotid, shaking my head. "No pulse."

Jerry locks eyes with mine, then he looks at Lisa. "We're gonna call it." Lisa and I glance at the clock. "10:43," we say, almost in unison, although he died before the ambulance ever reached him. He was a DOA. I peel the bulb away, exposing the bottom half of his face. His eyes are closed, long lashes pressing a crescent above the bony ridge of his eye socket. Now that I'm no longer holding his head upright with the AMBU bag, his face falls to the side, exposed. My heart stutters in my chest, pausing rebounding.

He is older than he should be, his face ravaged by the years since I'd last seen it.

"Do we have a name for this man?" I call out to no one in particular, hearing the sharp edge of hysteria riding along the rim of my voice.

"No ID. A John Doe."

I look up, seeing the medic who responded. They had stuck around the few minutes after they brought him in to know the results, although they undoubtedly knew. Miracles sometimes happen, but not tonight. Tonight is no night for miracles.

I shift from the top of the stretcher to stand at his side, to see his face in a more natural position, and in the shifting, I fully recognize him. The hairs on my body stand, and sweat beads at my hairline. This face is one that I still sometimes dream of, lying to the side on a pillow beside me, looking at me, talking, telling me about whatever happened at the bar that night, laughing at some grand joke.

"Al, you okay?" Lisa asks.

I nod. "He's no John Doe."

"Did you know him?"

"Yep, once." I pull the sheet up over his face, resting my hand on the bones of his chest, and I say a prayer for his soul.

She is beside me, her hand lightly on my shoulder.

"He was a hell of a drummer." I smile at her. "I'll walk him down."

The service elevator is down the hall and on the right. The morgue is in the basement. I angle the gurney through the doors and wait while they close. We travel to the basement, my hand resting on his chest. This ride is the last ride Warren and I will ever take together. I close my eyes and breathe. Trying to control the rising panic.

Maybe it's not Warren Robinson. Perhaps this is one of his many brothers or cousins. All the Robinson men looked so much alike. This shell of a man could be his cousin Don, who I bought my first and second car from, except for the tattoos. It could be him, except I know Don is no junkie. It could be Elliot or any number of brothers or cousins I lost track of or never met. They all have that same dark-haired look. They all look like they should dress in 1950s greaser gear.

It's not death that causes the panic to rise. I have seen much of that; it's the death of *this* man. It has been twelve years since I last saw him on a stage in Los Angeles at a New Year's Eve party. Thirteen years since he walked out of our apartment above Lola's Dry Cleaners in Greenville, Illinois. A few months more than that when we created a baby together. We never managed our ninth step. I always thought there would be time. We came close when he came to Life House, but there was still so much water under that bridge.

How will I tell our baby that he is gone?

Of course, I won't ever tell her. She doesn't know me. She is somebody else's daughter, people who could raise her and give her a better life than I had. I wonder if she even knows about me? Does she know she was adopted? Does she sense tonight that someone who meant something to her is gone? Did I do the right thing? If I had been stronger, could I have saved him . . . could we have kept her, together, and been a family?

2

I met Warren on Christmas Day during the last year of chaos with my mother. He came to the trailer for my mother's party with all of Cal's friends, Mom's new friends. He was Cal's brother. It had been a horrible day for me because this party with these people wasn't what I wanted for Christmas. These new people were druggies and drunks and loud. I was still mad that Mitch had left, that she couldn't hold it together enough to keep the only decent guy we'd ever had. I knew Mitch. He'd been with us a long time, and he never tried to have me. I'd gotten used to him, comfortable. He was the closest thing I knew to a father, and he hadn't cared enough to stick around. I knew, even if he wasn't perfect, that he wasn't going to touch me, and that was something. I felt safe with Mitch. Not so much with Cal; I didn't like the way he looked at me. I didn't appreciate him introducing drugs into my mother's daily dose.

I was doing my best to stay out of sight, locked in my bedroom at the end of the hall. It had been a long, lonely day when Warren had come to the end of our trailer. I can still hear the tone of his voice, the rhythmic knock of his head on the hollow door. He sounded so forlorn, so lonely; he seemed as defeated as I felt, and I opened the door. He had come in and sat on my bed, and I had stood by the door, thinking he was the most beautiful boy I had ever seen, with his dark hair and pale complexion. His lips were red and expressive in an almost unnatural way, the most arresting dark-fringed eyes the color of thunderclouds. He was more man than boy, though, and I should have been scared. But I wasn't. His body was maybe twenty-seven, but even then I instinctively knew his emotional development had stalled out several years earlier. He was just a guy who didn't want to be there any more than I did.

The memory stretches and rolls. We'd gone out to Warren's old blue car, which was parked in a mound of snow at the edge of our driveway. He opened the trunk, full of garbage bags and boxes of clothes, blankets, supplies. He dug through the piles and finally came out with a mess of lights. The stir we had caused as we came back through the house trailing strands of lights was nothing short of parting a sea. Out the back door we went and threaded the strands through the overgrown, snow-covered evergreen just beyond my bedroom window. We had laughed like we had known each other all our lives, and all my mom's new friends came out to join us, singing "Silent Night." My mother had held my hand, leaning close to me, an echo of the woman she used to be.

A tear rolls down my cheek, and I brush it away. It's the best Christmas memory I have, and it's from my worst Christmas.

It's almost embarrassing to remember how I was when I was young, how fragile I seemed. Warren gave me a leg up on getting tougher when he left me the way he did. I should thank him for that.

How can he be gone from the world? How could he waste his life with drugs? Wasn't my mother a big enough cautionary tale? Wasn't his brother?

A small quiver rolls through my stomach, and I close my eyes, feeling the narrow ribs in his chest beneath the thin fabric of the sheet. I will him to breathe. Breathe! I expect to feel a sign of his lungs drawing air; I pray for the rise of breath. He can't be gone. We never got to fix what was wrong between the two of us. We never got to make amends. We never did our ninth step. I stop the elevator and draw back the sheet from his face, needing to see him, to know him, as the man he became.

Time has ravaged his beauty; the skin is taut across the bones of his forehead and loose in the caverns of his cheeks. His neck, with its snake tattoo inking up under his ear, is corded and veined as if he was straining against some force when he died.

Anger wells, and I pull the sheet back up over his face. Warren is where he is because of the choices he made. I push my anger, my sorrow, down and away, uncomfortable feeling those emotions. He isn't the same boy who came to my room that Christmas any more than I am the same girl. Since the last time I saw him, I have spent every day trying to live a clean life, trying not to fall into the holes where my mother fell. There is no room for anger—maybe sorrow, but not anger. He is where he is because of the choices he made. I am where I am because of the choices I made. I have chosen to come to work when it's my time. I have chosen to make my bed every day. I have put my dishes away. I have decided to have just the things I need and not necessarily all the things I want. What did Warren choose? Rock and roll? Women? Drugs? Was he still chasing the dream of fame, the illusion that his life would be better if a record label deemed him good enough? It's hard to imagine, looking at the wreck of his body covered in a shroud. Did Warren ever settle down? Did he ever get a real job? Did he ever have children? Did he ever find love? Did he know who he was?

If my life ended today, what would the sum of my existence be? Would my roots define me, or would the small twigs I have grown since my mother died represent me? Would it be the chaotic girl I was that people would remember or the quiet, nearly invisible woman I've become? I know who I am. Remorse wells, and I lean back against the cage of the elevator, feeling the cold pressure like a hand.

I want to be loved! My soul cries for it. I bow down to my knees, trying to pull my pieces inward. Almost as soon as the thought flashes in my heart, I shove it away. I am not that person. I make decisions about my life; I decide. I don't let the chaos of emotion determine my path. My world is safe. It is clean; it is sterile.

I lived too much before I was twenty, and now I don't think I am living at all. I understand who I am. I am my mother's daughter. I have her weaknesses even if I never act on them. I have her blood in my veins, her restless, never-satisfied blood.

It's Warren. It's losing Warren like this that has sent me spiraling, and I finally catch my breath and stand to my full height.

Of course, I miss the electricity of being in love. Of course, I miss the quiet conversations in the night. Of course, I miss eating meals with someone else. I am human. But all the "getting to know each other," sharing likes and dislikes, the agreeing and then disagreeing, it's too stressful. The sheer thought is overwhelming. It's been so long since I had a relationship, it's like something from a different life.

Who would I be if I hadn't rushed to run away with Warren and had instead stayed with the McGills and given myself time to heal? Would I be whole now instead of just a facade? Would I be married with children, like healthy people my age? Would I be like my friend Charley who came from even more dysfunction than I did but has managed to live in the world while I am out of it?

Regret stands at my side, a constant companion, easing my loneliness while making me no less lonely. If I hadn't done the things I did, there would have been no pregnancy, no little girl named Emily Ann to be given to others to raise. Would I not have her in the world to have made better choices, to have made my life easier, more palatable?

No. I would not change my life. Sometimes, I wish I wasn't alone, or I wish being alone was less lonely.

When I pull all my pieces back in and think I am again in control of my features, I let the elevator doors open and walk Warren on his gurney down the hall to the morgue, no longer touching him, no longer thinking about it being him under the sheet. My face is placid. I smooth the lines around my mouth, a mask, as I tap the window to the morgue.

The door buzzes, and I push my backside against it, angling the gurney past the threshold.

"Got ya a John Doe here," I say, my voice calm, sterile, not betraying me.

Martin, sets down his sandwich, wiping his hands on a napkin, and stands to meet me at the edge of the gurney.

"Cause of death?" He begins pulling latex gloves over his hands.

"Heart failure . . . or overdose." We won't know for sure until Martin's toxicology labs come back. It doesn't matter, though. He's still dead. "He was a DOA."

He lifts the sheet, studying Warren's ravaged countenance as he pulls on a pair of latex gloves. He works his jaw and his tongue around the inside of his mouth, retrieving some lost morsel of the sandwich, then pushes Warren's lips up, revealing clean, cared-for teeth and no receding gums. Relief washes over me, which is crazy; it doesn't matter. I'm just relieved that his mouth isn't rotted, because he had such a beautiful smile.

"Hmm," Martin says, adjusting his perception. "Maybe not meth. He sure looks like it, though," he adds, taking in the desiccated body on the gurney.

"Yep, he does," I agree, but inside, my heart is breaking. His name is Warren, and he was a hell of a drummer, and back when I knew him, he tried to do the right things, even when it was hard—that's what I want to tell Martin, but I don't. I don't want to be the one to identify him; I don't want to admit what he once was to me. I'm ashamed of him, and of myself for being so sentimental.

"Somebody has put out a bad cook. He's the third one this week, probably not his normal drug." He takes the gurney from me and maneuvers toward the drawers—cold storage until somebody claims the body.

I make my way back down the hall, my senses on high alert, noticing the rings around the lights, the way my shadow bounces and shifts as I walk under them. I set my eyes on the elevator and walk, keeping my pace steady, not acknowledging the crazy sense that he is here, walking with me back down this hall, that he will follow me home and haunt me in the shadows of my clean, bare apartment.

I almost hear the shuffle of his feet, his "no longer tethered to the world" feet. I wonder if my mother had moments like this when the filament between the worlds evaporated. Did she hear voices, the way I sometimes do? Did she see things in the shadows, the way I do? Did she suffer nights when the ghosts screamed her into wakefulness, nights when she saw them crouched in the shadows of her closet?

Did she drink to numb herself to the presence of those who were not there?

I reach the elevator, turning back to face the empty hall, watching the doors close. "Go home, Warren," I say as the door seals, and I leave the strange sense of him below.

3

Around one o'clock, I make my way back to the room with the concussed girl. Dr. Kuhn has reviewed her films; she doesn't have a bleed, just a bruised brain. I'm to prep her to go home. "She's probably going to be tired over the next forty-eight hours. That's to be expected. She needs to rest, so no technology, no TV, no video games. I wouldn't recommend anything that requires close attention to visual details . . . and absolutely no physical exertion or roughhousing."

The mother nods, and I hope she understands. I don't tell her the primary concern at this point is a second concussion before the first concussion has had ample time to heal. Second Impact Syndrome can happen with seemingly minimal trauma and causes rapid swelling of the brain, which often proves fatal.

"You should follow up with your pediatrician tomorrow. Dr. Jackson?" I glance at the chart but pull the name from my memory.

"Yes," the mother agrees.

"I'll send a record to his office. If she starts vomiting or loses consciousness, we'll need her back."

The mother pats her daughter, where her head rests on her shoulder. She is tired; her eyes are rolling with weariness. "Should I try to keep her awake?" It's the one thing people think they know about concussions; we all sang about it as children. *He went to bed with a bump on his head, and he didn't wake up in the morning.*

"No, just keep an eye on her. She'll probably sleep a lot over the next few days, while her brain heals. She should take it slow for a couple of weeks. Dr. Kuhn is writing your discharge now. It won't be but another few minutes." I reach out and touch the girl's hair where it spreads down her back. "Did you hear all that, little miss? You need to be really calm for a couple of days, okay?" She nods, and her thumb slips into her mouth.

"Thank you." The father, who has spoken very little through the course of the night, leans in and takes my hand, not shaking it, but holding it in his like he's holding a small rabbit.

"Of course." I smile, drawing my hand back, caught by the intensity of his eyes on mine. "That's why I am here."

"Well, I mean it. Thank you, Alison." His voice breaks on my name, and something is suddenly familiar about him, something I know but can't place—the round eyes, the shape of the cheekbones above a face covered and hidden by a beard. I glance down at the chart and catch the last name, Jessop.

Derrick Jessop. My mind unfolds on a moment in time when his life and mine intersected. I was sixteen, during that worst, horrible year, and he'd run into me with his truck. It had already been a rotten week, and I was never certain if he had swerved to hit me or swerved not to. He'd had a bad week, too. His sister and nephew had been killed in a two-vehicle accident just days before, and my mother was the driver of the other car. I hadn't seen the truck until it roared beside me, and for a split second before impact, my eyes had locked with Derrick's before he jerked the wheel and we collided. It was the craziest year, unlike any I've known since then. My mother and I, stuck in a downward spiral, and every time we hit a new low, a glance around the bend showed something even more devastating coming our way. The officials cited slick road conditions as the cause of my mother's car sliding past the stoplight, but people knew my mother. Charleston is a small town, and nobody believed she wasn't impaired, least of all, me.

For a split second, I am standing again in the hall at the high school, days after he'd hit me, and Derrick is offering to replace the bike that he'd mangled under the tires of his truck. How insane? He bought me a bike, but his sister and nephew were still dead. What my family took from his could never be fixed.

Does he remember that moment, when we stood facing each other over our personal tragedies? Is he remembering that my mother killed his sister and then he had tried to kill me? Is that the look in his eyes, or is it just fatigue, a long night of worry and care?

Maybe I did give something back to him tonight, taking care of his daughter, helping her down the road to healing her concussion. After he had hit me, I had walked all the long miles back to the trailer, my brain bruised and swelling, and I had set our home on fire, with my mother sleeping and drugged on the couch inside. I say she was sleeping, but I had come back to the trailer and fed her vodka and half a bottle of the Vicodin she'd come home with after the accident, intending to send her to hell. I'm no angel.

"You're welcome, Derrick." The name falls from my lips, and my heart skips a beat.

All my damn ghosts are showing up tonight.

"Your daughter is going to be fine," I say, nodding to the wife, who has watched with a raised eyebrow the small interaction between her husband and me.

The door opens to admit Dr. Kuhn, and I take my leave, catching one last look at Derrick and his family before I let the door close between us.

I want a quiet room to sit and cry.

The morning crew comes on, and the night staff walks to the parking lot en masse. I laugh with Julia and Lisa as we march toward our cars, the way people do. I'm not listening, not part of the conversation. We are familiar with each other—I am friendly with a lot of people—but we aren't friends. When we reach my car, I peel away. The traffic on Lincoln Avenue is already flowing, vehicles moving in processions from one light to the next. As I change my shoes, I watch the road into town and the road out of town. It is the road to everywhere. I wave at Julia then Lisa as they leave the lot in turns.

Ghosts, ghosts, ghosts, they are everywhere. It's a small town; I knew when I came back that I would run into all the people I knew. I had dreaded seeing the kids I went to high school with, because I thought everybody had looked down on me, but the truth was almost nobody was even *looking* at me. I was the only one looking down on us—my mom and me. I thought I was going to have to prove something to everyone, that I'm not my mother. What I found was that I didn't have to prove anything to anybody except myself. I'm still working on that. I am my harshest critic.

Being in Charleston again has been good because I'm not alone here and everything else just felt like running away. The McGills are like family, and I am always welcome in their home. Tommy and Jay are both married, and their wives are like sisters. I don't think Keith will ever get married, like me. Tommy has kids, so I get to be an honorary aunt. My grandparents are just two hours away in the small town of Sorento. I make the drive at least once a month to see them, and I never need to be lonely on holiday again. If anything, holidays are hectic now, because I have so many people who want me at their house to celebrate. Uncle Steven married again, and his sons, Tyler and James, are grown. Tyler is married, raising three kids on a factory salary, struggling. His wife is hoping to go back to work next year. James, my younger cousin, who was awed by my stories of California, is living in New York, working on Broadway. He's Cogsworth in *Beauty an♦ the Beast* for the last four years. He doesn't make it home often, but occasionally he'll respond to an email and let us all know he's alive.

I'm glad to be here, even if sometimes there are ghosts.

How can Warren be dead? How did I not know he was around?

When I knew him, I could always tell when he entered a room because the electrical vibrations would change. He would touch me, and every hair on my body would rise toward him. I stare out through the frame of my steering wheel as I wait for tears. They don't come, and when I've sat for a minute longer, I know that there is something else I need to do.

Don Robinson runs a car lot in Mattoon, and I've bought both my cars from him. He's the right person to identify Warren. Don's lot has grown over the years, from forty used late-model cars, to seventy or eighty mostly new cars. He married into a Ford dealership and moved his business from 6th Street to Lakeland Boulevard, where he works with his father-in-law. He's all legit now, established and a member of the City Council. I pull into the lot and park in one of the customer spots reserved in front of the big glass doors. I sit for a long minute, staring at my hands on the steering wheel, seeing my car reflected in the mirrored windows, my face a pale blue in the reflection.

Warren isn't my responsibility; I don't have to go in there and bear this news.

It's the right thing to do.

I close my eyes and steel myself. "Don't be a river," I whisper. Rivers flow crooked and wild, always seeking the easiest course. I want to be a canyon, not a river. When there is a choice between the *right* path and the *easy* path, I always try for right. Ina taught me that way of looking at life when I lived in her family's basement the last two years I was in California. She talked in a way that made me believe she could see the future laid out. Ina knew the line between the worlds was thin. It had been Ina who placed the ad for their basement apartment to run for one day only. They had never rented it before, but she had insisted. She knew that a girl needed them and that the girl would be with them shy of two years. "She thought your name would be Alice, though," Vicki had confided to me after Ina had passed away.

"That was my mother's name," I had said, feeling awed that something magnificent had touched my life. Had my mother had some hand in my finding that apartment? Had my mother somehow given me the safe place I needed so I could grow the rest of the way up? Had my mother found Ina and somehow known that she could guide me? I had absorbed what Ina offered, from the benefits of a raw vegetarian diet to choosing right over easy, to not trying to use somebody else to make yourself okay. My mother had always thought the next man would fix her life; the next man would finally love her enough, the next man, the next man, the next man. I was probably on that path, but Ina helped me understand that nobody can fix you except you, and I haven't been on many dates since. I'm still trying to understand myself, and until I'm finished doing that, I have nothing to offer anybody else. Ina taught me that truth isn't just what we can see.

I push myself out of my car and watch my reflection in the mirrored front glass as I walk toward the doors. I look like my mother, walking across the lot. I have her eyes, her jawline, her high cheekbones. I am the age she was when she died. I've aged better than she did, either because of my diet or because I haven't put poison in my body every waking day. I am my mother, healthy. I look the way I remember her when I was young, before we moved to the trailer. I look how she did when she was room mom for kindergarten and all my friends were in love with her. I look the way my mother did when I loved her best, and we sometimes have lovely conversations through the bathroom mirror.

Ghosts.

The building has high ceilings, and there are three shiny new cars parked inside on the painted concrete floor. The vehicles are all red, bright and garish, against the white walls and black of the sun-shaded windows.

"Can I help you?"

I turn and face the man coming from one of the desks. "Is Don in today?"

"Yes. He should be in any minute. Is there something I can help you with?"

"No, if it's okay, I'll wait. It's personal." A look crosses the older man's face, and I realize how that must have sounded. "It's about his brother," I stammer, not wanting him to get the wrong idea.

"Okay. Can I get you coffee? I just made a pot."

"That would be great. Thank you."

He offers creamer and sugar, which I decline.

He leaves me, and when he returns, he hands me a small Styrofoam cup full of steaming liquid. I thank him again, and he heads back to his office, leaving me to wait.

I hover, looking through a side window into one of the cars, letting my mind roll backward. Warren was twenty-eight when we started dating. I was seventeen when I ran away with him. He was twelve years older than me; he'd be forty-four now. He had looked so much older with the life drained out of him, lying on the gurney. People do appear older in death, but I think he aged the way my mother had, because of all the poison he put in his body.

It should have all been different. We should have tried harder. Should I have encouraged Warren to walk away from the band when he came to me at Life House, when I was so pregnant that sitting was uncomfortable? The simple answer is yes. If we had made a family, built a life, I would have been able to keep him from the drugs.

Just like you kept your mother from them? The voice in my head is full of sarcasm, ridicule.

My mother had died in much the same way, overdosed with a guarantee at the end. She wasn't able to be whole because she had a family to look after. She had never been able to heal her wounds, and I wasn't enough to fill the holes in her soul. She could never stay away from the alcohol and, later, the drugs. *Nobody can fix you but you.* Ina knew.

I couldn't have saved him. In my head, I know that, but my heart is crying something different.

I did the right thing. I gave our daughter a chance. It was too much of a risk to try and then fail and tear up her life. I didn't know what I was made of then. I gave her a chance at a better life, but every single day I wish I hadn't. I wish I had held onto her with both arms instead of passing her over to someone else. I would have done better than my mother did. I would never have been a drunk. I would never have left her to fend for herself. But I didn't know that I could do anything. I was scared of everything back then. Life felt overwhelming, impossible.

"Isn't she a beauty?" Don's voice startles me, and I jump, sloshing a bit of the coffee out and onto the slick white floor.

"Hey, Don." I swoop down and swipe at the small splash of coffee with my hand, wiping it on my pants.

"Hey, Alison, what brings you over this morning? Your car all right?"

I paid my last installment in December. It wasn't new when I bought it, but it was newer than my old Volkswagen.

"Yeah. The car is fine. I need to talk to you. Like, private."

"Okay. Come into my office." He leads me back, and when he goes to close the door, I stop him. I don't want to give the old man any reason to think Don is up to no good, and I know a pretty girl showing up like this, saying she wants to talk "private" is sending out all the wrong signals.

"Sorry to come here like this, but . . . have you heard from Warren?"

Don's forehead wrinkles, his brows drawing low and together, his lip puckering out with a small shake of the head.

"Is he back in the area?" I ask as if I don't already know.

"Yeah, I heard he was. Living over in that trailer park out on Old State. He's got a woman over there, I think, but I've not heard from him. The last anybody told me, he was trying to stay clean, but who knows?" He shrugs, his face relaxing back into its more familiar lines.

"So, you haven't seen him?"

"No, Alison. I can't have that in my life." The look in his eyes is determined, almost cold, and I wonder exactly what his family has put him through over the years. How hard has it been for him to change the perception of the name "Robinson" in the area?

"I understand. How is Sherri?" I should have started with this, asking about his wife, the kids.

"She's good, about ready to pop." He smiles, his cheeks coloring with pride.

"Again? Is this three?"

He chuckles, nodding.

"Congratulations! That's wonderful. Is she doing okay?"

"Yeah. She's tired, but she's strong. Sarah's a big help with Maxwell."

"Sarah's six?"

"Yeah, and Maxwell's four."

"Wow. What a life. I'm so excited for you." I am tempted to ask him why his family had so many names from the early 1900s:--Sheldon, Warren, Calvin, Elliot, and now Maxwell—but I hold my tongue. That's a question for a different day.

"How about you? Anybody in your future?"

"Nope," I say, as if it's my choice to be alone, as if it isn't fear that keeps me from dating. Doesn't it make me strong that I am not afraid to be alone?

"You just haven't met the right guy yet."

I smile, letting it pass. I *have* met the right guy. I've known him my whole life, but we've never been able to wait for each other. He's married, coaching football at the high school in Neoga. He has a son, Daecus, named for the brother he lost. He would be the only right man for me. He already knows my history.

We sit for a long minute before he asks, "Why'd you ask about Warren?" I want to reach across the desk and take his hand, to give him strength for hearing and me strength for telling. I don't. I keep my hands to myself.

"He came into the hospital last night." Tears spring to my eyes, and I'm shocked, blinking hard to push them back.

"Is he okay?" His forehead creases, and he leans forward across the desk.

I shake my head. "No. He was DOA."

"What?"

"Cardiac arrest. We were unable to resuscitate."

"Well, shit." His voice sounds like a deflated balloon. He, like me, always thought Warren would find a way. Warren had such a big heart; he had such talent. How could Warren never find a path? Shouldn't he have been able to find a way to live a decent life?

I regret coming. Telling Don wasn't my job; I didn't have to do this. Why did I come here to bear this bad news? "He had no identification. They think he's a John Doe. Do you know who his next of kin is?"

"No ID? Are you certain it was him?"

I give him a steady look. There are many things in my life that I may forget, but Warren Robinson's face is not one of them.

"So you need somebody to identify the body?" he asks, moving on to the practical needs of the moment.

"Yeah, they will." It isn't about me. "I couldn't be the one, you understand?" I'm just passing on information, telling somebody who can tell somebody who can help.

He smiles at me, a forlorn spreading of his lips, blowing out a long breath. His head bobs forward into his hands, displaying the thinning spot at the back. "What a damn waste."

I push my hand over my face, trying to pull myself back together. I can feel my chin puckering as it always does before I break down. When I have composed my face and controlled my quivering chin, I take my hands away to see Don holding out a tissue to me.

My chin wrinkles, and my face crumples. "Could I have saved him?" I ask, reaching for the tissue, feeling the bones of my body turning to liquid, melting across the chair and pooling on the floor.

Don shakes his head and lets me cry. Don knows I'm not as tough as I pretend to be.

4

I cut the announcement out of the paper when it appears. Three sentences. "Warren Edward Robinson of Mattoon, Illinois, died on Tuesday evening at Sarah Bush Lincoln Hospital. He leaves behind a wife, Carla, and a son, Edward. Funeral arrangements are pending."

I stare at the print. So Warren did have other children. Emily Ann has a half-brother.

They couldn't rescue him, any more than I would have been able to. I feel justified that I made the right choice all those years ago.

I tape the announcement into my current composition book. I've written in the books since I came back home, and I try to write something every day. It's for her, the baby. Of course, she'll never see them, but I say the things I would tell her if I could. Early on, I wrote a lot about how much I missed her and how I regretted letting her go, but then I realized that I could only tell her that so often before she would close the book and move on. So I started saying things that happened around me every day, stopping short when my mind strayed too far into the dark corners of my history. I gave her the prettiest picture of myself that I could. Hoping she would believe that I was just too young and not that I was too broken. I told her little pieces about my mother, but not any of the ugly. She only needed to know that I was alone, that I had no support system, nobody to help me raise a child. I did the best thing for her; that's what she needs to know. I told her about California and about seeing Warren on stage, about how I fell apart and lost my way, then found my way.

I didn't tell her about being in the hospital, about cutting my wrists in the bathroom at the MTV party. Even though I know she'll never see it, telling her how weak I am, how hopeless I was, seems too much like making excuses. I don't want to play the victim. I don't want her thinking of me like that; it's too embarrassing. I did write about living in my car for a while and how I found the basement apartment and stayed there until I felt sane, grounded. I told her about the bird Cotton, who gave the best hugs. I told her about coming back home and staying with the McGills. I told her about standing as one of the best men in Jay's wedding, one of the biggest honors of my life. I told her about the day I heard Dylan had gotten married, and the page there is smudged and tear stained. We could never wait for each other, but by then, I had already begun to understand that I would probably never be ready.

My apartment is one of Mr. Billups'. Not the one my mother and I had shared, but a two-bedroom above the bookstore on Monroe. My front windows look out onto the courthouse lawn, and the rooms are open with high ceilings. The floors are two-inch planks that glisten in the sunlight. The two bedrooms are at the back of the apartment and overlook the alley. One room has my bed, and the other has all my art.

It was Dylan getting married that started me painting again. It broke my heart, letting him go for good. It has never healed, and I don't think it ever will. Dylan never could be alone; I always knew that. Just like my mother. He loved me, though, maybe even as much as I loved him. The two times we have kissed are among my most vivid memories. That last kiss, in the barn, was filled with hunger, even though we were both dating other people. Nobody else ever really mattered when it came to Dylan and me. What would have happened if I had kept my mouth shut, had I not said something snarky about him never waiting for me? Would we have worked our way around to being with each other instead of ending in the worst fight we'd ever had? I never saw him again. For months after I came back from California, I thought he'd show up. He had to know I was back; I'd run into his folks several times. A year after I came home, he got married to a girl he'd met in college. They lived in Neoga, and not long after, they had a son.

My heart is still broken.

My eyes travel down the page, reading what I wrote about the night Warren came into the ER, about the little Jessop girl and her concussion, about the chaos at the entryway and the odd moment when I recognized him. I see again the arcing of Warren's body, as his heart failed to start. I see still that moment when his head lolled to the side and I recognized him. I want her to understand that I tried. I even wrote about my small prayer in the elevator and about how I felt his spirit walking back down the hall to the elevator with me. She'll think I'm crazy, but he was my first lover. He was the first man I ever gave my body to of my own free will, and that means something. I wanted to leave out the telltale signs of his addiction, the cause of his heart failing, but I couldn't help myself and felt grateful when I finished that she will never see these words because nothing I have written is pretty, and all of it is honest. It's my memory on the page, and it is only for me.

When my mother died, she left a box filled with letters she had written to me. They were full of ramblings and inconsistencies. They gave me almost no answers and, except for the first letter that led me to my grandparents, they left me frustrated and annoyed. What was the point of rambling about some boss I didn't know? What was the point in complaining about Eddie, Mitch, or Cal when what I wanted was answers? Why did she drink? Why did she never go home to her family after I was born? Who was my father? Why didn't he want me? It's that box of useless notes that makes me write for Emily. If she ever reads my journals I want my words to make sense; I want them to provide answers, as much as I am able. I want her to know the truth as best as I can offer.

My phone vibrates on the table beside my hand, and the name "Charlotte" flashes with the vibration.

"Hey, Charley." I smile at the phone because Charley always makes me feel grounded. She's my best friend, like a sister.

"Hey. You still gonna make it this afternoon?"

"Of course." I fold the notebook closed, my finger tracing the edge of the book. "Three o'clock?"

"Could you stop and get the cake?" Her voice is stretched high and thin, and I can imagine the frazzled state of her hair.

"I can," I say, pitching my voice low to keep from adding to her escalating stress.

"It's paid for, I just . . . Carmi got called into work, so I'll have the kids. It will just be chaos."

"No, that's fine, I'll get it. Is there anything else I can do?" Dan and Leslie McGill are celebrating their fortieth anniversary, and we've all worked hard to pull a party together, but Charley has done more than the rest of us combined.

"No, that's it, I think."

"Okay. Is everybody good?"

"Oh, yeah, just, you know, kids." The phone seems to shift away from her face as her voice becomes muffled, speaking to someone in the background. "Sorry," she says when she comes back to the phone.

"No. It's fine. You okay?"

"I want it to be perfect, you know?" Charley has a big heart, just like Leslie, and I'm only sometimes jealous that she is so like her and I am not.

"They are going to be thrilled. You've done a great job of pulling this together," I say standing up from the table, replacing the journal amongst its companions on the bookshelf in my closet.

"They've just done so much for me; I want it to be special."

"It's gonna be special. Forty years is a long time."

"I feel like I've forgotten something. What am I forgetting?"

"To relax."

"P-shaw. What is that?" She laughs but in a tense and frazzled way.

"What else can I do to help?"

"Just get the cake." The phone muffles again, but I hear her say, "Brooke, put the cat down!"

"I'll let you go."

"Okay. Love ya."

"Love you, too," I say, but she is already gone, dealing with whatever her youngest has done to the cat.

I head to the bathroom and shower, washing the hospital from my hair, standing a long minute in the stream, letting the heat sting against my skin. When I finally turn off the water and step out of the tub, my skin in steaming and red. I pull on sweats and a t-shirt and go into my bedroom, with the blackout curtains already drawn. I pull down the sheets and slide between them, setting my alarm to wake me at 1:30, so I'll have plenty of time to get the cake on the way to Leslie and Dan McGill's fortieth-anniversary celebration.

5

When I was seventeen, after my mother died, I moved in with Leslie and Mr. McGill. I wasn't an official foster kid, but they took me in until the court could work through the paperwork of getting me placed. I was too old to be entering the system, and Leslie helped me to file the paperwork to get emancipated. She is a person who brings home strays, and Charley was one of them before me. It was Charley's rose-exploded room that I moved into when my world blew apart like a nuclear bomb. God only knows where I would be if Leslie hadn't taken me home and given me a taste of something akin to a family. She was the first of my other mothers. She made me feel that I could make something useful from my life.

I didn't know Charley until after I came back from California, but when I met her, it was like we were a double-faced coin. She gets me, as nobody else does. I sometimes wonder, if I had met her before I moved to Greenville with Warren, would I have come back after the baby was born instead of running away to California. If I had known Charley, would I have been so desperate to have a friend in Cici? Would I have gone all that way, chasing after someone who turned out to be in disguise? I try not to have regrets; the life I have lived has made me the person I am, good and evil. If I had to do it over again, would I choose not to have known Trey? Would I have chosen not to have the experiences modeling? Would I have chosen not to meet Vicki and Ron and the girls? Even Shirley, Ron's daughter, who reminded me so much of my mother? Would I have chosen not to know Cotton, the beautiful white cockatoo that still holds a chunk of my heart? By not knowing Cotton, I would not know that birds give hugs almost as satisfying as a horse's?

No. I wouldn't have done anything differently. Except for the baby. I would have kept the baby.

If I had kept the baby, none of the rest would have happened. Cici wouldn't have invited me to California, and she would never have let me stay if I had shown up with a baby. It's almost laughable to imagine her reaction, that California Cici. Everything would have been different. My mind spins.

I park in the lot at the small regional airport and scan the black asphalt for vehicles I recognize. Leslie and Dan McGill are not here yet, but Charley's van is two over, and three down, I see Jay and Serena's 4-Runner. I lean into the passenger side of my car and bring out the cake, closing the door with my hip. There is Tommy's car, and down the way, Keith on his motorcycle, just pulling into a spot. I pause, waiting for him so that we can walk in together. He removes his helmet and plants it on the seat, smiling and coming toward me at a lope. He reaches under the cake and lifts it from my hands. "I'll get that."

"Thanks," I say, letting my shoulder bump against him. "Nice bike."

"Like it?" Heat is rising from the pavement, late June heat that, from a distance, causes the air to waver above the ground.

"Yeah. It's nice." He steers me toward the bike, and we stand for half a minute, admiring the sleek lines, the chrome, the bell of the tank, before we turn and head toward the airport again, feeling the heat like a weight. Small planes are parked along the fence demarcating the runway, and I scan above to see if any are up right now, but the sky is crystal blue, unmarred by planes or clouds.

I open the door, and Keith angles past me with the cake. The door falls closed, pulled in on the vacuum of the air-conditioned lobby. The sweat on my scalp chills, and a shiver runs down my spine.

It's a country airport, and black-and-white photos of the planes that have flown in and out decorate the walls. Models hang, suspended by fishing line, from the ceiling, and they could be high in the sky, navigating some aeronautical move. Charley chose the airport because Leslie and Dan had their first meal as a married couple here. She knows all their stories.

"I ha● the elephant ear." I can almost hear Leslie's voice, reminiscing about the lovely life she has had. It's not an actual elephant's ear, thank God. Instead, it's an enormous deep-fried pork tenderloin slapped between two hilariously tiny pieces of bread. The loins are the size of a platter. I've never eaten one; the thought of eating the flesh of another animal always makes my stomach churn. I have known cows with a better sense of decency than many humans I've encountered. Pigs are incredibly intelligent, too. Once I met Cotton, I recognized all animals as sentient beings; I could never think of eating them again. It was a gift from Ina. I hope a spinach leaf never tries to communicate with me, because I'd die of starvation.

A hostess is waiting as we pass through the lobby, where model airplanes hang above our heads. A banner spans the entrance to the restaurant and reads "Happy Anniversary, Leslie and Dan!" I smile seeing it, remembering helping Charley and her kids color in all the letters using a tub of broken and much-loved crayons.

The noise from the restaurant is rolling out toward us, and Keith waggles his eyebrows as we step into the crowd. Charley rushes us, inspecting the cake, rumpling Keith's thinning hair. She is such a big sister. He shrugs her off, and she smiles, leaning into me for a hug. "Thank you for picking it up."

"No problem," I say and ask if they are here yet. Charley shakes her head, taking the cake to display it on a table toward the wall. Keith and I move into the standing-room-only dining area. He stops to talk to a man I don't know, his beard hanging long and bushy, and his hair tied at the back of his neck in a gray-streaked ponytail. I see Jay and his very pregnant wife, Serena, and make my way over to them.

"Alison!" Jay says in his punctuated speech, articulated to remove all hint of his parents' accent. I reach them and kiss him on the cheek as we hug, patting backs like long-lost brothers. When he releases me, I turn to Serena and give her a side-armed hug,

"Look at you," I say, delighted. She is well into the later third of her pregnancy, their first. She has gained no weight anywhere except for the watermelon-sized growth protruding from her stomach. She is carrying the baby low, I think, and I try to calculate when she is due, because she has the look of someone ready to deliver. I'm sure she's not due until next month, but I could be wrong. I haven't seen her in a couple of weeks, so maybe she's only bigger and not carrying low at all. It's hard to tell. "How are you feeling?"

"I'm good." Serena is always good. She does not complain, although I can see by the way she is standing that her back is aching, the way it does when your body is ready to release its burden.

"You're such a trooper." I tilt closer to her and kiss her cheek. Serena is not a touchy-feely girl, but she tolerates my affection. I love her because she makes Jay happy. Serena loves me because I love Jay. A lot of women would be jealous, but not Serena; she knows her place, and she knows mine, and we both understand that we are not interchangeable. They are a good team. She is strong where he is weak, and he is strong where she is weak. Of all of my friends, as I've watched them get married, it is only Jay that I ever felt jealous of, maybe because he and Serena were such a matched set. I wanted that for myself.

Tommy and Rachel have twin seven-year-old boys, Jacob and Jordan. I scan the room, looking for them, smiling and nodding as I see the men from the firehouse, a couple of people I knew from school. Tammy Bridges is here, dressed in her uniform because she's probably on duty. She catches my eye, and we smile. Just like Tommy has followed his dad into the firehouse, Tammy followed her uncle into the police department. None of us fall far from the tree. I'm not yet like my mother, but that doesn't mean I won't be.

I leave Jay and Serena to pass a little time with Tammy. We see each other out at the hospital sometimes, running drug tests on perps she has brought in. The drugs have gotten bad. I thought I had it rough when I was young, but it seems that even good families are being touched by meth use now. Two weeks ago, a two-year-old was found in a car with his parents, known druggies, who had overdosed, right there in front of their dealer's house. The dealer was cleared out by the time the medics arrived after receiving an anonymous tip, and last I heard he is still on the run.

"Hello, Officer," I say, and we shake hands like old men.

"Hey, Al. How you been?"

"I'm good. Just working," I say, the same as I always do. Tammy's dark hair is cropped short, like a pixie. She has masculine mannerisms—the way she holds my forearm as we shake hands, the sidelong way she looks out from under her eyes. She was always tough, even back in school, but she has perfected her shell now. I have a mask, too—I know I do—we all have costumes we wear. Tammy does what she has to in order to fit in with the men on the force. She's good at what she does, like me. If she ever gets tired of being alone, she doesn't show it. Tammy has always had a special spot in my heart. She was one of the people who tried to help me when I was a teen. She warned me about the man my mom was dating, and she did it without making me feel like she pitied me. If ever I'm in trouble, I want Tammy Bridges on my side.

I see Tommy's family coming in from the lobby, and I make my way toward them to catch the boys. Jacob and Jordan are slapping at each other, both of them with their hair wetted down. They got their mother's springy curls, but Jacob looks just like his daddy from the eyebrows down, and Jordan has the small thin bones of his mother. They are night and day in personality, too. Jacob has a book; Jordan probably came with a soccer ball but was forced to leave it in the car.

"What you reading, Jacob?" I slide between the boys, angling them off and away from their parents, one arm over each narrow shoulder. Jacob holds up his book. "*Runaway Ralph!*" I exclaim. "That's a classic."

"How about you, Jordan? What you up to these days?"

"I scored three goals in the game today," he says, puffing up with pride.

"Three?" I say, letting my voice rise high, enthusiastic. "Is anybody else even on your team?"

Jordan blushes, taking the praise as his due. It was hard when the twins were born. I had to figure out how to be happy for Tommy and Rachel and not sorry for myself. My life is what it is, that is all. It felt big, enormous when I found my happiness in being happy for them.

I don't know that I could live the life Charley has, with her chaotic kids and a full house. I'm not cut out for that. Other people with loud and happy lives isn't a reflection or judgment on my quiet one. Just because I'm not a mom, or married, doesn't mean Rachel and Serena shouldn't be. I babysit for the boys now and then, and it's almost enough. After I let the baby go, I thought I would never be able to be around kids, that it would rip my heart out. They aren't Emily, though, and in some ways, being around the boys has helped because I've watched the twins grow up, I've seen all their stages, and can imagine her growing up along the way.

A hiss whispers through the room. "They're here. Shh. Shh." We all freeze, and the boys scatter toward the door to be first in line to see their grandparents. Charley comes up beside me, her nervous energy rolling off of her like the heat rising from the asphalt in the parking lot. I hear the door open, feel the air shift as it sucks toward the closing door. They are talking, not even aware of the anticipation in the building. Dan laughs at something Leslie has said, and his hand slides down the curve of her back. Then they are looking forward, seeing the banner stretched across the entrance to the dining hall. Leslie exclaims with an intake of breath, a gasp of excitement, and my stomach flips with such an intense need to see her reaction that my feet, like Charley's beside me, ratchet up and down, the hooves of prancing horses. She squeezes my arm, and we glance at each other, bursting.

Then Leslie and Dan are walking beneath the banner, registering the crowd, understanding. Tears are streaming down Leslie's face, and Dan has his arm around her, holding her, supporting her. Charley breaks formation and rushes to them, joining others to hug them, to congratulate them on their beautiful life together.

The room erupts, Leslie wipes her eyes, never one to contain her emotions. She buries her face in Dan's shoulder. Tears spring to my own eyes, and I wipe them away. Jay bumps against my shoulder, and I know he has caught me. I laugh. His dark eyes are narrowed and amused, but none too dry.

I am so lucky to have these people in my life. I step forward in my turn, to hug Leslie and Dan, to tell them how grateful I am. Leslie, who knows almost as many of my secrets as Charley, stands in front of me, and now I can't keep the tears back. She is crying, and I can't help myself.

"Did you do this?"

"No. Not me. This was all Charley."

"You helped!" Charley calls from Dan's arm.

"Well . . . all right. I colored an 'A' and a 'P' and part of a 'Y' but everything else was Charley." Leslie pulls me in and squeezes me, her body shaping around me like warm dough. "We love you!" I say into her ear.

She releases me, and we are both soggy.

"We love you, too, Mr. McGill," I say, not wanting him to feel left out. I haven't called him Mr. McGill in years; once I got comfortable with him and began feeling less like such a child myself, I stopped calling him by his surname. I only say it now as banter, a quiet joke between us. He offers a quick squeeze, and I move out and away to let everybody else come and talk.

I'm heading toward the bathroom to wash my face and pull myself together, but stop in my tracks when I hear a voice calling to me above the din.

6

"Alison!" My stomach lurches, and I turn on a heel to see Dylan walking from a table toward me. A young boy, probably seven years old, follows. Dylan Winthrop, a man I haven't seen since he became a man. My first crush. My first, most true, love. The man I've always known was the right one, but forever at the wrong time.

"Hey!" I say, smiling, glancing past him to see the woman, but I can't see past his shoulders. When I knew Dylan, he was narrow, tall, and lean. Now he is thicker, not heavy, but built like a grownup and not a child. He could have transformed entirely, and I would have known him, though. I would recognize his eyes anywhere.

"I thought you'd be here," he says as if he has been looking for me.

"Yeah. They are amazing people. I wouldn't miss it."

His presence makes all the noise and chaos of the room diminish. I hear less; I see only him. I have not been in the same place with Dylan in ten years, and yet I feel my cheeks burning at the memory of him. I feel like I've fallen backward through time and we are still together in that barn, in the moments before our lives detoured away from each other. I look away, breaking the hold of his eyes on me. I am not that girl anymore. I'm not the kid from down the street with the second-hand clothes. I'm not that love-struck girl who threw myself at him one desperate night when my mother kicked me out of the house.

I'm not that girl, but I swear, I can almost feel the pressure of his lips on mine. I drop my face, letting my hair fall in a curtain and catch the eyes of the young boy staring up at me. He is thin with heavily fringed, light eyes. "You must be Daecus?"

He nods and draws his hand toward his face, and for a second, I think he's going to suck his thumb, but he only scratches a spot on his cheek. Of course, he's too old to suck his thumb.

"Yes, ma'am," Dylan says, a correction, an admonition.

"Yes, ma'am," the boy repeats, and I squat down to be more at his level.

"Well, what are you? Like thirteen now?"

"No. I'm seven." He cocks an eyebrow, and I see the humor in him in the way he takes my banter.

"Oh, well. You're so tall," I say to the boy, laughter bubbling under my words. He is thin and lanky, the way kids are when they've just passed through a growth spurt. I extend my hand. "I'm Alison. It's good to meet you."

"I'm Daecus," he says, then blushes when he realizes that I already know his name. Or he may blush simply because an adult is talking to him. "Nice to meet you."

"Your daddy and I used to be great friends."

"I know. He told me. I have a best good friend, too. She's a girl. So it's okay."

I laugh. "I'm glad it is." I stand up, expecting to finally meet the wife, the woman Dylan chose, and my stomach fills with dread as I pull my mask down, putting all my features in the proper place.

"Where's the missus?" I ask Dylan when we are face to face again. There's no sense in beating around the bush, so I bring up the thing I don't want to talk about, to get it over with.

His brows draw together, and his lips compress. "She couldn't make it."

"She didn't come?" I ask, relief washing over my shoulders. I don't know that I'm yet ready to meet the woman he married. I'd do it, but it doesn't mean I'm looking forward to it.

"No, she's visiting her folks." His voice is flat.

"Oh. That's a shame. I would have liked to have met her." It's the proper thing to say, and anything else would admit to my jealousy.

"Another time," he says, but his voice sounds strained. For a split second, I imagine that all is not well in his marriage, that he may yet be mine. He tilts his head, studying me. Has my mask slipped? Can he see the girl inside me?

I close my eyes, forcing my face to stabilize.

When I open my eyes again, he is looking away from me, down at his son. What did he see on my face? What did I give away? He's a married man.

While he is looking away, I drink in his lines and etch his face in my mind, overlaying this older version with the boy I remember. They don't line up in a precise way, but the points are the same—the arch of his brow, the interrupting scar, the jut of his chin, the line of his jaw, the blue of his eyes. He looks up and catches me studying. The red of his lips.

I draw a deep breath, trying to slow the rhythm of my heart.

He glances down at his son; worry etches across his face. He is not the same boy I remember. He's a father; he's a husband. He's a grown man, and from the look on his face, his life is maybe not perfect.

"Actually, I'm moving back to town." He rubs his hand over his son's hair, and Daecus leans into him, dropping his face.

"Well, that's exciting," I offer, but from the expression on their faces, I suspect they are not excited.

"Yeah. Life's an adventure," he says, and that look crosses his face again.

"When are you moving back?" My stomach is shifting and flipping, and I try to hold my features steady as I wait. Just having the opportunity to run into him again is worth anything.

"Looks like the first week of August."

"Jake and Vaude retiring to Florida finally? You guys taking over the farm?" I ask, feeling unsettled thinking of his family living there. It's like slipping back through time and closing a door. Vaude has told me often enough of their desire to move south. She has developed arthritis and the cold months of Illinois winters are hard on her.

"Nah, I'm renting a house over on Foxglove Lane. It's small, but we don't need much."

"That's nice. So, how's work?" I ask, needing to move past this awkward moment.

"Oh, it's been good. I like teaching."

"I bet you're good at it."

"I hope I am." He sounds so humble that I narrow my eyes. I've never known Dylan to be unsure; he was always confident, always competent. What has happened in his world to make him only *hope* he is good at what he is doing?

"Of course you are," I say. "You were always so smart."

He glances away, then back, uncomfortable with praise.

"What are you up to?" he asks, leaning close not to have to shout, and I can almost feel the warmth of his skin radiating toward me.

"Still nursing. I see Vaude now and then, at the grocery store, usually."

"Yeah, she said that." The volume of the room has increased, and I lean closer to hear, turning my ear toward his mouth.

Then I smell him, and the scent is like every good memory I have from my childhood. I close my eyes and let the sensation fill me. It has been a very long time since I remembered him in such a visceral way.

Cheers erupt around a table, and Dylan turns toward the celebration. "Anyway. I'd love to catch up sometime. Maybe not here, I guess."

"Yeah, it's pretty loud." I laugh.

"So, we could get together sometime, have coffee?"

I nod and feel the heat rising in my face, the one part of my mask I cannot control. "That would be nice. I'd like that."

Every alarm bell in my head is singing, my flight impulse rushing through my veins. These are words that lead to trouble. "Let's have dinner" ends up with "Why don't you come back to my place," which leads to invitations for uncomfortable sex that I don't want to be having.

But this is Dylan, and he is the only right man. . . and still wrong because he's married. We're just friends. We've always been just friends.

"Can I call you?"

"Of course. You can call me anytime." I smile, feeling better, the alarms downgraded to a Code Yellow.

"I've missed you, Al." He steps closer, looking down at me, knowing me too well. His scent envelopes me, and I have the intense urge to touch him, to place my hand on his chest, to press my face against his shoulder, to kiss him. He's married, but I don't even care.

"I've missed you, too." He is just a breath away. He's close because it's loud, but my blood is racing through my veins, hitting checkpoints through my heart.

"Ali!" Tommy is rushing to me. His face is panicked, and suddenly the sounds in the room come clear. There is excitement, shouting, a woman calling out in pain.

I turn, and my shoulder brushes across Dylan's arm. The electric jolt of his flesh against mine sings, even as Tommy is pulling me away.

We reach Jay and Serena. She is sitting on one of the chairs, bowed forward, and Jay is folded protectively above her.

The noise inside my head calms, as it does when emergencies hit the door. My eyes take in the fluid pooling beneath the chair.

"How many weeks?" I ask Jay, pulling my phone out, dialing 9-1-1.

"Thirty-four," he says, fear making his voice rise in a question.

"This is 9-1-1. What is your emergency?"

"I have a woman, thirty-four weeks. She's going into labor." I'm kneeling beside Serena, one hand on her belly, feeling for movement from the baby. The muscles of her stomach contract, she calls out, and I see the bulbs of Jay's fingertips going a darker shade, purple to blue. I can't feel the baby through the turgid wall of her stomach. When the contraction passes, I feel a small motion under my hand, a small "high-five, baby." When I was pregnant and Cici and I were at Life House, she used to always say that when the babies moved: "High five, baby," and her voice calls in my memory. I feel a pang for that long-lost Cici who wasn't quite the same person when I'd found her again in California.

"We're at the restaurant at the airport," I say, realizing as I say it that the hospital is right across Lincoln. "We're on our way."

"Do you need me to send an ambulance?"

"No. I'll bring her. Tell them we're coming." I disconnect the phone.

"Serena, honey, we need to get you to the hospital. Jay, call her doctor, let him know she's in labor. Honey, can you walk with me?" I keep my voice low and calm, needing everybody to stay calm. I need them to be as relaxed as they can; I need them not to panic. Serena grits her teeth, and I recognize the terror on her face. I remember. I swallow hard.

"Serena, darling, you have to look at me." She nods, opening her eyes to see me. "This is okay. You're going to be okay. You're having a baby, that's all, okay?"

She nods, and I see her pulling her strength together.

"I need you to walk with me to my car. I'm gonna drive you across the street. They're gonna have everybody waiting for us when we get there. Okay?"

She starts to drop her eyes, but I lower my face, catching her descent. "Jay, you're gonna help me help her, okay?" He nods, looking stricken and petrified.

"Okay, Serena, honey, you with me? On the count of three, we're gonna get up and walk out of here. Okay. One, two," I lock eyes with Jay and nod, "three." He lifts her under the arms. As light as she is, her fear and pain make her unwieldy, and we move from the chair across the lobby and out to the parking lot. Tammy blazes the trail in front of us, opening the door, helping to guide us. I dig into my pocket and bring out my keys, clicking the button to unlock the car. I open the back door and take Serena's hand as Jay slides in, ready to receive his bride into his arms.

I drive from the lot, and when I reach the stoplight, Tammy turns on the lights of her patrol car, leading us. The siren wails as we pass through on red.

We reach the emergency room before the next contraction hits. I'm out of the car running toward the doors as they open and the day crew comes out with a wheelchair, I point, and they follow my finger to the passenger side of the car and open the door.

"How far apart are they?" John, from the day crew, asks without ever looking at me.

"Last one about seven minutes ago," I say.

"She's only thirty-four weeks," Jay is saying, and I hear the rise of panic from the back seat as another contraction hits.

"This baby's coming," John says, glancing my way as he opens the door. I stand back and let him do his job, although every impulse in my body wants to push him back and help Serena out and to the wheelchair myself.

John looks like a puff of wind would send him flying across the fields, but I have seen him pick up grown men and carry them like children when needed. I'm glad John is on duty, even though I moved to the night shift so I wouldn't have to see him. He was too persistent.

We get inside, and Lucy meets us then rushes ahead to get Serena to a private location to be assessed.

"Go." I push Jay's shoulder

He looks at me, his eyes glazed over, "Oh, God." His voice is a whisper, a prayer.

"She's your wife, man. Go and be with her!"

"I'm gonna be a daddy." His broad face splits in that smile that I love so much. His eyes narrow to slits, and everything in his face glows.

"Yes, you are. Now go." It's when he is gone that I realize I am crying.

7

Brenna Rose came into the world at 5:34 p.m. on June 20th. She is small, a mere four pounds twelve ounces, but beyond size, she has an excellent Apgar score. I breathe a sigh as the news spreads and look around the waiting room, where almost everybody from the airport has gathered, somber and waiting. Dylan did not come. Jay is nobody to Dylan.

Leslie had thought to call Jay's parents, who have just arrived when the news came. A cheer rises, and we break into hugs as if we have had some hand in delivering this healthy child into the world. I am crying again. Nobody seems to notice, except for Leslie, who wraps her arms around me and pulls me in.

"You did good," she whispers against the side of my face, her breath warm, sweet from the cake.

Leslie knows the truth of the life I have lived. Leslie knows about the little girl I gave up for adoption. Leslie knows about the empty hole in my heart that never closes, that only oozes and bleeds.

"I am so proud of you."

I choke back the tears, pulling myself together, and when she feels the shuddering in my frame lessening, she peels her body slightly from mine and puts her large, square hands on my face. I smile, sniffling, uncomfortable being the center of her attention.

"Do you hear me, Alison Hayes?" Her voice is just a whisper.

I nod but can't look at her.

"You've done well." She embraces me again, and I know she isn't just speaking about today, when Serena's water broke, knowing what to do to get her here safely, keeping her calm. She is talking as much about the life I have lived, the clean, quiet way I live, the lonely life I have built.

I'm not alone. I have a family. I have Leslie and all of them. I even have Mitch, the closest thing I ever had to a real dad. I have Mr. Billups, and Rob and Faye, who are still together. My life is so full of people that I almost don't miss being in love. Almost.

Then Dylan shows up.

I've lived a decent life, and if this is all there is, then that's okay. If I never get to be a mother, in a real way, then I'll be happy being an aunt. I'll keep believing I did the right thing in letting her go, even though in my dreams she is always here with me. My stomach flips at the secret wish, the illicit dream. I shake my head and push the thought down.

Emily would be almost a teen, and I have missed all but the first day of her life. I wouldn't even know her if I ran into her somewhere. I laugh—a small, fractured sound—pulling all my features together, facing the family I've collected around me and claim as my own, and cheer with them over the birth of Jay and Serena's daughter.

Everybody wants to see the baby; they are all settled, waiting until the happy couple invites them in. I hesitate but, ultimately, decide to leave. I'll see her when they have had a chance to breathe. I have someplace I need to be.

***

The Crisis Clinic is an outreach center funded by the Catholic church on 7th Avenue. I got started volunteering a couple years ago when Dr. Jerry mentioned they were looking for a nurse to be on their team. He always has his finger on things happening in the community. For me to volunteer, to have something of value to offer somebody else who is maybe struggling makes me feel like I've done something right in a world full of easy wrongs.

The clinic puts me in mind of Life House, although it doesn't have full-time residents or an in-house physician, and we aren't only dealing with pregnancy counseling. We work with the domestic violence shelter and run a suicide prevention hotline. We organize a Fun Run every spring to help support our various interests. The Crisis Clinic does good work in the community, and no crisis is ever turned away.

I work the morning shift on Fridays, heading straight to the clinic after my hours at the hospital, but tonight I'm here filling in for Joan, who is visiting her sister in Virginia. I don't mind filling a night shift at the clinic. It will give a chance to see Mary, a retired bank teller, who works almost every night. She lost her granddaughter to suicide two years ago, and she felt "called" to be here. She is the best I've ever seen on the suicide line, and I know it's her granddaughter she is trying to save.

The clinic is a small, white-sided house with a black roof. There are no signs, no indicator on the outside that the clinic is here, next to the church with its stained-glass windows and seventy-foot steeple. Those are the directions we give when somebody calls looking for us. "Next to the giant steeple on 7th Street." Everybody in town knows where we are anyway.

It's rising toward nine o'clock when I reach the door, and Mary glances up, points to the phone, indicating that I should be quiet.

"Do you have a relationship with God?" she asks, and I know instantly from the tone of her voice that it is a suicide call, and my stomach rolls. There are no right answers for a suicide call.

My mother committed suicide for any number of reasons. She had lost control of her life; she never had control of her life. She had killed Cal Robinson, and she probably knew she'd be found out. She had failed as a parent, failed as a human experiment. She wanted the booze more than she wanted life, and that was too big of a shame to bear. She wanted to set me free. I don't know all her reasons or any; it's just what I tell myself to make it okay that she is no longer here. Of course, it isn't okay. I wish I knew then what I know now. I would have been able to help her through that horrible year instead of just making it worse.

Even now, I'm not sure, in my heart, that somebody else didn't have a hand in it, that it wasn't murder. The police even investigated Warren because they found a gun registered to him in our apartment.

I'll never understand why she finally did it; nobody ever understands a suicide. Maybe she was only trying to turn off the noise inside of her head, the way I was trying to when I landed in the hospital in California.

I don't hover and listen to Mary's call. Instead, I make my way to the kitchen to grab my mug. There is a large A on it. Joan's has a J, and Mary's has an M. There are others, all with their initials, but only a few ever get used. It's not an easy thing, giving up your time for something that you won't earn money for. Although a lot of people come to help, very few volunteer for long. The glow of good deeds lasts for a couple of visits before it begins to feel like weight, and they stop coming. It's not a fun place to be. It's not happy times to tell a sixteen-year-old she is pregnant and that she has three choices: parenting, adoption, and abortion. It's not happy times to talk a suicide off the ledge. It's not happy times to try to find safe housing for a woman who is running and hiding from a violent husband.

The coffee is thick, like sludge. I drain the pot in the sink and set the coffeemaker to drip a new one.

We try always to have two of us here during the day and early evening, but at night, it's usually just one. Mary will leave when she is finished on the phone, and then I'll lock the doors and man the hotlines. All of us have had a good sleep on the couch on a quiet shift.

Mary is still on the phone when I get back to the front of the house. She will stay on the phone until the caller wears out and says he, or she, is going to bed, too tired to do anything about it tonight. I start tidying the room, picking up magazines from the coffee table and placing them on a rack. I empty the trash, about half full of tissues, and check the bathroom for testing supplies.

Mary is leaning over the desk, her head propped up by her hand. She is looking down, holding the phone to her ear with her shoulder.

"Will you pray with me?" I hear her ask, and I stop moving, bow my head. I will always pray for a suicide watch. Suicide is never the best answer. It's an answer, for sure, but never a good one. When Mary's voice, soft and melodic with a Southern twitch, rests, I again look up, watching her from the side, seeing the weariness in her posture, grateful that it was she who caught the call tonight.

She looks up at me with vacant eyes and lifts the old rotary-dial phone from the desk and walks, tethered by its long cord, into a side room, where she will switch to a different phone. It's important not to be distracted while on a suicide call. We never leave dead air on a suicide call. We never ask them to hold, while we change phones. Mary will only hang up the first phone when the second one is on her ear. We use corded telephones here because we can't risk one of the new wireless ones losing battery during a call.

The door opens, and a girl who could be thirteen or seventeen walks in. Her hair is pulled up over her head and in a messy knot.

"Hi," I say. My voice is thin after the emotion of the day. I clear my throat and try again. The girl twitches, looking back through the window at the front of the house, and I see a Camaro pause then move off, back into the street. "How can I help you?'

"I need a test."

"Okay. I can help with that."

"Good," she says with all the attitude of youth, rolling her eyes as if I've said something stupid. There was a time when I would have reacted to such hostility with a share of my own. But I'm older now. I understand. It's just a mask, a camouflage to not show the bruises on her skin. Her attitude is nothing different from the leather bracelets I wore to cover my scars. She's just a stupid kid, a scared girl. I don't know her story. I don't know who has brought her to find out if she is pregnant and left her to deal with it on her own.

Her manner reminds me of Cici, who had the same way of walking in and demanding attention. She doesn't look like Cici. This girl is plump and round, with a smattering of freckles on the left side of her face, as if she has suffered sun damage already, or a burn.

I walk with her to the bathroom, unlocking the cabinet where we keep the tests. I give her a small cup to urinate into and explain that she can leave the container in the little metal receptacle beside the toilet.

"Can you tell me when the first day of your last period was?" I ask, and she shrugs, already reaching for the ridge of her waistband.

"All right. Let's see what we find out." She closes the door between us, and I head back to the front. I check the desk, looking at the calendar. Dr. Maguire was in earlier, so the schedule is full of ultrasounds, each name crossed out as the girl was called from the waiting room. We always want them to see an ultrasound. More importantly, we want them to *hear* the ultrasound. If a girl comes in, saying she wants an abortion, eight times out of ten she will change her mind once she listens to the beating heart.

It's a sound that I never grow tired of, that beating rhythm. The first time I heard my baby's beating heart, it had ruptured me. I remember how Janice, the lady who ran Life House, gave me time to pull myself together before coming in to talk. I remember, to this day, that sensation of knowing that the baby was me and I was her.

"Hey." The girl is calling from the bathroom, standing in the door, holding the cup of pee in her hand, looking semi-disgusted.

I know two things about this girl by seeing her standing there. The first, she doesn't follow directions, and the second, she isn't comfortable inside her skin. I accept the cup from her, smiling, asking if she'd like to join me or wait in the lobby.

"I don't know." The attitude drops, and she follows me into the exam room where I set her cup beside the sink. I tear the packaging of the test and dip the tip into the urine. She watches with her fingers by her lips, picking at a small red patch on her chin.

"Do you have a name?" I ask, trying to sound young, like a contemporary.

"Amy."

"I'm Alison. Nice to meet you."

"Yeah."

"So you don't remember your last period?"

"No. I'm not very regular." Her voice drops low, uncomfortable talking about such things. I judge her to be closer to the thirteen side of the spectrum. I'll be surprised if she is anything more than that.

We wait. We don't waste breath on small talk. I ask Amy if she is familiar with contraception, and she shrugs. "You may want to try something different than what you are using now," I say, cocking an eyebrow at her. "Would your mother sign for you to go on the pill?" She doesn't meet my eyes, just stares at the test, shaking her head when I ask about her mother.

A small smile quirks on her lips. "I wouldn't mind being pregnant," she says, almost in a whisper.

"So, you have a steady boyfriend?"

She nods.

"How does he feel about being a daddy?" I ask, thinking about the sporty car that she had climbed out of, not a vehicle for a family man.

She shrugs. "He's gonna take care of me."

Warning bells ring through my head, and now I know something else about Amy. She is looking for an escape.

"You've graduated high school?"

"I don't care about school."

I nod. "Well, if you're not pregnant, is there anything you think you might like to do with your life?"

She shrugs, and we wait. The lines of the test appear, as if by magic and I feel a riot of emotions for her.

"Well, it looks like you are pregnant." I heave a low sigh, and a smile flutters on her lips. I watch the cascade of emotions marching across her face, and the last one to settle is relief.

"You sure?"

"Yes. I'm positive. The test is accurate at two weeks past conception."

"What's that mean?"

"It means that you're early in this pregnancy, and you still have all options available to you."

"Oh." A small nervous laugh escapes. "We're keeping the baby."

It's my turn to feel flustered. "Okay. Perhaps you'd like to have your gentleman come inside so we can talk."

"No. Not necessary. We'll be okay. He's going to take care of us."

Her words are confident, but the shell washes away from her for a split second, and I see the girl beneath it. She is not like Cici, brash and bold; she's like me. She smiles, a little quiver of her bottom lip. There is something in that quiver that I recognize, in a very extreme way, of myself when I was her age.

"How old are you, Amy?" My voice drops into its clinical mode, detached, judgment-free.

"Fourteen."

I swallow. Emily would be nearly that age. I have held her every day in my heart as an infant, but that baby is long gone. I hope sex is not already a part of her life like it is for Amy. I hope she is still a child.

"You're young. You have your whole life ahead of you." I've deviated from the script and keep my voice low, not to carry. "Do you have parents who will help you raise this baby?" How do I say that her boyfriend is probably not going to stick around? "Maybe we should talk about your options. Adoption is a wonderful gift to give a family." I always start with adoption, although it is more often they choose abortions, especially when they are young.

"You don't understand. He loves me. He gets me. We'll be fine."

"Is he fourteen as well?"

She laughs, a barking cough. "No. I don't waste my time with boys."

"So your boyfriend is what, in high school? College?"

She compresses her lips, and I wonder how much older he is than she. Is he a grown man? Has he warned her not to say anything about him?

"Are you safe?" It's not part of the script, but that shift in her eyes has taken me back in time, when I'd needed somebody to ask me that question. They frown on us going off script.

The mask is back. "Yeah. I'm fine. It's good news; I'm going to be a mommy," she says, but the small flood of tears at the rim of her lashes suggests that she feels more conflicted than what she is letting on. "I'm fine," she whispers, turning away, wiping her eyes so I won't see. But I've already seen.

"Yes, indeed," I agree. Had the test been negative, my next step would be to talk about options for protection, one of my least favorite parts of volunteering. I am not comfortable with sex in any of its forms, verbal and otherwise. It's preferable only compared to discussing termination, which is where I must go next.

But she is rising, pulling the door open.

"Thank you. Don't worry about me. I'll be fine." Her words are a mumble, rolling over on themselves, and I suddenly see the shape of her differently.

"I have some literature up front," I offer, keeping my voice steady.

She rolls her eyes and looks down the hall toward the front of the house. She's not interested in my literature, but she nods.

"I have to ask, because you're under eighteen . . . ?" She nods, and I continue. "You have protections against unwanted sexual advances. Nobody has a right to touch you against your will. Is there anything you would like to report today, anybody who has forced himself on you?" I try to make it sound like a standard question, but it isn't. We aren't supposed to pry, but the vibe I'm getting from this kid is screaming for help, and I can't let her leave without giving her at least a small way out.

"It's not like that. We're in love."

"So, you don't have anything you need to report?"

She doesn't meet my eyes but shakes her head.

"Nope." She looks at me then quickly away, pushing through the door. "Thanks for your help."

I follow her down the hall.

I don't want her to leave. I don't want her to go back to whatever life she has where she is confronted by sex when she should still be nervous about holding hands.

"Your whole life is ahead of you. You don't have to be in a hurry."

She blows a puff of air through her nostrils. It is familiar, like a memory. "Yeah, I'm fine."

I close my eyes, hearing my voice from some distant past, remembering very clearly how I didn't have any choices about anything. It is easy for grownups to spout these things, because it is the way it should be, but in the real world, the child has no more rights than what the adults around them respect. I had no rights. I had no rights to keep the men in my mother's life from touching me. I had no voice.

"We are here to help. If you're in crisis, we can help you find a safe place." It's the script, the carefully composed words to offer the right level of comfort without infringing on the privacy of those we seek to help. It's wrong. All of the scripted words don't mean anything to these girls. We're not speaking to them; we're talking at them.

She stands, glancing out the front window. We have both heard the Camaro pulling back around to pause in front of the house. "Seriously, I'm okay. We're in love."

She opens the door, and I watch her running down the sidewalk. I try to catch a glimpse of the man in the driver's seat, but the car is too far forward, and he is in the shadows.

I'll ask Leslie if she recognizes the girl when I talk to her tomorrow. I check the intake form, and she has written "Jennifer Aniston." I laugh. I probably would have chosen Marilyn Monroe or somebody like that, but Jennifer Aniston works just as well.

Even though the night started out with a suicide call and a walk-in, the darkest hours pass in silence. At one o'clock, long after Mary has gone, I lock the building and sit at the desk to wait for the next call, flipping through the paperback novel Mary left behind. Nobody comes to the small building after midnight. Pregnant girls aren't out looking for answers in the middle of the night, and hopefully all the potential suicides have given it up for the night and gone to bed.

8

"The fair's coming to town in a couple of weeks," Dylan says, his voice echoing across a bad connection.

"Yeah," I say, moving through the bedroom to the living room to get better reception.

"Well, we were thinking of going, wondered if you'd go with us?"

"Yeah, I don't know, Dylan." I can just see myself trailing behind him and his wife and son, the whipped puppy I used to be. I did say I wanted to meet his wife, but surely he understood that was just something people say.

As if he can read my mind, he says, "It will just be my son and me. Mandy is still in Chicago." It sounds strange, Dylan saying "my son," and the years behind us stretch. We've been apart for more years than we knew each other.

"Still? Is everything all right?"

"It's a long story." His voice falters, and I catch the hesitancy I saw in him at the McGill's party. Where has his confidence gone?

"I'll be out at the fair on Saturday morning." Charley and I have a booth at the crafts barn reserved.

"Oh, so you already have plans?"

I smile at the disappointment in his voice. "No. Well, I do, but I can get away for a bit. It's just that Charley and I will be selling stuff in the craft barn."

"Oh, maybe we could meet afterward?" He sounds hopeful, and my stomach flips.

"Okay." I hate the sound of my voice, like a little girl talking to her first crush. I clear my throat. "Yeah, I'll meet you guys. Since I'll be there anyway, you know?"

"Yeah." He laughs. "It'll be good to be with a friend. Bumper cars, cotton candy, and corn dogs."

"Yeah. It's been a long time." I want to ask, "Why now?" Why is he suddenly so interested in catching up with me when he hasn't come to find me in ten years?

I'm standing at the front windows overlooking the square, watching cars moving, watching a man sitting on the bench in front of the courthouse in a vacant way, feeling the roiling of my stomach. The man stands up and shrugs his shoulders back, holding the phone to his ear.

"Where are you?" I lean closer to the window, watching through the glass, recognition sparking through my body. He looks up at my window, a small smile spreading his lips.

"Care for lunch?"

I can't help it—my lips spread into a smile and heat rises to my cheeks, I'm still just a giddy girl when it comes to Dylan.

***

"It's been a long time." I bump into him as we walk down the sidewalk, past the bookstore, past the jewelry store, past the bar that was one of my mother's favorite haunts.

"Yeah. Too long."

"I'm sorry about the way we ended things," I say, trying to keep my voice steady, working to sound grown up and mature.

"Me, too." His arm falls quickly across my shoulders, squeezes, then drops away. "I wish I had done a lot of things differently."

I laugh. "Me, too." We walk a few paces, awkward and unsure. "Well, Daecus seems like a great boy."

"He is." We turn the corner, and he motions toward the restaurant in front of us. It's more of a bar than a restaurant, but it serves food. I've never been; I don't eat out often, and when I do, I don't choose bars. He holds the door for me, and I pass through. "How about you? Are you seeing anyone?"

I laugh, glancing over my shoulder, shaking my head. "No. I don't date."

"Ever?"

"No." The word sounds harsh and final, and I almost regret it, but it's true, and I don't offer anything more. The interior of the restaurant is not what I expected. It is light, with a beautiful, polished bar curving away from the door. The back half is a dining area, and several other couples are already seated, enjoying their meals. It's not like the Ice House that my mother used to frequent, and my estimation of the place rises. The hostess leads us to a table, past the bar and toward the back, where the bright daylight pouring through the front windows doesn't penetrate. Small lanterns flicker on the tabletops.

We sit and look at menus, then make the waitress come back twice because we've gotten caught up talking about his parents, about his new job, which is a step back from a full coaching job to an assistant but in a more prominent school district. We talk about my work at the hospital. We talk about Daecus.

Every word is like a zipper being drawn down, exposing us to each other. There is water under the bridge. Lots of dark, murky water rushing between us, and I'm scared to look for too long, afraid I might yet see the monsters lurking there.

The waitress comes back a third time, one eyebrow arches high on her forehead when she realizes we still haven't chosen.

I quickly make a decision. "I want a salad. Do you have a balsamic?"

She nods, and I say, "Great."

Dylan glances at the menu and orders a burger and fries, something quick and easy. The food doesn't matter; it's just an excuse for us to have a quiet place to talk to each other.

"So, why don't you date?" he asks when the waitress has gone.

I look at him for a long second, trying to decide the best answer. Could I tell him the truth of my life without imploding? Could I admit to him all my dark secrets without coming unglued? Would he still want me to meet them at the fair? Would he want his son and wife to know someone like me? I shake my head, answering my question.

"You know how people say it's better to have loved and lost than never to have loved at all?"

"Sure."

"I disagree." I laugh, trying to make my voice light.

The things I have lost in my life because I dared to love are profound, and the wounds left on my soul always fester and never heal.

"I can see that. At least I have Daecus."

I nod. "Yeah. You have Daecus." I don't have my daughter, though. I have nothing but scars and emptiness to show for my failed relationships.

The waitress returns with my salad, promising to be right out with his burger.

Dylan doesn't know about the baby I gave away. He doesn't know anything about my life after my mother died. When I came back from California the last time, I had spent half the drive playing the conversation in my head where I told him everything. I played out his different possible responses to the story of Warren, how I had run away with him and how he had left me alone in Greenville, pregnant. I played the conversation telling him that Warren was running from the law, thinking they were going to pin my mother's death on him. Then I played the conversation again, without suggesting that he left because he was on the run, and the Dylan in my head still loved me after I finished both times. I told him, in my pretend conversations about Trey—the boy I knew in California, the one I was never really honest with and how my lies came back to haunt me—how I broke down and fell apart when the truth came out. The Dylan in my head still loved me after that, but maybe a little less. But when I told him about the child that I gave away, Dylan in my head turned cold and distant. I never told him, even in my head, how I had slashed my wrists and ended up in the psych ward.

"I'm not good at relationships. I am my mother's daughter." I run my tongue over my teeth, hoping it is enough of an explanation, playing it safe in the not telling. The waitress returns and places a platter in front of him, and when I finally look back at him, after the waitress has gone, his eyes are warm and bright on mine.

"Apparently, I'm not either," he says, a small, sad smile scudding across his face.

"What does that mean?"

"Mandy isn't just visiting her parents. She lives up there now," he says, not looking at me, shrugging his shoulders.

"Oh, Dylan. I'm sorry." I reach out and take his hand. "Are you okay?" Suddenly I understand why he has reappeared. He needs a friend. Of course, he would come home when he needed a friend.

He squeezes my hand and pulls free. "Yeah, I'm okay.

"When did that happen?"

"A while ago. But she filed about two months ago." He holds my eyes, looking less shattered than I would expect. When Warren was gone two months, I was a wreck; it's been twelve years since I last saw Trey, and I still can't think about going on a date without getting hives.

"What happened?" Now that I understand my role, I relax, the tension slipping from my neck. I steel myself to be a listening ear, to finally be the friend I should have been all those years ago. I'm not a narcissist anymore, and it's important to me that he sees that.

He lets out a long breath. "I think I wasn't a very good husband to her. I don't know. She's a city girl and hates the country. I'm a country boy who hates the city."

"Your marriage fell apart because you couldn't settle on where to live?"

He laughs, hearing the absurdity of it. "No. There's more. We aren't very compatible."

"But you have a kid." I let out a long breath, looking away, feeling hollow and ill.

"I know. It sucks."

"Maybe you can work it out," I say, trying to be the friend.

"No. I think it's too late for that. We've been to therapy. We both realize that we rushed into being married because it was the next thing to do. It's been going south for a long time, even before Daecus was born."

"Oh." Some of the glow comes off of him in my mind, and I see him not as the Adonis of my youth but as the fractured man he is now. "So why did you have a kid if it wasn't good between the two of you?"

"We thought it would fix things." He chuckles, a hollow sound sliding across the table.

"How did that work out?"

"You know how that goes. Relationships are hard anyway; it's just the thing to add a baby for more stress." He must realize how that sounds because he is quick to add, "Not that I ever regret having Daecus. He's the best part of my life." He pushes the hair off of his forehead, and the motion is so familiar to me that I bite my lip to keep from smiling.

"How about you? Are you seeing anyone?" he asks, changing the focus back to me. My stomach flips, and I glance away from him, betrayed by my desire.

"No. I'm not." My eyes touch on his again, and his look feels weighty, earnest, sincere.

"That's right; you don't date."

"No, sir. I don't."

He studies me, chewing, a small quirk at the edge of his lips. "What has your life been like, since that day in the barn?" The last time I saw Dylan was before he got married. I had come home from California carrying all the stories of that big life, showing off my modeling pictures like they actually had something to do with me. He had kissed me, even though we were both dating other people. Then it all went wrong, he was holding me, and then, in the next breath, we were angry. How did we go from kissing that way to being angry? It had all gone wrong so fast. He had called me a narcissist, and I didn't understand what that meant. I know now.

What would my life have been like if we had let everything else go instead of each other?

"Oh, just living the big life," I smile, my best modeling smile.

"Seriously, Vaude told me when you came back to town. She's kept me updated." He smiles, and there he is: the boy I used to know.

"Oh, that's good to know." I laugh. "She kept me updated on you, too."

"I know." We laugh together, and some of the tension eases.

"Well, after the barn, I went back to California, and it all just fell apart. I wasn't cut out for that kind of life, you know? I was always pretending to be somebody I wasn't, and that was exhausting, trying to figure out who everybody else needed me to be. So I just dropped out. I blew my modeling contract. I lived out of my car for a couple weeks until I found an apartment with this family. I lived with them for two years. I did a lot of growing up in their basement."

My words flow, and I tell him about Ina, about Vicki and Ron, Shirley and the twins. I tell him about Cotton, the white cockatoo, and his beautiful hugs. I tell him how much Shirley made me think of my mom, and how knowing her helped me see my mom from a different angle. Shirley helped me understand that Mom was broken, not evil. "When Ina died, I just knew I needed to come home, or I would always be running away from something."

He nods as if he knows something about running away from things.

"No boyfriends since then? No way!"

I imagine saying, *"I think I was always in love with you, an• if I coul•n't have you, I •i•n't want anybo•y."* I don't say it; I bite my tongue instead. He is still married. They may yet work things out . . . and then where would I be?

"No, none," I finally say when the silence becomes too long and uncomfortable. "I don't think I know how to love."

"Of course you do." His hand folds over mine, and I look at the point where my flesh is devoured by his, the faint shift of color. My complexion is nearly iridescent compared to his summer tan.

"No. I don't. I am my mother's daughter, after all," I say again, hoping that is enough, and from that, he will understand I am not able.

"I don't see that in you at all. You've always loved, maybe you've loved too much."

Tears spring to my eyes, and I am thrown. I chuckle and sniff, blinking them away, hoping he is not familiar enough with me anymore to recognize. The small fray in my stomach lurches, and the drumbeat of nerves, of uncertainty, of fear of the unknown, set a cadence, and I remember who I am. I wrinkle my nose and draw my hand free. I'm not a fragile little girl anymore. "Dating makes me feel crazy. It's too . . . terrifying." The drums rest with my honesty, and I stir dressing into my salad, understanding the power of saying truths. "I don't date because I'm too scared of the consequences." I've spent the better part of ten years perfecting my solitude. I've dated, some, but as soon as I felt that chaos was beginning to roll inside of me I closed the door. The last time I got serious about a man I nearly killed myself, and the time before that, I created another human. Relationships are too much. I'm not willing to take the risk.

More weight shifts, and the tension in my shoulders lessens. I am a grown woman, paying my way through the world and not doing a bad job of it. I am not that same insecure girl who came back showing off beautiful pictures, when I was really still the trashy kid from the trailer. Sometimes it is hard to remember how chaotic my life was.

"So, is your divorce going to be amicable?" I ask, shifting back to listening-friend mode.

"Are they ever? It's not like we hate each other. It was never like that. We're civil."

I remember the girl's name that he had been dating, that last time I was home. Amanda. Wasn't it Amanda? Mandy? A pang washes through me. "That's nice," I say. "Is she the girl you were dating in college?"

I catch his eyes and look away, embarrassed at my need to know.

"That is her."

I nod. What did I expect?

"We both agree that it's the right thing to do. It's hard, her being in Chicago. It makes it harder for me to see Daecus."

Every impulse in my heart tells him not to break up his family, not to let his son be away from him. Those are minutes and hours you can never get back. What difference does it make, where you live, when there is a child in the picture? I want to tell him to make it work, for Daecus, because he's selfish not to. He doesn't get to choose his life anymore, because he has a child . . . and that child is more important.

Hypocrite. I shake my head. Who am I to judge anybody on their life choices? I made my decisions and lost everything. Dylan has the right to do the same thing.

"Do you get to see him often?"

"Right now I get him every other weekend. It's tough, the days in between. That's why we stayed together as long as we did, but it just wasn't good."

"You don't think you can make it work, even for Daecus? Divorce is hard on kids." I regret saying it as soon as it is out of my mouth. His face shifts, and he swallows, looking away from me, his teeth clenching. "I'm sorry." I can see how difficult this has been for him, how much strain there is around his eyes.

"No, you're right. I wish I could have, and if it were up to me, I woulda stayed to be near Daecus. God knows I would. But not Mandy; she is done."

"I'm sorry," I say again.

"Me, too."

"So what does she do?"

"She works with the airlines. She was working out of St. Louis for a while, but last year she got the transfer to Chicago and took it. So we had tried to work things out on her days off, but even after the counseling, we both realized it's not ever going to work."

"Do you think you could move to Chicago?" I ask.

"No. We tried that last summer, but it just made it clear that she's moved on. She doesn't want to try anymore."

"I'm so sorry, Dylan." If he tried moving to Chicago last summer to keep the family together, then they've had more than a couple of months apart.

He nods, and I can see that he is resolved to his fate.

"Which brings us back to the fair," he says, brightening. "Interested in trolling with us? I'll have him the weekend it opens."

"Sure. It'll be fun."

"So what's this about a craft booth?"

I explain that Charley and I rent a booth every year, and she sells her soaps, and I sell art. "They call it the Art Walk."

"Wow. So you still draw?"

"Yeah." A smile spreads because I don't think he has a concept of what art has been to me.

"That's awesome. You were pretty good, from what I remember."

I smile, blushing, looking away, my eyes falling on the TV mounted in the corner of the room.

The anchor is speaking, her expression contained and serious. An image appears in the corner of the screen, and the blush that was rising in my cheeks blanches, washing back down my neck. Dylan is saying something, but I stand from the table and walk away, past him, looking up at the TV and reading the captions as the anchor speaks.

Every hair on my body stiffens, and I feel like a ghost has just walked through me. The picture is nothing special, a school picture of a brown-haired girl, missing since Saturday afternoon, according to the closed captioning.

"You okay?" Dylan is behind me, his hand on my shoulder. "Do you know her?"

"I think I do."

The bulletin is over, and I face Dylan. "When did it say she was last seen?" I ask, needing confirmation.

"Saturday afternoon, I think."

"I saw her Saturday night." I tell him about the clinic, about her coming in, about the Camaro coming back to get her, how wrong it had felt to let her go. I speak in a whisper, unwilling to let anybody else hear me. "She was pregnant."

"You need to talk to the police."

9

The police station is on the opposite side of the square and down a block. The sun is high in the pale-blue sky, ducking behind cotton-ball clouds. Our shadows are small pools beneath us as we jog past the storefronts toward the police department. It is a perfect day; the air is fragrant with cut grass.

Dylan is pacing me, and when we reach the station, he opens the door, ushering me through. The dispatcher sits behind a wall of glass, probably bulletproof, and she looks up when we burst through the door. The room has changed since the last time I was here, the night my mother died, the night I met Leslie McGill. The night my life truly began. The night my life ended. The folding chairs that I remember are gone, replaced with long metal benches with bright-orange plastic seats. The walls are white, where before they were gray. I rush to the counter, and Dylan stops next to me, his long fingers splayed on the countertop.

The woman behind the glass puts a finger up, saying, "Let me transfer you." Then she turns toward us expectantly.

"Is Officer Bridges in?" My breath comes in gasps from the short run across the square.

"She's on patrol."

Should I wait to talk to her, a familiar face, someone I know and am comfortable with, somebody I would want on my team, somebody I want on Amy's team? No, I can't wait. "Who do I see to talk about the missing girl?" Dylan's hand settles on my back, between my shoulder blades, and I feel the rhythm of my heart shifting to a slower cadence, my breath becoming less labored. I do not move out of his touch but glance at him, catching the pale blue of his eyes. How had I forgotten the exact color of his eyes?

"You have information about Amy Kent?"

"I think so."

She pushes a button on her multi-line phone and speaks into her headset. "Detective, I have a lady here who has information about your case." There is a brief pause. "Yes, sir."

She faces us again. "Detective Daniels will meet you in the back. If you step out here and go around the building, he'll meet you at the door."

"All right." Dylan's hand slides from my back as I turn away, remembering that there is a side entrance to the actual department. My back feels cold where Dylan's hand had been, and for a split second, I wish he would put it back, I want him to touch me again, but then I am through the door and walking toward the side entrance, which opens as we approach.

"Miss Hayes, good to see you again."

His familiar manner throws me. I don't know this man and don't think I've ever met him.

"How do you know me?" There was a time when I would have pretended familiarity and spent a quiet length of time tormenting over the holes in my memory. I haven't had so much as a speeding ticket since I've been back in Charleston. I've been reticent, very under the radar. I've been invisible. He knows me from the hospital probably, but that doesn't seem right. I recognize all the cops who come out there, and I'm sure this man is not one of them.

"Oh, we met once before, years ago. I never forget a face."

"Oh. Nice to meet you, sir." I shake his hand and then introduce him to Dylan. They shake, and I speak. "We were having lunch and saw the girl on the news." I keep my voice pitched low.

"Do you have information?"

"I might." We are moving through the station, and he opens a door for us to come into his office.

"Have a seat, and tell me what you know."

"I volunteer over at Crisis Clinic. Are you familiar?"

"Yeah. You guys do good work."

"I don't usually work nights, but I was there last Saturday, filling in, and I think she came in. Her hair was different from what I saw on the TV. Do you have any other pictures of her?" My heart is sputtering again, and I'm talking too fast, saying all the wrong things.

Dylan's hand darts across the desk as he reaches to take the offered photographs. We look down at the images, the smiling girl with her thick eye makeup and red lips, snapshots from her friends and family. The smattering of freckles on the side of her face is the same as the girl who signed in as Jennifer Aniston. I hadn't been able to see them on the photo on the television.

"I'm sure that's her." I glance from Dylan to the detective and back again at the image. "She said her name was Amy, but signed in as 'Jennifer Aniston.' She's only fourteen."

"Do you mind if I record our conversation?"

"No, of course not." I reach out, and Dylan takes my hand, his long fingers intertwining with mine. I squeeze, grateful he is here.

I recount the details of Amy's visit to the clinic, how the test was positive and how she kept saying that he loved her and was going to take care of her.

"She was pregnant?" Detective Daniels asks, after glancing through his file, double checking his notes.

"Yes. It was early, I think, but the test came back positive."

"Well, that's definitely new information. Did she say anything about the father, give you his name?"

"No, she didn't, but I don't think the father was a kid." I try to remember what she had said, exactly, that made me think he was an adult . . . something about not wasting time with boys? Wasn't it? I am unsure, the words are a blur. "She clammed up when I asked about him." I shake my head. "I should have never let her go. I knew she was in a bad situation. I should never have let her leave."

"Did she say something that made you think she was in a bad situation, or was it just a feeling?"

I try to think back, to remember all the pieces of the conversation we had together. "I guess it was just a feeling." It was me projecting my remembered self onto her. "But clearly something has happened to her." She had said they were in love, that she wouldn't mind being a mother.

"Maybe, maybe not," the officer says, leaning back in his chair, folding his hands over his stomach.

"Well, she was pregnant, and now she's missing," I insist, annoyed that he can be so nonchalant.

"Yes, but that doesn't mean she hasn't just gone off somewhere and will show up when she is ready."

"I don't know," I say, squeezing Dylan's hand.

"Do you remember how she arrived?" the detective asks, drawing me back to myself.

"Yes. I do. Some guy dropped her off and then drove off around the block. We could hear the car coming around the front every time he circled."

"Nobody came in with her?"

I shake my head.

"Do you think you'd recognize the person who dropped her off?"

"No. I never saw him. I just saw the car." Detective Daniels asks for a description of the car, and I tell him what I can: it was a late-model Camaro, some dark, flat color, with no gloss at all. "It was old and loud. It had a dent in the front fender." It comes to me in a flash, the way the light caught along the front fender, dipping into darkness at the fold in the metal. I hadn't realized that it was a dent at the time.

"So, a woman could have dropped her off."

"What?"

"You didn't see the driver, right? It could have been a woman."

"I guess." I'd assumed it was a man.

"All right. Is there anything else?"

"No."

"Well, I appreciate your coming by. We'll get this information out to the team. It would be best if you don't tell anybody about this, so we can keep it close and hope that somebody slips up and mentions it." He rises from his desk, and Dylan follows suit. We walk together down the hall and back into the day, and I keep my hands pushed down into the pockets of my jeans as we walk back toward the square, because all I want is for him to touch me again. I can't let that happen because if he touches me, I will be sixteen all over again.

10

On Thursday, when Amy Kent has been missing for five days, I join a search party to walk through the cornfields in search of her. The police have not released the information I gave them, and I understand what Detective Daniels meant about hoping somebody would slip up. If the official word is that she was seen walking toward the cornfield at around two in the afternoon, the person who saw her later may also have seen the person she was with, or better yet, be the person she was with. They are holding my information close to their vests.

Amy had been living with her mother and her aunt and uncle in the small white house on Locust Avenue, where the search party is gathering. The garage is closed, and the curtains are drawn on the house. I park my car across from the house and steel myself. We won't find Amy Kent in the field, unless she was brought back here later, but it's part of the police tactic, I think, to give the abductor a sense of ease. If we are looking here, then we are not looking for a dull-colored Camaro. Upwards of thirty people are already in the yard, and I walk into the street to join them, fighting the urge to go and peek in the garage, to see if the uncle has a project car.

Halfway across the street, I catch sight of Anna and Henry LaDieu. I've long since gotten used to bumping into my old skeletons, and Anna smiles and waves, nudging her husband. I join them, exchanging hugs, grateful to not be alone in this crowd. When we were in high school, we were the two awkward girls in gym. Anna always seemed angular and fuzzy. Her curly brown hair was untamable, and she was made mostly of elbows and knees. One of Anna's legs is slightly shorter than the other, which makes her limp. The limp is part of who she is now, something she has embraced and incorporated and made hers. She's come into her own over the years, cropping her hair close to her head and forsaking the glasses for contacts. She's not a beauty, but she's cute in a quirky way. She's also brilliant and is the features editor at the newspaper. I always thought she'd follow her mom into writing.

Henry is a professor in the math department up at the university. He was such a geek growing up, studious and intense. He hasn't changed at all. He's tall and somber, always with thick glasses and disheveled hair. I wonder if Anna and Henry were together when we were kids, but I don't remember. Ending up with people you grew up with is one of the side effects of living in a small town, of never leaving, of having only a tiny pool to choose mates. They are a good fit, though—both of them intelligent and odd.

"What a nightmare," Henry says, his arm folding around Anna's shoulders as Detective Daniels climbs up onto the porch to face us. Anna's hand rests on her stomach, the way mothers do when their children are inside. I notice but don't say anything, seeing the round mound of her belly protruding. Everyone is having babies. I turn to face Detective Daniels, and my hand travels to the flat plane of my abdomen, where once I carried a child, remembering her there when she shared my blood and our hearts beat on the same rhythm. Grief weighs against me, pushing me to the earth.

"Thank you all for coming out. As you know, Amy has been missing since Saturday afternoon. She was last seen walking in westerly fashion toward the edge of town, on this road." We all turn, in unison, to look down the road to where it ends, blocked by a low gate with a stop sign mounted on it. At the road's edge, the cornfield begins, narrow shafts rising thigh high into the air. The sunlight is still at a slant; I've come straight from the hospital. Moisture flashes and sparks in the sun.

"Isn't it true that she was seen later?" the question erupts from the back of the crowd, and when I turn to look, I see a woman dressed in a lavender top and a black pencil skirt, standing at the edge of the crowd. She is holding a voice recorder out toward the group.

My stomach plummets. Behind her is the news truck from the local television station, and when I turn a little more, I see the cameraman standing to her side, framing her in his lens.

"I am unaware that such information has been released to the public."

"Well, my source says that a worker from the pregnancy counseling clinic has come forward and said Amy was there late in the evening on Saturday night."

I jerk around and catch the detective's eyes. I fold in, making myself small, guilt rising along my spine. I never thought it would be a secret, but now that people might know that I saw her and let her go I feel like I am the one who stole her away.

"Was she pregnant?"

"I'm not in a position to make a statement on that at this time," Detective Daniels says, sounding very curt and annoyed.

"I'll take that as a strong maybe," the reporter says, the smirk in her voice sounding like *"Gotcha."*

A buzz of conversation erupts around me, speculations and perceptions adjusting to incorporate this new information.

"Somebody should talk to the boyfriend. He probably knows where she is."

"I don't think she was dating anybody. I know her mom."

"I think she probably just ran away."

"Things like this just don't happen here."

"You know she's already dead," someone whispers nearby. I turn and try to catch sight of the man who said the last and see the bulge of tobacco roosting along the line of his lower front teeth. Would he be the type of man to drive a Camaro?

"So that means she was pregnant," the woman beside him says, catching the juicy gossip, and suddenly Amy is not someone's lost child. She is a tart, a slut, a floozy. They think of her as a different person with this new information. I hear the judgments. She is no longer just an innocent child; she's now a wild teen who had gotten herself knocked up. Didn't she get what she had coming to her?

The man who had said she was dead holds my eyes. His hair is dirty blond and thin, flying above his head in wisps caught in the morning breeze. He winks, a smirk lifting one edge of his mouth. I shudder and turn away, taking a step away from him, stepping closer to Anna and Henry, trying to tune out the mumbled conversations. I focus as Detective Daniels explains how we will search the field in a grid pattern.

It's true, though . . . what the man said. Amy is probably dead. Didn't I hear that after the first forty-eight hours, missing persons are usually not found alive? Had the man sounded like someone with knowledge, or was he the same as everybody else, speculating?

"The last time something like this happened was back twenty years ago," a woman says, and I catch her eyes. It wasn't twenty years ago since someone went missing in Charleston. I don't offer my input, though, not wanting to admit my proximity to that disappearance, either. I look back at Detective Daniels, wrapping up his instructions.

The news team walks toward the field with us, talking with those nearest, and I make a point of finding a path far away from them. I try not to look at them, try not to get caught looking at them.

It was sixteen years ago, for sure, the last time they mounted a search for someone from the town. That had been Cal Robinson, a man my mother was dating at the time of his disappearance. I had not participated in that search and had only felt relief when they found him dead, weeks later, in a field outside of Neoga.

Sixteen years ago.

Time stretches like a band, and I'm afraid the past is going to snap back and catch me up. Then it will drag me through time with it. All my ghosts are coming home to haunt me: Warren, Dylan, all the babies coming into the world.

"Alison." I turn and see Kelci Delaney coming through the crowd. She is another one of my ghosts. We've had our ups and downs, but over the years, she's been steady, and although we aren't great friends, we are friendly.

"Hey," I step across the gravel, and she leans in to give me a small hug. "I'm glad you're here. Can you believe this?" We are in the middle of the crowd, now waiting at the edge of the cornfield.

"No. I can't. I know the family. *I know her*. She worked for us last summer, and I thought she was going to this year, too. She's a good kid." Kelci's family owns the Bancroft Market, and even though Walmart coming in has impacted their business, it's still where we locals go. We support our own, and Mr. Walton doesn't need us to make him any richer.

"What is she like?" I am careful not to speak of her in the past tense.

"She's just full of life. She's always laughing." Kelci shakes her head, and a bright red splotch appears on the bone of each cheek. She blinks hard to push back tears. I try to picture the sullen girl who had come into the clinic laughing, and I can't even find a smile that fits her face, even after seeing the red, glossed lips in the snapshots Detective Daniels had shared. "What if we don't find her?"

"We'll find her," I say, offering assurances that I don't feel. "Do you think she might have run away?"

"No. Not Amy. She wasn't that kind of kid."

Kelci isn't as careful not to put her in past tense, I notice, and it's odd that she doesn't think Amy was the running-away kind of kid when it seems that the police think she is.

"Was she seeing anybody?"

Kelci shrugs, "I didn't see much of her when school was in session. Just when she came by to shop or help out over holidays." Her complexion is blotchy, and she looks like she could cry. "Growing up is *so* hard."

"You can say that again," I agree.

"Don't you work over at the Crisis Center?" She drops her voice low, leaning close, looking for the scoop. She must have been here in time to hear the newswoman ask her question, level her allegation.

"Friday mornings," I say but can't look at her. I can feel the red heat rising in my cheeks the way it does when I lie.

She must see it, but she doesn't say anything, and I'm grateful when she changes the subject. "I heard Dylan is coming back to town. Did you know?"

"Yeah. I saw him over at the McGills' anniversary party. Last week." I don't mention having lunch with him, not wanting to see the knowing look, the suggestion that we will get together now that he's coming back.

"Oh yeah? How was that? I meant to make it over, but you know . . . Life."

"It was really nice." I ask if she knows Dylan's wife.

"Yeah, our folks are close, so I've met her over the years. You know, they are getting a divorce."

"I heard."

Kelci blows a puff of air through her nostrils. "Hopefully the third time is the charm."

"Oh, they've split up before?" I ask, and my stomach plummets, my hope washing down through the soles of my feet.

"Yeah. She's 'too good for him.'" She taps the side of her head, indicating that it's all in Mandy's mind.

"That's a shame," I say, surprised at how much I mean it. I see the little insecurities I recognized in Dylan with new clarity, and anger flares. The idea of anybody making Dylan feel small boils my blood.

"Yeah. She's not nice. She works with some airline and thinks she's some big deal." She is leaning toward me now, like a conspirator.

I hold her eyes for a split second before looking away, blushing. How did I hate her for all those years? "That makes me so sad. Dylan's such a good guy, too."

"Yeah. His boy is sweet, too," she says, and I nod agreement, my mind rolling in on itself. How could Dylan have chosen somebody who would treat him poorly?

Our conversation falters and moves to other things: David and the kids, her life.

A hand lands on my shoulder, and Dylan stops beside us, startling me, "Sorry I'm late," he whispers, his breath smelling of coffee.

"Speak of the devil," Kelci whispers. We are waiting at the edge of the field, to be cut loose to search for clues. Detective Daniels is cautioning us not damage the crop.

"How are you?" Dylan asks Kelci, drawing her into a side-armed hug.

"I'm fine," she says, squeezing him.

"How's David?"

"He's good. He's got a little bit of arthritis in that knee, you know? But he's okay." I catch Dylan's eye and have to look away to keep from laughing. When did we all get so old? The turmoil building in my soul because of the newswoman's question, her accusation, subsides, calmed by Dylan's presence. As long as they don't know who I am, as long as they don't come asking me questions, it will be okay.

When I can look back at him without laughing, I say, "I didn't know you were coming."

"Of course." There is tension around his eyes, a set in his jaw.

"We were just talking about you," Kelci purrs. She hasn't seen the strain on his features, apparently. Or if she has, she doesn't seem concerned. I watch him, trying to figure it out. Did he fight with his wife? Has something happened to Daecus? Has his lease agreement fallen through? Or has something happened with the new job? Has something fallen apart in his world more than what I already knew?

"You were? Good things I hope?" The strain lessens, and he smiles at me, probably seeing my concern.

"Just trying to get the two of you hooked up," is what I think she says, but she is turning away, with a little wave of her hand. Her words are low and under her breath, and there is a rustle up toward the front of the crowd, drawing my attention.

He bumps against my shoulder, like old times. Of course he came. Dylan isn't the type of man who doesn't help; he isn't the type of guy who can go about his life when somebody is in trouble. When I glance up, he is looking forward. I notice a small nick on his chin from where he shaved this morning, and I want to reach up and touch the wounded flesh. We all have scars. I rest against him, letting my arm ride alongside his and refocus on the search at hand. "You okay?" I ask in a whisper.

He looks down at me, his features softening, his tongue flicking out to wet his dry lips. "Yeah, just puts me in mind of Dake." For a second, I think he is talking about his son, then my memory spreads, and I remember his brother.

"Yeah." I lean into him. "I'm sorry." When Dylan was eight, his dad and his older brother, Dake, were involved in a boating accident while on a camping trip. There had been a search party then. Jake, his father, had been found miles from the lake, drunk and passed out. His brother had been found at the spillway three days later. Of course Dylan would have been part of that search; of course this reminds him of his brother.

For all the years we were growing up, I thought his life was so comfortable and perfect. It's now when we are grown and have been away from each other for so long that I can see the scars. His arm slips around my shoulder and squeezes, then drops away, careful, knowing that I am touchy about being touched.

"All right." Detective Daniels is calling out through a bullhorn, finally finished with his directions, his cautions, his answering of procedural questions. "There are four staging areas, heading into the field. Split up, and the officers will guide you to your search zone. When you reach the far side of the field, we'll bus you back. If you come across something, don't touch it or move, just stop where you are and call one of us over."

We migrate in a group, voices murmuring. I want to speak to Dylan. I want to say something that will matter, but my tongue is thick and numb inside my mouth. I want to tell him that the media has caught wind of Amy Kent being seen later on Saturday, at the Crisis Clinic, but I'm afraid someone else will hear. Instead, I hold his eyes and think how glad I am he is here, how happy I am that he is coming home, how much I have missed him.

We spread out through the field, each taking a row to walk along, keeping our eyes trained on the ground. We are looking for clothes, keys, jewelry, body parts. We are looking for the upheaval of earth that may suggest a struggle or a burying place.

The dew rolls in drops down the slick ridge of the corn blades, and my scrubs and shoes are wet in minutes. We make our way through the field as the sun rises, and the cold moisture on my legs become sticky with heat. The sun is high by the time we reach the three-quarters point, and our shadows pool around our feet, lost in the rows, when a shout comes from the left. The whole procession stops, and we turn to watch as an officer makes his way.

They've found a necklace. It is silver with a small, ornate key pendant, I don't see it, but the description passes through the search party in whispers. The rest of us continue our forward march, a slow stampede, as they stake the area where the jewelry lay undisturbed. Yellow tape stretches around the stakes, and the click of the camera combats the buzzing of the insects, jangling my nerves.

When we reach the far edge of the field, I am weak and exhausted. I've not eaten, and my twelve hours at the hospital through the night are catching up with me. There is a bus at the other side of the field to take us back to our cars, and Dylan and I sit side by side, our legs pressing against each other, the way we sat as children before he stopped riding the bus to school. I let my head rest on his shoulder, weary and sad, trying to remember if Amy Kent was wearing a silver necklace when she came into the clinic.

"What do you think?" Dylan asks when we are standing beside my car, watching others drive away but somehow unable to leave ourselves.

"I don't think she was wearing a necklace."

"Maybe she lost it earlier?"

"Maybe." I shrug. "Maybe it isn't even hers."

"Maybe." He opens my car door for me. "Lunch?"

I look up at him, the car door between us now. I open my mouth to say, "Sure," then close it again. I shake my head. "I need to get to bed." If I say yes, we'll go to lunch and talk and talk . . . and hours will slip past. I don't want to hear the story of his dissolving marriage; I don't want to be that friend. He should have married me. He already feels so familiar, how could he ever have married anybody else? A small wheel of frustration rides in my heart, and I push it down and away. I don't know anything about his life, who he is or where he has been. All I know is who I am and where I've been. I can't risk falling in love with him again, as if I ever stopped.

Yes, he and Mandy are separated, but according to Kelci, it isn't the first time they've worked things out to stay together. I cannot get caught in that, or I will fall apart. Every time I look at him, I remember his lips on mine, his hands inside the bathrobe against my flesh. The most intense sexual encounter of my life was that night with him, and we didn't even have sex. He is trouble for me. He may be just looking for a friend, someone he is comfortable talking to, but I have always wanted more. I know me well enough—when it comes to Dylan, I can't just be his friend.

He folds his lips in, and I see the disappointment like a flag. "All right. Another time?"

"Sure." I slide down into my car, and he closes the door behind me and turns. He walks away. I bite my lips and turn the key, refusing to call out and bring him back. He is dangerous.

It's safer to be alone.

11

My phone is ringing, and I push the button to answer the call. "Alison?"

"Yeah," I slide up in my bed looking down at my watch. It's only two o'clock. I'm not late for anything.

"This is Chloe Chandler. I'm on the board with the Crisis Clinic. I think we've met?"

"Yeah, hi, Chloe." We'd met when I interviewed, although I couldn't say which of the three austere women she was. "How are you?"

"Well, to be honest, we're all in a bit of a tizzy over here."

"Oh?"

"Yes. Yes, we are."

"How can I help?" Dread flows through my veins, and I leave my bedroom to get a better cell-phone signal at the front of the apartment.

"Have you seen the news today?"

"No. I work nights. I was sleeping."

"Oh. Well, did you work with Amy Kent the night she went missing?"

"I did."

"You didn't feel we needed to know that?"

I remember Chloe Chandler very clearly all of a sudden, her bleached-blond hair pulled back in a severe ponytail.

"Well, yes, but I haven't been in since, and only just realized it was the same girl a couple of days ago."

"What did you do when you realized?"

"I went to see the police."

"Oh, Alison." She breathes a long, disgusted breath across the phone line, and my irritation rises. "We have procedures."

"You have procedures for when somebody goes missing?" I try to keep my voice neutral, but I hear my mother sneaking in, my back getting up, as she would say.

"Well, yes, dear. We assure our clients that their visit to us is confidential, of course. You know that."

"It seems that a girl disappearing might mitigate the need for confidentiality." Calling me "dear," as if she knows me, sets me on edge and now my back is full up. My voice is cold.

"Well, Alison, we really wish you had come to us so we could have handled this appropriately." I seethe, setting my teeth, biting my tongue. "Now Amy Kent's secrets are all over the news, and our clinic is no longer a private place. Do you understand how that might be a problem?"

"I don't believe that's my fault. Detective Daniels didn't release the information, somebody else did."

"Either way, dear, I think it is best if you not come to the clinic for a while until this all blows over." She is so smug, so full of condescension, that I want to scream.

"Are you kidding me?"

"No, Alison, I think it's best. The board would like for you to come over and give an account of your dealings with this girl. You understand, don't you?"

I do not respond, anger raging, and the things I want to say are so out of character that I feel sideways. I disconnect the phone without answering, and sit, seething, staring out at the afternoon street. What the hell?

I am tempted to go to the police, to find out how word got out, to ask Detective Daniels which of his policemen is leaking information to the press. It's not that I requested anonymity, but when he asked me not to share it, I thought nobody would know that it was me who saw her last. I don't even care. None of this matters if it helps find Amy.

I finally catch the news later in the afternoon, and my anger shifts from Chloe Chandler to the woman on the screen, spouting her innuendos, indicating that the clinic has something to hide. No wonder the board is upset. The image pans out from the clinic, and I turn the volume up.

"What do they know? What are they hiding? Was Amy Kent pregnant, and was she alone? Why is the Crisis Clinic not coming out with the information that the public wants? Why are they hiding the truth of what happened to Amy Kent?"

My stomach rolls in on itself, and I turn the television off, angry, furious at Miss Thing spouting her innuendos across the airwaves. How dare they put something like that on the news? That isn't helpful; that isn't going to help us find Amy. Even I know that the spike in ratings and viewership is all the reporter cares about. She isn't interested in Amy Kent, and she doesn't care if she damages the Crisis Clinic's reputation and ability to help people in need.

When I leave for work later, I am stopped by the woman. She has been waiting for me, I see it in the way she startles when I open the door from the stairway. How long has she been pacing the sidewalk, waiting for that door to move? "Are you Alison Hayes?" It's an ambush.

"Can I help you?" I say, still feeling the internal heat from the events of the day. Feeling the flood of disgust coursing through my veins.

"I'd like to know what you know about Amy Kent. Why isn't the Crisis Clinic cooperating?"

"I have no comment. Everything I know, I've told the police." I make haste down the street, toward the corner of the building, anxious to get to my car, determined not to run or look guilty.

"So you were the one who helped Amy that night?"

I stop in my tracks and turn to face her.

"I have nothing to say to you. You are disgusting. What you said on the news, is reprehensible. The clinic does good work in this community, we help a lot of people, and you trying to cast it in a bad light is irresponsible and bad."

"Is it true that Amy Kent was pregnant?" She holds a tape recorder out toward me, and it takes every bit of my willpower not to bat it away. "Why did you let her leave?"

I stare at her, numb. How can she manipulate this into something it isn't? I did the best I could in the moment, and it's either not enough or too much.

I turn and walk away, only realizing later that I've confirmed that I was the one who let Amy Kent go. I should have said I didn't know what she meant. Stupid.

12

The night is busy at the hospital, and the hours fly, leaving me little time to dwell on my encounter with the newswoman. I half expect to see her outside my door when I turn the corner from the parking lot, but the sidewalk is empty. When I glance down the street, I see no sign of her or her news van. I breathe a sigh of relief and open the door to the stairs going up to my apartment.

I am startled by a woman sitting on the bottom step. It is not the newswoman, but the shock of seeing a person there makes my hand nearly slip off the handle of the door and let it fall shut. Her hair is long and limp, hanging like ragged clothes across her thin shoulders. The deep hollows beneath her cheekbones suggest more skeleton than person. A hundred thoughts pass through my head in the split second that I first see her. I am reminded of my mother, during the horrible months when she was using, getting thinner and more wasted as each hit took her further down the rabbit hole. I almost let the door fall closed without going through, unwilling to approach her. Fear flashes in my mind like a beacon and the cadence of my heart slams an arrhythmic chant against my ribs. Is this Amy Kent's mother, come to ask me why I let her daughter go?

I'm exhausted after my shift, and the confrontation with the news reporter last night has left me feeling on edge and disconnected. There should have been more I could have done. I should have paid closer attention to the details. Was she wearing a necklace at the clinic? Why didn't I keep her from going out into the night? Why didn't I press her for the name of her boyfriend who was going to "take care of" her? Does that have a sinister meaning now, in light of everything that has happened? I knew something was off, but I still let her go. How could I have made her stay? Should I have gone out to the car to make sure she was with someone who would keep her safe? How could I have done that and been within the guidelines of the clinic?

"Excuse me." I step over the threshold and mount the steps, shifting to the side, so I don't bump into the woman. There is another apartment in the building—we share this stairwell—and after the first shock of seeing her, I know she isn't here for me.

I skim the steps, pulling myself up using the rail, feeling drained.

"You Alice Hayes's girl?"

I make two more steps before the words sink in, before I make sense of what she has said. Amy Kent's mother wouldn't have asked me that.

I stop and turn back, looking down the stairs at the woman. She is standing and looks less bedraggled now that she is upright. She is clean, her clothes are buttoned and tucked, and her lank hair is thin but not dirty. It was only the shadows that had made her seem gaunt. Her arms are exposed, thin and unmarred, passing beyond the sleeves of her shirt.

"Excuse me?" I repeat.

"You Alice's daughter?" Her accent is thick and Southern with long vowels and dropped consonants.

"Yes." The word draws long from my lips, sounding like dread. "Can I help you?"

"I hope you can." She comes up the steps, and we stand looking at each other for a split second before she speaks again. "My name is Stella Hayes. I'm married to your father."

My vision narrows, closing on her mouth. I sit down hard on the landing, my hand still holding the rail. "I don't have a father."

All my life I have wondered about the man who fathered me. My mother would never talk about him, she never even gave his name. The only thing I have of him are two photographs that I got after my mom had died. One image from some dance and another of them on a motorcycle, young and in love.

"Well, dear, we all have a father." She chuckles a little, but not un-kindly.

I look at her, taking in the brown eyes, the softness of the expression in them, the lines stretching around her mouth, worry and strain etched there. I notice that her clothes, more than just being clean, are of nice quality, expensive even. It isn't my mother she makes me thinks of; it's Vaude, Dylan's mother, with her quiet voice and warm eyes.

I must look fractured because she kneels on the step in front of me and puts her hand on my shoulder. "I'm sorry. This must be a shock. I haven't presented this well."

"Why now?" I look at her face, finding my strength to speak.

"Well, honey, he's wanted to reach out to you for a very long time."

"Then why didn't he?"

"Well, he did try, but he never heard back from you. He didn't think you wanted to hear from him."

"What do you mean that he 'tried'?"

"He had an investigator seek you out when you was little, but when he came to see you . . . well, there was an argument, and the police was called. Later he sent a bunch of letters, but they all came back, and he just never heard back from you. Then he just gave up a little, I guess, figured your mama done poisoned you against him."

I laugh, a small bark at the absurdity.

"I never got any letters. Are you sure I'm who you're looking for?"

"If you is Alice Hayes's daughter, then you is who I'm looking for.

"Well, I am Alice's daughter. That is true enough."

I look at her, my mind reeling, thinking how it's a little late now, wondering if my mother would have refused letters addressed to me. I know she would. My mother was a believer in the "If I can't have him, then neither can you" line of thought. "So why didn't he come himself?"

"We thought you might be more open to a woman showing up unannounced on your doorstep."

I nod seeing the sense of that. "So what does he want from me now? Does he need a kidney or something?"

She laughs, a sharp staccato belt of sound. "You is definitely your father's daughter. That sounds just like something he would say."

"Sounds like something my mother would have said, too." I am none too ready to give any credit to a father who has never been a part of my life, even if it is just for my sarcastic, jaded sense of humor.

"I reckon it does, at that," she says, nodding her head, a soft smile parting her lips.

It's in that smile that I see the spreading of a fond memory, and I have to ask, "Did you know my mother?"

She nods. "I was real sad to hear how she went. Must have been a terrible way to die."

"Certainly was a terrible way to live."

"No doubt there," she says.

We nod at each other, and I say a silent prayer for those who have gone before us.

"My mother never talked about him, never would even tell me his name."

She shakes her head, making small tut-tut sounds with her tongue. "It's not right to keep a child from knowing her daddy."

"She did the best she could." I pitch my voice low, unwilling to hear criticism from this woman.

"Oh, heavens, child, I'm not saying anything bad about your mama. I'm not one to speak ill of the dead. God knows I loved her well when I knew her." She talks like an old woman, but she can't be even to fifty yet.

"How did you know her?"

"I was friends with Camille, your daddy's sister." She smiles, and the years slip off her face. "Camille and I thought she was the prettiest girl we'd ever seen."

I nod, my weariness rising again. "Well, if he doesn't need anything from me and I don't need anything from him, maybe we should just leave well enough alone."

"Oh." Her voice is flat, deflated and I know this isn't the response she expected. She expected excitement or a fight, maybe, but not disinterest. "You understand, he's just trying to make things right. He's come to the Lord these past several years and is trying to atone for his sins."

"So he's making *amends?*" The word rolls long and slow across my lips. All those amends. Everybody is working the ninth step.

"I reckon. He's trying to."

"I am not one of his sins. He doesn't owe me anything." The little wall I surround myself with is fractured, but I slap more mortar in place, adding another row of bricks. I feel strength returning to my legs, and rise from the landing. The past few weeks have felt like too much chaos and adding this one last thing is one thing too much.

"He'd just like to meet you. You're his only daughter."

"I'm nobody's daughter anymore."

"I understand that he's not been a daddy to you," she begins, and I can hear the rhythm of a well-rehearsed speech, something she has probably said a hundred times while she's been sitting waiting for me.

"No. He hasn't," I say, interrupting, not wanting to hear the justification for my father's absence, the blaming of my mother. I look down the stairs at the woman—her soft eyes, her nice clothes, her pleading manner. I raise the sign of the cross toward her, the way a priest does, thumb to forehead, chest, each shoulder. Finally, I turn my palm toward her outstretched, as if some magic transfers. "Consider him absolved." I turn and head up the stairs.

When I reach the top, I turn and look back. She is still staring up, her face glistening. Is she crying, or is it just a trick of the light? She isn't going to beg me; she isn't rushing after me, and I respect her for that. "I do have one question."

"Yes, ma'am?" she asks, her manners restored and intact.

"What is his name?"

A breath wallops out of her, and it almost sounds like a sob. "Tom. His name is Tom Hayes."

"Thanks." I unlock the door to my apartment and step past the threshold. When it is locked again behind me, I head to the bathroom and set the water to run. My mind is numb; I am too weary to think or feel. I'm too strung out on the emotion of the week just passed. I have too many ghosts, and the one out in the stairwell is one I never expected to appear. I got over not having a father years ago.

I stand a long time under the running water, feeling the heat like a second skin. When my hair rinses clean, when I'm washed, I step out, wrapping myself in a towel, my head turbaned. I make my way from the bathroom down the hall to my bedroom, sliding into the bed, still damp.

Sometimes you just have to do the things that need to be done.

Right now all I need to do is sleep.

The towel bunches at my hip as I slide down under the covers, and I close my eyes and will myself to drift.

I dream of my mother sitting across the table from me out at the trailer. She is as she was that last year, and I am sitting opposite her, grown, a woman myself. We are similar in so many ways. It is almost like seeing myself reflected in a mirror. She is laughing, a small contagious chuckle.

"She just kept telling me to go and get the turtles from the back step. She wanted to make turtle soup. Alison, is that even a thing?"

"I don't know," my dream-self answers, and my voice sounds young, like a child's, but the hands before me are my hands—grown, thin, skilled.

"She just kept saying that, about 'Papa' leaving the turtles on the stoop. She was utterly *flustrate*." She shakes her head. I had forgotten that was a word she used to say, a word that isn't a word, just a mash-up of two emotions. The dream kitchen melts, and I am standing on the cliff at La Jolla Cove overlooking the ocean. The wind is blowing, and the spray covers my face with salt.

I reach my hand up to wipe the water away and realize that I am crying. I am back in my bed, in my room, in my apartment, in my hometown, and I am crying for all the people I have lost, and all the ones I never knew.

I catch a hold of the memory of the dream and am unsure if it was a conversation we really had or something I created. Mom did sometimes to talk to me about the residents at the nursing home, the little old people, during that worst last year. I was so angry at her by then, though, I don't think I ever stopped to listen.

I would give anything to have one more conversation with her.

***

Outside my door, a small, white envelope is propped against the doorframe for me to see when I come out. The woman left it there, a letter, begging me to reconsider meeting my father—I'm sure that's what it will be. I fold it and stuff it into my purse, unwilling to look at it, reluctant to admit that it is even here.

13

When Amy Kent has been missing for two weeks, and when Warren has been dead for a day more than that, I find myself sitting in my car in a parking lot at a bar called Blind Billy's. Warren's family has planned a celebration of his life as a benefit to help his wife and son through this hard time without him. When he was young, Warren and his brothers had a band they called Elliot's Child, and they used to play in the bar on Friday or Saturday nights, so Blind Billy's offered up the space for the event. I've seen almost as many signs for the celebration as I have for the missing girl, Amy Kent. It has been a horrible two weeks.

Amy Kent's mother went on the news, begging for her daughter to come home, and the clip that they keep playing over and over is her weary, thin face filling the screen. "I just wish somebody," meaning me, "had been paying attention and helped keep her safe." The camera cuts to the newswoman, her face drawn in her makeup as she attempts to wear the appropriate expression of concern. She doesn't pull it off and only looks phony, trying to force her face into a frown. I feel like I should be in the Witness Protection Program. Everybody seems to be pointing at me as if I am the one who took her. I haven't been to the grocery for a week, and the jar of backup peanut butter finally got its seal cracked. I hate peanut butter. I go to work, and I come home; that is all. I am about two prank calls away from changing my phone number. Everybody is talking about it, I think, behind my back—how I let her go, how it's my fault that Amy Kent never made it home. I have made an absolute pest of myself calling Detective Daniels every day hoping they've discovered something, offering tidbits of memory that are not any more useful than not knowing what color the car was or whether it was a man or a woman driving.

I had no intention of going to the Celebration of Life planned for Warren, but at seven o'clock, I find myself parked outside of Blind Billy's, where we had our first date. Warren brought me to hear his band, and I still remember the thrill I had felt at being on the dance floor, setting the beat with Warren on the bongos, how alive I had felt. I sit, watching as people walk through the door. I see his son, with all those same Robinson features, red lips, dark hair, his pale skin as yet unmarred by the tattooist's gun.

I am not doing this. I start my car, unable to pull my eyes from the window where I can see his son, his wife, who is not what I expected. She is plump but not fat, with a clear complexion. She doesn't look like a user. She looks like a child, her hair wrapped up in a messy bun at the top of her head. I can't reconcile her with him. How could she be with someone on such a self-destructive path? How could she have loved him when she had to know he was an addict? Was he a practicing addict, or just a man who fell off the wagon one too many times? A shudder washes through me. Elliot reaches the door, and my heart skips a beat. They all look so much alike. Elliot's khakis and polo look new, or at least freshly pressed, his dark hair close-cropped and streaked with silver. I turn off my car, trying to remember Elliot's wife's name, but can't. She forced him out of the band, I remember, and now he looks like somebody who golfs on Sundays. Apparently, putting away the music was a good thing for him. He is arriving alone, though. Did she choose not to come? Did he end up resenting her for forcing him out? Did it destroy their marriage the way I had been afraid it would ruin Warren and me if we had tried to make a family?

I pull the keys from the ignition and drop them into my purse. I am here and dressed for a wake, so I might as well stay. I need to do this, or he's going to walk with me forever. My hair is contained, braided down my back, and I have come with a clean face, even if my soul isn't entirely unblemished. I walk across the lot, the click of my heels echoing against the glass-fronted building.

The first time I had walked up to this door, I had felt such disappointment, thinking Warren had misjudged me, mistaken me for someone like my mother. I thought we were going on a real date, but he brought me, a sixteen-year-old kid, to a bar, when all I wanted was a real meal. Then we had come in; I understood that he was part of the band. I had sat and watched, starstruck, and finally been taken with the music enough to dance, to join him at the edge of the stage and try to catch the beat, laughing, feeling alive.

The memory is a ghost, walking with me through the doors into the dim interior. The bar has not changed. It has the same wooden benches facing Formica-topped tables. I take in the crowd, a broad mix of people, some looking like they just came in from the curb and others wearing pricey button-down shirts. Mr. Billups is sitting at one of the tables, his red suspenders cutting a line across his pressed shirt, and I stand for a long second as my eyes adjust, trying to understand why Mr. Billups would be here. Across from him is Rob and Faye, and I am relieved to see them, people I can share this night with and not be alone. Did they come for me? Did they remember that Warren was once somebody important in my life?

I rent my apartment from Mr. Billups, and once a month, I go into the office at his store and enter the stack of invoices into his accounting program. I would do almost anything for that man. Without him, I wouldn't have survived that worst last year. My job in his store, his encouragement and faith in me had kept me moving from one dark day into the next until there was finally some light filtering through. He was maybe the first person who ever believed in me. Faye was my mother's best friend, and Rob is her fourth husband, the one who finally stuck. I make my way through the crowd and join them at their table, leaning in to hug Mr. Billups. He moves his four-pronged cane to the other side of the bench and pats the space beside him. I slide in, and he puts his arm around my shoulders, holding me for a second and then just letting his arm rest there.

I touch hands with Faye, who rises and leans toward me, offering an air kiss. She is looking old; her hair is teased and frayed until it looks like a halo around her head. Her makeup is too thick and makes the lines around her mouth and eyes look like grand caverns. Rob grasps my hand, smiling, looking sad.

"What are you all doing here?" I ask.

"It's such a tragedy," Mr. Billups says loudly, because he is hard of hearing when there are crowds.

"Yeah. It is." I agree. "How did you know him?"

"Warren tended the machines at the store," Rob answers because Mr. Billups hasn't heard my question.

"What does that mean?"

"The vending machines, you know?"

"No way, was he still doing that?" When I met Warren, he had owned or worked for—I was never really sure—a small company that ran a vending machine route; it was called the Vendor Tender. The memory makes me smile. I never thought he would have come back to that.

"Oh yeah, for several years now," Mr. Billups says, his words slightly slurred from a stroke a couple of years back. His speech has never quite recovered.

"Hm. I didn't even know he was in town," I admit, feeling something close to jealousy. How could I not have known he was near? How could we have been within ten minutes of each other and never run into each other? My schedule doesn't put me out in the world much, and when most people are heading to work, I am heading home. I like my hermit life; it's comfortable, it's safe. But still, it jangles me that I didn't know he was in the area.

It's hard to reconcile the emaciated, wrecked body that came in as a John Doe with somebody Mr. Billups would think was a good man. Maybe he wasn't a junkie. Perhaps he was just on a bender that went one day too long.

We sit in silence, and the crowd draws to attention when Elliot mounts the stage. He clears his throat and taps the ball of the mic. The sound bounds through the room, and Elliot smiles, a small, chagrined spreading of his lips.

"Thank you all for being here. We're here to celebrate my brother, Warren. We'll be doing a silent auction to help cushion his family through this time. If you can donate, it would be appreciated. Carla is planning to take up the business to keep it running, but losing Warren cost a price." He looks down, and I see he has a stack of index cards, a list of what he wants to say. "We're gonna have an open mic here through the night, and I hope some of you will share stories about Warren. Eddie is gonna never know what a great man his daddy was unless we all tell him."

"Great man" seems like an exaggeration. The man who came into the hospital wasn't a great man. He was a man strung out and wasted. I push that thought down and away. What a horrible thing to think when I'm here to celebrate his life. We are all flawed, nobody is perfect, and who am I to judge him? I don't know what his life was.

Then I remember him, the way he was during those first months when we dated. He was so shining and beautiful, with that smile that felt like a summer day. What could we have done differently? He wasn't a great man, but he was a decent man. I remember how he waited until the night I was emancipated to make love to me when we'd been seeing each other for months, and I was more than willing. He had waited, explaining that we needed to take our time to make it right. I thought he wanted me to be sure, but looking back, I know he just wanted me to be legal. I remember farther back, to when he came to the hardware store weeks after I first met him at Christmas, how I knew then that he had tried to protect me from Cal that Christmas night. He had a freshly healed scar above his eye proving it. Then I remember seeing him on stage, and I see again how the hard thrum of the music seemed to wrap him in light.

I'd run away to be with him, needing to be out of this town, needing to find a new place to start where nobody knew my mother or our stories. He was just a road for me, a way out. I had used him to get away. He left me when things started getting hard, when the police were searching for him, closing in, to question him about my mother. I'm still not completely convinced that he didn't have something to do with her death, that it hadn't been a suicide after all. When he came to me at Life House, I was hormonal and getting bigger by the day, and my thoughts were spinning. I was convinced of it by then. That's when he told me the story of that last day and the week that led to it. He had fallen to the floor and pressed his face against my belly, whispering to the infant I carried, our baby. I remember his face when he said he'd give it all up and do the 'right thing,' that we could be a family. I was stubborn, set in my path, unwilling or unable to believe that he could stand by me. Even if he had stayed, I would have just been repeating the same mistakes my mother had made, making my daughter live through all my failures. He couldn't have stood by us. He would have resented us and left; he would have been just like my father, gone. The words hiss in my head because it's what I have to believe.

Tears spring to my eyes. It was a mistake to come.

Elliot's eyes land on mine, and he stumbles on his words, falling momentarily silent, then he starts again. "... With that, I'm gonna turn the mic over to Warren's wife, Carla, who has a few words to say."

She climbs the steps, her eyes rimmed in red. Her son walks behind her, his little face closed and stoic. Elliot folds her in a hug and kisses her cheek, then ruffles Eddie's hair and steps to the back of the stage. Warren had stayed for them, my mind rolls.

"Thank you all for coming. Many of you probably knew Warren longer than I did. I met Warren when he came back from Los Angeles. Some of you probably know that he played with Lemon Squeeze for a couple years before they broke up. I have one of their CDs over on the auction table, signed by the whole band. I don't know if it's worth anything, really, but, um, I think Warren was a really talented man." Her face crumples, and she looks down at her son. "Anyway, I know he wasn't perfect. He had his demons that he struggled with," she sighs, and her breath ratchets through the room, amplified, and her next words are broken by a sob she can't contain, "but he had a really kind heart, and most the time, he beat his demons."

"Hear, hear!" A cheer rises from a small pod of men, celebrating that most of the time Warren beat his demons. A quick glance tells me that they are men who know something about demons. They know the struggle is real. A full set of teeth is barely present in the three skulls combined, and a plume of smoke surrounds them where they stand by the auction table. A nervous laugh spreads through the crowd, and Carla takes the interruption as an opportunity to regain control of her emotions. She smiles down at the men.

"You know, don't ya, Jerry, and Mark, Steve?" she says away from the mic, talking directly to the small group of men. Were they men that Warren had become friends with as they tried to beat their addiction? Were they all part of the same anonymous group, sharing their stories the way my mother had when she was finally going to get clean? Does anybody ever manage to beat the call of the drugs? My mother hadn't. Warren hadn't. I watch the men nodding their heads, comrades in the program, working whatever step they've come to. The small exchange is exactly what Carla seemed to need because when she finally looks back out at the rest of us, her eyes are dry and she is composed. "Well, I would love to hear your stories about Warren. If you knew him, and he somehow touched your life, can you share that with me? Share it with Eddie." Applause erupts, and Carla and Eddie walk off the stage.

The evening progresses, and stories of parties, misadventures, and kind deeds pepper the crowd until around nine.

"I think I'm gonna go," I say, loud and toward Mr. Billups. Hugs pass around. I stand up and walk toward the door, feeling again the haunt of Warren walking beside me.

I step out into the night, pausing before crossing the parking lot.

"Thank you for coming." A voice jars me, and I turn to see Carla and Eddie standing just past the edge of the window, a cigarette in her pudgy fingers, glowing in the night.

"Absolutely." I smile and step toward them, drawn by civility, social niceties, an obligation to be polite. "Warren was a good man when I knew him."

She drops her cigarette, grinds it beneath the flat of her sandal, and offers her hand to shake. "He tried." Her hand is warm, moist. I nod, standing as straight as I can. She is older than I first thought, probably forty. She is not at all the woman I would have expected him to marry. "How did you know him?"

I am drawn up short and almost stammer. I blow a long breath out between my lips as my mind ratchets back. How did I know Warren? I shake my head, glancing down at the boy.

"My mother once dated his older brother, and one Christmas, they were having a party. I was sixteen, I guess, and I didn't really like Cal, Warren's brother, so I was hiding in my bedroom, being angry. Well, Warren came down the hall and talked to me, and he was just really nice, a good guy. He kinda understood that I wanted something different, you know?" I laugh, feeling self-conscious, knowing that my story isn't conveying what I want to convey. "Anyway, we went out to his car, and in the trunk, he had a string of Christmas lights. We went out back behind our house and strung those lights all over this evergreen that I could see through my bedroom window. Everybody inside figured out what we were doing." I have to stop; my throat is closing, my nose is running. I look again at the boy, and I wipe away the hint of a tear.

I clear my throat and continue. "They all came outside, and we stood around that tree singing *Silent Night.*" I laugh because I don't want to cry. "That's it. It's just my best Christmas memory. You know. My mom died that next year."

She smiles. "That sounds like something Warren would do." There is pride in her voice, that her man had been kind even if he was broken.

I nod.

"Thanks for telling us." She ruffles the boy's hair, and I nod again. Warren had stayed for them.

"I"m sorry he's gone." I lean in and hug her, smelling the stale smoke in her hair, a scent I always associated with Warren.

When she releases me, I kneel down in front of the boy, "You doing okay?" He nods. "I thought your daddy was an extraordinary man." He nods again, leaning into his mother's hip. I offer a hand, and he reaches out, putting his small fingers into mine.

I rise, meeting Carla's eyes. "It was nice meeting you," I say, ready to go.

"I'm afraid I didn't catch your name."

"Alison." I clear my throat, nodding, looking away.

"Oh." There is recognition in her voice. I catch it and step off the curb, not looking at her again. I need to get away. Why would she recognize my name? What had he told her? Did he tell her about the baby? She kept her son. He stood by her. He tried to do the right thing.

"Good luck," I call back and walk across the parking lot, not looking over my shoulder, tears streaming down my face, as the Fourth of July fireworks erupt over the campus pond.

14

I dig my phone out when I am safe inside my car, fighting to control the puckering of my chin, the flood of emotion roiling inside of me.

"I've been a horrible friend," I whisper when he answers the phone.

"Alison?" His voice is thick, and I only now think about how late it is and that I've called him on impulse and probably woken him up.

"I'm sorry. I shouldn't have called. I forget normal people sleep at night."

"It's fine. I wasn't asleep. Are you okay?"

"No," I say and let a small, defeated laugh roll against my teeth.

"The day we searched the field you asked if we could have lunch, and I said no because I'm afraid of how I feel when I'm around you. When really you may have just needed a friend. I'm still such a narcissist."

"What's happened?" He is alert, his concern broadcasting across the airwaves.

"Are you busy?" I ask, turning the key in the ignition and calling the engine to life. My voice steadies, my hysteria abates.

"No."

"Can we meet for coffee?"

He chuckles. "Sure. Where?" We settle on a truck stop on the other side of Mattoon, about halfway for both of us. I would have driven all the way to Neoga to talk to him, but he suggested the truck stop, and I agreed.

I arrive before him and sit in a booth in the back, away from the windows. I stand up when he walks through the door and hug him, feeling the hesitation in his arms before they fold around me. I stand too long, breathing against his chest, but when I step back and sit down, I feel better, holding his hand across the table. "You always had that effect on me."

"Hmm?" he asks.

"Calming," I say, folding my fingers between his.

"So, what's going on tonight?"

"Nothing. It's been a crazy couple of weeks." Now that he's here, I don't know how to offer my ear to him. "I know you're going through a lot, and I want you to know that I can be a good listener if you ever want to talk."

"That's nice." He nods. "I appreciate that."

"Even if it's about your wife, you know?" The words "your wife" catch in my throat, and I wonder if he can hear the strangeness in how I say it. He has grown whole new dimensions in our absence from each other, and now I don't know where his edges are.

"I pretty much told you about her."

"I know. I just want you to know that it's okay for you to talk about what is going on in your life. I'm here to listen."

He lets out a sigh and leans back, pulling his hand free of me at the same time. He stares at me for a long second as if he is trying to read something on my face. "Did something happen tonight?"

I came here to give him the opportunity to talk, to prove that I'm not only interested in *me*, and he's making it so difficult. "Is this the first time you've been apart?"

"No." He shakes his head. "We've not been good for a long time."

"So you may be able to work it out," I say, hoping I sound hopeful, encouraging. It feels like a charade, and I know he sees through it.

"Nah. We're not going to work it out. We both thought the other would change, and people don't change like that." He looks so much older than thirty-four, with stubble on his chin, his ball cap casting his face into shadow.

"I'm sorry. That's hard."

"Yeah, the hard part is Daecus. I hate for him to have a broken family."

I nod but have no words, feeling guilty about pushing him to talk about something he clearly didn't want to talk about.

"Relationships are tough. Being married is hard. People think it's just about caring for each other, but it's more than that. Jake told me before I got married that I should marry the person who annoys me the least."

"That sounds like something Jake would say."

"Yeah. It was good advice."

"You didn't, though, did you? Marry the person who annoys you the least."

"No, and I annoy the hell out of her." We sit for a long second, and my hands ache to reach out and touch him, to connect with him. "What about you? I know you said you don't date, but surely you've had boyfriends."

"Not in a long time. You remember Warren, who I moved to Greenville with?" He nods and I continue. "He passed away a couple of weeks ago. That's where I was, at a celebration of his life." I shake my head, hearing how absurd it sounds.

Dylan leans forward again, closing my hands in his. He is a grounding wire in an electrical storm, tethering me to the earth. "I'm so sorry."

"I didn't even know he was in the area. He was a John Doe when he came into the hospital."

"Were you on duty?" he asks, and I am impressed that he would get that—that he would put those pieces together and know.

I pull one hand free and press the heel into my eyes, trying to push down the vision of his head lolling to the side, slack-jawed and hollow. "We couldn't bring him back. It reminded me of my mom. He looked like he'd been on a bender." I slide my hand back into his and study where our skin connects. "I don't do very well with a lot of chaos. I like to be in control of my world."

"I can see that, how you like to be in control. You were always kind of like that. Determined. That's why you don't date?"

"Yeah. You showing up really threw me for a loop." The honesty shocks me, but with his eyes cast in shadow from his cap, I can't tell if it is too much. I don't care. It is a night for telling truths, and when the next words cross the table, I'm not even surprised. "I always had a crush on you, and you . . . just all this, kinda threw me a bit."

"Oh." He cocks an eyebrow, but something in my face discourages him from mocking me. "So, you've only dated one man?"

"Two, I guess. I dated a man out in California for about six months. His name was Trey. He always made me think of you," I say, more truths, "When it came time to share my story, my history with him, I imploded."

"After that?"

"Nobody after that. I felt like I needed to grow up a little, and when I'd done that, dating just seemed too complicated." Three dates with John Kinney doesn't feel worth mentioning.

He nods as if he understands, and the waitress freshens our coffee.

"I just wanted you to know I will always be there for you, even if it's just friends. Life is too short."

He looks at me for a very long minute, and I begin to feel uncomfortable, a blush rising in my cheeks. I've misread him, I know. He wasn't thinking about me in any other way, and I just projected my desire onto him.

"So let's be friends. Okay? I have missed you." His voice is so soft, so familiar, so open to any possibility that I wish he would take off the hat so I could see his eyes, so I could know how he really feels.

"Okay. Let's be friends," I agree, and then I tell him that I found my father. It doesn't make any sense to say it, without any preamble, without any explanation, but he takes the shift in conversation without batting an eye.

"Oh, God," he says, and it sounds like a prayer.

I tell him about Stella Hayes sitting on my steps, coming to find me, and all the while, his thumb rubs along the base of my wrist.

"She left me a letter," I say, remembering. I jerk free and dig through my purse to find the envelope that I had folded and tucked away.

He moves into the bench beside me, and we read it together. It's just a simple note, an introduction, an apology for showing up unannounced, and a phone number if I choose to reach out. I sit, holding the sheet in my hands.

"Wow, Al. What are you going to do?"

"What do you mean?" I ask, not able to comprehend anything I should do.

"Are you going to meet him?"

"I don't know. I'm used to not having a father." I hand him the sheet and watch as he reads through it again.

"You may have brothers and sisters," Dylan says, and finally I feel the beginning of awe, something akin to what I felt when I first started the search for my grandparents.

"She said I was his only daughter."

"But brothers, you may have brothers."

I laugh, finally catching his excitement. "You think I should meet him."

"I don't know, but if I found out I had somebody else in the world, I'd want to meet them." He hands me the envelope after he has folded the sheet of paper and placed it inside.

"I think I should talk to my grandparents before I do anything."

He agrees, and we sit for another hour, letting conversations bloom and fade before we finally say goodbye in the parking lot. I drive back toward Charleston feeling more right in the world than I have in a long time. I'd forgotten what a decent person he is; I was so wrapped up in all the emotions he draws to the surface that I forgot that Dylan was first my friend.

15

Nobody recognizes the necklace that we found in the cornfield. They put a picture of it out on the news channels with hopes that somebody will know something about it. They are trying to keep her in everybody's thoughts, but the news marches on, and without any leads, Amy Kent begins to drift from the town consciousness. Of course, her mother is still out there, pleading for her to come home, with her other daughter at her side, looking so much like Amy that it is jarring.

I've not been sleeping well, and the nights when I don't work are the worst. Last night I talked to Dylan for an hour on the phone, and then I spent the rest of the night in my studio. When I sleep, I dream about Amy and relive the night she went missing, and never in my dreams do I manage to keep her from walking out the door. If she is dead, it is my fault, and I'm not the only one who believes that. I am becoming obsessed, and there seems to be nothing I can do to curb the obsession.

After a fitful night, I am pulled out of the depths of a dreamless sleep by a phone call from Detective Daniels, asking if I can come to the police station. It's then that I realize the sun is high; I finally did find sleep, empty and opaque, borne of pure exhaustion after hours spent restless in the studio. There is paint in the creases around my nails. My eyes feel bulbous with the night.

"Of course. I'll be over as soon as I've showered."

"Great. Come on around to the back."

"Yes, sir." The phone goes dead in my hand, and I set it down on the counter.

I wait for toast, staring at the sky through the window that overlooks the alley, picking flecks of paint from my skin. I roll the toast inside my mouth and try to get it down, but my throat closes, and I cannot swallow. I spit the masticated wad into the trash and drop the rest in behind it. Have they found something? Did they discover her body, the way the farmer found Cal in his shallow grave all those years ago? Is she dead?

I have thought about that last year with my mother a lot since the girl went missing. The story Warren told me about the week when Cal disappeared, has never settled inside my mind. He said my mom killed Cal, using a gun she had gotten from Warren. That's why the police were looking for Warren, because it was his gun that shot the fatal bullet. I've tried a thousand times over the years to understand how that might have played out. My mother wasn't a big woman, five-four standing straight up in tennis shoes, and at the end, she couldn't have been any more than one hundred fifteen pounds. I see her in my mind's eye, her jaw ratcheting the way it did when she was coming out of the drug. How did she get him to the back of that field? How did she shoot him? I'd never known her to touch a gun, let alone know how to fire one. How did Cal let that happen? He didn't look like much, but I know he was tough.

"He's got a mean hook." I hear the words and jerk around, half expecting to see Warren standing behind me. Of course, he isn't there. I am alone, and the voice is only a memory. Words I remember hearing about Cal. How would he let my little mother, my broken, pathetic, weak mother, get the jump on him? Then, how did she bury him, shallow grave or not? It doesn't make sense. It's hard to imagine her having the strength in her hand to pull the trigger, let alone drag a body.

They found Cal's car on the side of the road in Neoga, not far from the field, and the logistics have never worked for me. How did she get back to town? If she was driving her car, I guess, but how did she get him that far back in the field? Did they walk together, and then she turned and shot him? Was he chasing her and that's where she fell, and she shot him to keep him from killing her? I think she must have been in the car with Cal; they probably got in a fight, and she jumped out of the car, and he chased her. That's the only way I can make it work. But still, there's the gun.

When they found Cal's car, everybody thought he'd just broken down and gone off with a friend. He had quite a network back then. But how did my mother get back to town? She couldn't have walked, not from that distance. Did she call Warren? Or was Warren already there, waiting in the field? Had they planned it; was it an ambush? There was no love lost between the brothers. Did Warren shoot Cal and, then kill my mother because he was afraid she would tell? Did he plant the gun in our apartment? The neighbor heard my mother arguing with a man the day she died. I thought it was Cal when I heard, but later, the neighbor told me it was Warren's car she had seen leaving. Had Cal already been dead by then? It was Warren in our apartment the day she died; he admitted that much to me when he came to me at Life House. Did he stage the elaborate suicide, planting the gun to cover his tracks? Was the story he told something he constructed or the truth?

Was that the demon that haunted Warren through his life, the dark secret that never set him free?

I believed the version he told me because I was exhausted from being alive. I was pregnant with his baby. I needed him to be a good guy. I didn't question him; I took the words he said and stuffed them into one of the boxes in my mind and never looked at them again. I never allowed myself to doubt him. I simply closed the door and let it be. I couldn't fix it; I couldn't make it right. What's the difference, in the end, who pulled the trigger?

Irritation tightens my frame, and I make my way to the bathroom to shower. All of my freaking ghosts are walking with me. My life has exploded, and I am completely off my beam. For ten years, since I came back from California, and two before, my life has been quiet. When I left Cici's condo, it was like I stepped from the bustle of a busy city street to the alcove of a protected doorway. I've sheltered there, in my quiet world, ever since. I work nights, so I don't have to be part of the day.

Dylan flashes through my mind, one of my many ghosts. I want to call him, to ask him to come with me to the police station. He would come if I asked. I lose several long minutes thinking about Dylan, wondering what he is doing before I finally remember that I have somewhere I need to be.

I stand in front of the mirror, drying my hair, hearing the roar of the hair dryer but seeing my mother reflected.

"What really happened to Cal?" I ask my reflection that looks so much like my mother that it almost feels like she is here.

She doesn't answer, even when I ask several different ways. She has no words for me, sometimes she does, but not today. I turn off the dryer and stare at my own reflection, now just a faint echo of my mother. I wrap the cord and put the dryer away.

There is a gift waiting on the table beside the door, wrapped in pink with a yellow ribbon. It's for Jay and Serena's baby, and I grab it on my way out the door. I should have taken it to them a week ago, or more, but I keep making excuses not to go. Babies are hard. I put the gift in the trunk of my car and drive over to the police station. I could walk, but the day is already hot, and I don't have the energy.

I try to remember when I would have met Detective Daniels. It has bothered me ever since he said, "Nice to see you again," as if he knew me, as if I should know him. It had to be that last year before my mother died. I was questioned at the station after she died, but that wasn't him. That man had been freakishly tall, a caricature of Ichabod Crane. I let my mind roll back, trying to place him as I walk to the door.

"I'm here to see Detective Daniels."

The officer presses a button and speaks into the phone. Then, to me he says, "He's ready for you." He didn't even ask who I was, but I heard him say my name on the phone. How does he know me, too? He's about my age. I probably went to school with him, one of the many faceless people from my youth. My skin crawls down my back in the artificial chill of the station house. That's the only way he should know me if he remembers me from the past . . . because, in the present, I am invisible.

I walk around the desk and toward the office I know is Detective Daniels's and tap on the door when I reach it.

"Come in."

"You wanted to see me?"

"Close the door."

I do and sit down across from him at his desk. "Have you found Amy?"

"No. Not yet. But I wondered if I showed you some photographs of some cars, you might recognize the one you saw."

"I don't know. It was dark."

"Willing to try?"

"Of course."

He reaches to the table behind him and comes back with a manila folder.

I am unable to restrain the edge in my voice. "So, how did the word get out that I had seen her later? That reporter has been following me around like she thinks I had something to do with the disappearance. I thought we were going to keep that quiet."

"Yeah. I'm still trying to figure out who let that slip. It would have been better if we could have kept it quiet." He looks frustrated, disappointed, and I wonder how hard he is trying to figure it out.

"Well, it sure would have been better for me. I got this with my mail yesterday. Thought you might want to see it." I reach into my bag and pull out the note. It has no envelope; it was shoved through my mail slot for me to find when I got home.

He takes the paper from me, and his eyebrows do a dance, as he studies the typewritten words, pressed in and indenting the sheet. He is careful to touch it by the corners, and only barely. I've not been cautious like that and had even dumped it in the trash at first. I dug it out after he called.

It's why I didn't sleep well.

"You have no idea who left this?"

"No. It was there with my mail when I came home yesterday."

"No envelope?"

I shake my head, and he puts the note into a bag, its black words staring up at me from his desk: *Why •i• you let her go?* The "g" is misaligned, and I wonder if they could discover the typewriter that made the impression based on that.

"We'll dust it for prints, see if we get a hit."

"I just figured it was her mom; she's pretty vocal that she thinks I should have kept Amy at the clinic. Or the reporter."

"It might be, but we'll look into it. It's probably nothing, but it's good that you brought it in. Have you noticed anybody else following you? Anything out of the norm."

"No, just the reporter, but that's plenty enough. I feel like I'm a suspect or something." I wish I hadn't come forward. I wish I had just stayed in my world and not intersected with this other world.

"I'll talk to her. She's just looking for her next story, I'm sure."

"That's what I figured, but it's still uncomfortable." I nod and sit down, relief washing down my arms. I was afraid they had found her body and that we hadn't worked fast enough or hard enough to save her.

He holds my eyes for a second, and I suddenly remember how I know Detective Daniels. I am sixteen, my lungs are full of smoke, and vomit is on my pants leg where my mother chucked up the contents of her stomach. It is the day the trailer burned.

The day I was hit in the parking lot by Derrick Jessop.

The day I had walked from school home, my bruised brain swelling, distorting my thoughts.

The day I had poured alcohol through the trailer and set it alight.

The day I had tried to kill my mother.

My stomach rolls, and for a second I think I'm going to be sick, sweat prickling along my hairline, erupting over my lip.

I suck for air.

"Are you all right?"

"Yeah. I'm fine." I pause. He waits. "I just remembered when I met you."

"Oh yeah?"

"Yeah. I couldn't place it before. It was the day the trailer burned."

"Yep. That was it. You rescued your mom from the fire."

I nod. *Yes. Let's let that be the official record.*

"So let's look at some photos."

There are twelve 8x10s in the folder; each car offers some form of damage along the front driver's side fender. I sort through them, discarding all the ones that are too shiny or where the dent is too crumpled. I remove nine of the twelve, leaving three. Was there pinstriping? Racing stripes? I lay out the three in front of me on the desk and close my eyes, trying to drop back in time to that night when I watched the car pull away from the curb. The fold in the frame was dead center above the wheel well. I open my eyes and choose one of the photos.

I lift the image. "Maybe?" I offer.

"How sure are you?"

"I'm not. But this is closest. I think? I don't remember pinstripes, but I don't know that I would; it just seems too bright. I don't know how to describe it," I say. I feel like I've let him down by not being confident.

"All right. That's all we need."

16

Jay and Serena live in Champaign, and the thirty-minute drive to their house is just what I need to pull all the fraying edges of my soul back in place. Their home is a small ranch with a basement. I park in front and wait, having sent Jay a text, not wanting to disturb them if they are not ready for company. I watch the door, and within minutes, it opens. Jay smiles across the lawn to me.

"How is everybody?" I ask, handing him the gift.

"Sleeping," he whispers ushering me inside.

"I don't have to stay." I don't want to keep them from resting.

"No, it's good. We're glad you've come." He says "we," although there is no sign of Serena or the baby in the room beyond him. "I'm so glad you were there."

I laugh, letting the tension wash out of me. "Me, too. Serena would have done fine, though."

"But you knew just what to do."

"That's what happens when you're a nurse," I say with just a hint of dismissal. I know what he's trying to say, and I accept the compliment, but only because it's Jay. "How is fatherhood treating you?"

"It's amazing. Exhausting." We laugh, and he tells me how she wakes up to eat every two or three hours, how Serena is trying to sleep every time she sleeps. We are walking down the hall toward the bedrooms, and when we reach the nursery, he opens the door a breadth, and we slip through to stand at the side of the small crib.

The baby has dark hair and an olive complexion, her mouth tucked in like a bow, one little fist hovering in the air.

"Oh." My breath washes out of me at the sight of her. I put my arm around Jay's waist and squeeze him. "She's so beautiful. She is so tiny."

His face is just a proud smile, his eyes squinting to the smallest of slits. We exit the room, and he brings me to the kitchen where he pours me a cup of coffee. He talks, telling me everything they have learned, about changing diapers and belly gas, and how important it is to burp Brenna halfway through a feeding. I listen, having nothing to offer, no experience to share. Except for the one, and that one is only for me.

Ten minutes pass, and the monitor that Jay has carried with him chirps. He jumps up and heads for the nursery, and when he returns, his bright-eyed daughter is awake and burbling in his arms.

"Hold her?"

I hesitate, terrified that she will break. The baby looks fragile, with her tiny fists and feet flailing in the air.

"Serena's been pumping between feedings so I can let her rest when she can. I'll get a bottle." He passes her to me, and my heart stutters and stalls.

"Hello," I whisper, cradling her in one arm while my other hand catches her waving fist. She is warm and soft and cooing. "Look at you," I whisper, making my way with her into the living room to sit on the sofa.

Jay finds me and hands me a bottle, already warm. Before I can protest, I've placed the bottle in her mouth, and she is drinking, swallowing in long draws. Jay comes to sit beside me. He guides me, adjusting the tilt of her body, handling the burping himself before passing her back to me. We talk. Then she drifts to sleep again, and we sit in silence, looking down at his beautiful daughter. We study the lashes on her cheeks, the moist pucker of her lips.

It isn't until Serena comes from down the hall, her eyes puffed with sleep, that we even become aware of the room around us. She sits beside me, her hand cupping Brenna's fuzzed skull.

"You did good," I whisper, leaning into her.

"She is beautiful, isn't she?" Her pride drips from every word.

I nod.

"You need one," Serena purrs.

"Not me." I chuckle, and the baby shifts, reaching toward Serena even in her sleep as if she knows her mother has joined us. She stretches, her body arcing, a little muscle pulled tight. I pass the baby to Serena, and she nuzzles her. My arm is wet where Brenna's body had rested, sweating against my skin, and I can smell her, the sweet smell of baby powder and milk. "Is there anything you need? I can run to the store."

"No, we're fine." We sit.

"Was that Dylan Winthrop?" Jay asks

"When? At the McGills' party?" I clarify.

Jay nods, and I ask him how he knows Dylan. "I did go to high school with you," he says, a hint of laughter in his voice.

"I guess you did." I never knew Jay when I was in school. We met after I moved in with the McGills, and I never really went back to school after that.

"He seemed pretty happy to see you."

"We used to be good friends, back in the day."

"You were cute together," Serena says, and I hear the question in her voice.

I glance at her, shaking my head. "We're not dating."

"Maybe you should," she says, winking. It's all well intentioned, I know. Everybody thinks I need to get out of my shell, and they all want to help me.

"Hm." I blow out a noncommittal breath. "He's still married."

"Of course I mean you should wait till he isn't married." Serena clarifies, sounding offended that I could have thought she would mean anything else.

The television is on, the volume low, and I turn away to look at it, hearing the shift in the news. I know Jay and Serena surely notice the nervous flush rising in my cheeks at the mention of Dylan. I'm thirty-two years old, and I'm still such a child. I don't know if I'm angry at

Dylan for walking back into my life or terrified that I'm going to fall in love with him all over again—or even worse, that I never stopped loving him in the first place. My heart has been through too much; I don't think it can handle another break. It's still not healed from the first time, from all my first times.

The image of Amy Kent fills the screen, and I lean forward to listen. Another photograph replaces it, of a man, middle-aged, average-looking. I click the volume up another notch. "Police are looking for Shawn Mallory in connection with the disappearance of Amy Kent."

"Have you been following this?" I ask when the bulletin is over.

"No. Not really," Jay says.

"I saw her the night she disappeared. I was one of the last people to see her." It has had the desired effect, and they drop the subject of Dylan Winthrop.

***

When I leave their house, I feel hollow and empty. Holding their baby has made me ache. I sit through a green light, and another red, not wanting to go home, not knowing where else I can go. I keep checking my mirror, looking for the news van, wondering how far they would travel to follow me and why. I could go to the mall. I could go to a movie. My phone vibrates in my purse, and I dig for it.

I find it and answer the call. "Hey!"

"What are you doing?" Charley's voice is quiet, almost a whisper.

"Nothing."

"Can you come see me?"

"Sure. Are you okay?"

"Yeah." The word draws out in a long breath, a sigh.

I flip my blinker and wait for the light to turn again. "Charley?"

"My brain is turning to mush."

"On my way. I'll be there in thirty minutes." She has no idea how badly I needed a place to go. She does it a lot, opens the door when I need it, when I would never open it for myself.

17

Charley, like me, has baggage. Both of us tend toward depression; both of us have histories and scars like a minefield. Where my mother was broke, Charley's mother was selfish. Where my mother was neglectful, maybe, Charley's mother was spiteful. Where my mother could never find a man to keep her, Charley's mother inspired obsessions. Where my mother's relationships were verbal, filled with conflict and fight, Charley grew up with fists and belts and locked doors. She once spent a weekend locked in the closet because her mother went to Vegas to meet a man while her father was away on business. My mother rotated men through our life; Charley's mom rotated men through her marriage. Where my mother committed suicide, Charley's father murdered her mother in a jealous rage, and that's how she came to be at the McGills' Home for Lost Kids. Hers is a story you read about happening to somebody else—you never actually know the people involved. Her father is still in jail, and she gets letters from him once a month, and she always writes back.

Charley now is a woman at peace with her life, secure in her family, confident of her choices. Her youth was much harder than mine, and somehow Charley has stepped out of it and built a beautiful family. I don't know how she has done it, going straight from that to Leslie's and then to marriage, but she did, and it worked. She was younger than me when she came to the McGills' and had more time to grow up there, with all the positive influences of that typical, healthy family surrounding her.

Why haven't I been able to do that? I have no delusions about the life I live, the quiet, hiding-from-the-world life I live. When John Kinney started asking me out, after several weeks, I finally said yes. We have things in common; we're nurses, we both take care of other people. He's handsome and kind. He doesn't know my history, didn't go to school with me, and never met my mother. He thinks I'm normal. I tried hard to make myself okay enough to date, to take a chance. He is a nice guy, and I believed that if I could learn how to date, then I would finally be okay. We went out three times, and it was okay, enjoyable even. Then, at the end of the third date, he took me in his arms and kissed me solidly on the mouth.

He had wanted to come into my apartment, and I made excuses, pushing away, trying not to offend him, but not inviting him inside. Finally, he had left, and I could see that he was confused and hurt. We had a good time together, hadn't we? The next day I walked onto the hospital floor and saw him down the hall, smiling, seeing me. I'd waved but turned into the HR office and requested a shift change instead. I never explained it to him. I never told him my history. I just removed myself from his orbit and hoped it would be enough. He had looked so happy to see me that day, and that's what did me in. He thought I was "perfect," and the pressure of keeping up that pretense was more than I could handle. He was too much like Trey, and if I dated him, I would be pretending not to be who I am, and I would always be waiting for that next skeleton to drop out of my closet and onto the floor in front of him.

He caught me in the hall, later, after he'd seen that I was switching shifts, annoyed but polite.

"Switching shifts?" he had asked.

"Yeah, I think it will work better for me," I said, unable to look him in the eye.

"Hmm. 'Cause it feels like you're kind of avoiding me. Did I do something to upset you?"

"No. You didn't do anything. You know, I just can't date."

"I thought we had something. I mean, I really like you."

"It was fine. It's just me, not you, John. You're a great guy, and some woman is going to be very lucky to have you."

"Just not you?"

"Not me. It's complicated." How could I possibly explain all the dark ridges in my life?

"Gonna make for a lonely life, but all right." He stood a second longer, looking down at me. "You know, you could have just told me that you didn't want to go out with me. I am a grownup. Maybe you should try that next time." A small flash of anger welled and ebbed across his face.

The implication that I was not a grownup, that I was still a child, running away and pushing things under the rug, rang out clear and loud in the hall.

He had turned and walked away from me, forgot me entirely, as far as I could tell. After that, every time his eyes caught mine, I looked away in shame. I should have handled that differently.

I park behind Charley's Odyssey and walk the sidewalk to her stoop. She opens the door and lets me in. A red bandana hides her hair. She only wears a bandana when she's due for a color or a cut. "What's going on?" We hug, and she draws me across the threshold. Music is pounding from one of the upstairs rooms, and her middle child is standing at the dining room table studying a set of Lego schematics for some ship from Star Wars. I never saw any of those movies, so I don't know. "Hey, Smith!" I call, and he nods, too intent to speak. He is nine and tall for his age. Charley leads us through to the kitchen and offers coffee.

I accept and settle on one of the stools at her counter. She stands; she almost never sits still. Heavy footfalls punctuate the music from upstairs. "Sounds like they're going to come through the ceiling."

"I know." Charley makes her eyes wide. "They're working on a routine."

Her oldest is in high school and is part of the dance squad. "I guess all those years of ballet are paying off."

"Pfft, there is no ballet happening up there. That's Tea Diddy or Joe Bangles or Mouthpiece. I don't know. I've gotten too old. I can't keep up," she says, and I laugh.

We talk, in a general way, catching up about her married life. Her mother-in-law is coming for the week, and I can tell with a quick glance around the house. Even the baseboards are clean. I can place the faint scent of vinegar. Charley is organic, all natural. There are no toxic chemicals in her home, and even her laundry detergent is homemade, with baking soda and Borax or something. The counters and kitchen table are lined with cooling trays filled with Charlotte Suds, her specialty soaps. The vinegar scent is mixed with patchouli and vanilla and lavender—musky, sweet, and aromatic.

I select a tray and lean in to sniff. I love Charlotte Suds. We split the cost of booth rental for most of the festivals over the summer. I sell my art, and she sells her soap. She is a better salesperson than I am, and my most significant sales always happen when I've stepped away from the booth.

"I just met Jay and Serena's little girl."

"Aww. How are they?" I tell her how tiny and precious the baby is, how Serena is trying to catch up on sleep, and how Jay looks like a peacock, proud and protective.

"How'd you do?" She knows about the baby that I let go.

"Okay. Baby's are tough." The conversation rolls.

She talks about Carmi getting a promotion to foreman at the plant. She talks about Cheyenne, the daughter upstairs, planning to do the county-fair pageant. We talk about Smith; he has decided to play the alto sax in band next year. We talk through all of "life" as her youngest, Brooke, lies on the kitchen floor coloring, the cat curled at her side, one amber eye trained on us. Finally, we get around to the upcoming festivals. From the count of her soaps, she's expecting a lot of business.

"That's a lot," I comment, indicating the number of soaps cooling and others already packaged.

"I have two bulk orders. Twenty a piece."

"That's great," I say, excited for her, because selling homemade soap isn't an easy business.

"Yeah. Both from the university. One of the counselors gives them as welcome-to-the-floor gifts, and another . . . well, I don't know what she does with them, but she keeps buying them."

We talk about the prints I'll have, the new works I'll hang to promote my portrait work.

"I think you're missing the boat, not putting *The Baby* into the mix."

She's talking about the painting of Emily Ann.

"I'm not putting her up here," I say, and Charlotte shrugs. It's not the first time she has said that I should include *The Baby*. She's right. I always get commissioned to do family and kid portraits when Emily Ann hangs, but I don't want her displayed here in town. It's too personal where people know me.

"You'll take her to the big show in Springfield, though?"

"Yeah. Of course." I always take her to Springfield.

I relax, sitting in her kitchen, feeling the rhythm of her life around me. "How do you do it?" I ask when my coffee is gone and all the stress of the past week lies like dust on the floor.

"Do what?"

"This?" I spread my arms and take in her home, her full life, her healthy children.

"You mean my *chaos*?" she coos. "Chaos" is my word.

"Yes."

"I think, um, you just have to be willing to let there be a little mess."

"I don't think I'll ever be able to do that."

"Maybe not," she admits. It's one of my favorite things about her; she doesn't try to sugarcoat it.

"Do you remember Dylan Winthrop?" I ask.

"Of course. He was a good kid. Wasn't he the 'big crush'?" I forget sometimes that Charley knows him from when he stayed with the McGills after his brother died. It was a short-term situation, but Dylan is pretty close with them, still.

"Yeah, him. He's moving back to town."

"I saw him at the party." Of course she would have noticed.

"Yeah. He's getting divorced." I drop the words, trying to sound casual, hearing the failure.

"Oh." She gets my meaning. "Be careful. *Getting divorced* isn't the same as *divorced*." Her gimlet eye sees through me, and a fluttery smile plays at my lips then scampers away.

"I'm not going to do anything. We're just friends."

"I'm sorry, honey. Someday it's all going to work out for you. I know it will."

Charley is an incurable romantic. "I know. I'm okay. Better alone."

"You are not like your mother." Her voice is little more than a whisper. "You're not."

"How do you know?"

"Because I've met you." She puts her hand on my arm. "You can't live your whole life like this; you can't imagine what you are missing."

"I know what I'm missing, Charley," I say, and my voice is colder than I mean for it to be.

She leans and hugs me, and a tight knot swells in my chest. I know what I'm missing. Every second of every day, I know what I am missing.

"It's been a tough couple of weeks," I say, and a small shudder washes through my frame. We've not had a chance to talk in a long time. Her life is busy with kids and family and making things happen, like the party for the McGills.

We spend the next hour and then another catching up. I tell her about Amy Kent coming into the clinic and let the story fall out, trying to work out the details.

"I know her family. Her mom works at the plant with Carmi. Good lady. She makes an incredible apple crumble."

"What about her dad?" Nobody has mentioned him at any of the pressers.

"I don't think he's in the picture. Not for a long time. I don't know the story there." She refreshes our coffee. "Was that your Warren in the paper?"

"Yeah, it was."

"That's tragic," she says, resting her hand on my arm. "You definitely have had a crazy couple of weeks."

I nod.

Our conversation stalls, and I begin feeling the need to push off, to move on. A thump rebounds from upstairs, and we hear laughter. Charley rolls her eyes, and I laugh. I love her chaos. I tug my hand out of hers and stand up to go.

Her life is loud in a happy way. Is that even something I want?

Part Two: Summer

18

The town is plastered over with fliers. Amy's aunt and mother are less visible but still trying to keep her in the media after twenty-one days. The news cycle churns, and although she doesn't get mentioned on every newscast, she is mentioned sometimes. The town came together and offered a reward for information, and I donated a thousand dollars. "She's just a child," they say, and "Please come home." It is incongruous, to see their faces on the TV, pleading for Amy to "come home." Does that mean something, that particular choice of words? Do they think Amy is a runaway and not an abductee? When she came to the clinic, she said that he was "gonna take care of her"—doesn't that suggest willingness? She was only fourteen.

Is. She is only fourteen.

Was she in crisis, when I let her walk away? Nobody was paying attention to her until she was gone, except the wrong people, or is that just me? Am I projecting the person I was at that age, how isolated and uncared for I felt? Is it me, the memory of my former self, that wakes me in the night? Is she locked in a basement somewhere or just hiding from her family because they don't approve of her boyfriend?

The search had the whole town on edge for about a week, but now it's just part of the fabric of our lives. It's slipped off the radar as if we've given up, or just lost interest. People are moving on with their normal routines. Entire days slip past without a single mention of her. Humans are fickle. They get excited about the next new thing and forget everything that came before.

Detective Daniels told me, in one of my many phone calls, that Shawn Mallory, who owned the car I picked out of the photographs, was a complete miss. They questioned him, but he was at work that Saturday night, a solid alibi, with plenty of people to corroborate.

Carrying my canvases down to my car, I pass one of the many fliers of Amy. Up and down the stairs, I pass it eight times, there on the door to my apartment building. I wonder if it was placed there for my bene-fit, as a judgment about my failure to keep Amy from leaving the Crisis Clinic that night. Did that horrible reporter woman put it there? The flier is getting worn, faded by the elements, and I try not to look at her ghostly image, her pale countenance. I stack the canvases, which are not for sale, in the back seat. I only sell prints at the festivals; the paintings are displays for my custom work. The bread and butter of my work. Custom work takes time and effort, and I no longer feel guilty asking my due.

The 4-H barns are already full when I arrive, and the smell of horses and livestock is thick in the heat. I drive past them to the vendor build-ing and park in the loading zone. Others are here as well, preparing to sell everything from crocheted doilies to pottery. Charley is already in-side, setting up our booth. I prop my canvases along an edge of the table and then give her a hug. She follows me out to get the rest of my art.

***

My bestseller is a print called *Tumult*. It's the oldest piece that I've kept in the rotations. It is based on an art project from when I was still in high school—three horses in a storm. I can't look at it without feel-ing some of the turmoil from that last year with my mother, but it feels nostalgic now, looking at it with one eye closed. It's been a long time, and when I finally painted that piece, I was in a good place by then, so it also feels like hope. I'm not as creative as I used to be—my art is more precise, more skilled now. The energy is different. I've gotten better at the "skill" of painting, but my newer works lack passion. People don't want "passion" on their walls, though; they want a pretty scene. I've al-ways done my best art when the rest of my life is in crisis. I display *Tu-*

mult in the highest central peak and two portraits on each side. I set the photo album out, open, ready to be flipped through. Charley keeps a stream of conversation rolling as we set up.

"He's gonna have to have surgery," she is saying, and I realize that I've lost the thread of her words somewhere along the line.

"Who?" I ask, and she rolls her eyes, knowing that I've only been listening with half an ear. She has known me a long time and is used to me being distracted.

"Carmi." She lets the "i" stretch out long.

"What?" I stop positioning prints and turn to give her my full attention. "Why is he having surgery?"

"He was up on the catwalk night before last, and damn thing busted through," she says without inflection, as if he stubbed his toe going to the bathroom in the night.

"Oh, no!"

"Yep, nearly tore his leg off."

"Why are you here? You should be home with him."

"No. He's quite glad I finally left. He's sleeping."

"What if he has to get up for anything? What if he has to pee?"

"He has a bottle." She giggles.

"You are so wrong! You should be there."

"Nah. His brother is two doors down; he's probably hanging out already. He came over last night with some video game, and they played that stupid thing for three hours."

"Is he in a lot of pain?"

"He's on a lot of medicine. So I hope not." I ask her which doctor he is seeing and she says, "Dr. Ahmet? I think."

"Oh. He's good. He's a great surgeon." I relax. Carmi will be fine. Dr. Ahmet is competent and diligent about his follow-up care.

Charley goes on, talking about workman's comp, how the crew leader came by, looking like a whipped pup. "They're scared he's going to sue them."

"He probably could." I reach into my purse to bring out the money I pulled from the bank for the cash box. The envelope Stella Hayes left at my door flutters from my bag and lands on the table. Charley and I both watch it; the moment freezes in time.

"What's that?" she asks, snatching the envelope from the table before I can move for it.

"Nothing. So is Carmi going to sue them?"

"No. We're not *those* people." She says it with disgust; she is proud that she and her family doesn't ask for anything.

She looks up at me, her eyes curious, questioning. I should have told her about this letter already, but I liked it being something between just Dylan and me.

Charley is holding the envelope up to me, and I can't help but see Stella's slanted, hurried words: *Your father just wants to meet you.*

"What is this? You found your dad?"

"No." I shake my head, and she lets me take the envelope. "I didn't find him. He found me."

Her excitement at this news makes her feet dance. "This is great news, Al." I'm not as convinced that it is great news, but now that she knows, it feels less like a secret and more like a fact. "When did this happen?"

"I don't know, a couple of weeks ago? His wife showed up, was sitting on my steps when I came home. I was kinda rude, you know? I asked if he needed a kidney."

"Oh, heavens. You and that mouth. How did she respond to that?"

"She said I was my father's daughter, 'cause that sounded like something he'd say." My mother used to say that I was like him when she was mad at me and wanted to insult me. Stella hadn't meant it as an insult.

"Are you going to meet him?"

"I don't know. Probably. I want to talk to my grandparents first. I feel like they should know."

"He's your dad. Of course you should meet him."

People are beginning to filter down the walkways. I want to tell Charley that it's complicated, but she already knows. We are interrupted by an elderly couple who stop to admire the soaps. "My husband has this rash, you see?" the old lady says, lifting the tail of his shirt.

"Yes, ma'am," Charley says, smiling. The old man pats his wife's hand away, and his shirt falls back into place. He mutters under his breath as he lifts one of Charley's soaps to his nose and sniffs.

Charley slips into her sales routine, talking about the hypoallergenic nature of her soaps. "They have less water than soaps you buy in the store, which are mostly water, so my soaps last longer." While she is distracted, I stuff the envelope back into my purse and finish setting up the cash box. Their conversation is close and quiet, not airing the poor old man's business to the world. When they have selected a trial set, I step out of the way for her to handle the transaction.

"Well, Mrs. Funkhouser, if these work out for him, I'm happy to deliver right to your home in the future, save you from getting out."

"That would be a good thing, then. I hope they work. They sure smell nice."

"This here is my business card, you call me anytime and let me know how things are working out." This is one of the many things that I love about Charley, her ability to make everybody feel important and special, and it didn't cost her a single cent.

Charley turns back to me, her eyebrows raised as if we are still in a conversation.

"What?"

"I was thinking . . . you shouldn't go alone when you meet him, and you should probably meet in a public place."

"Yeah, I thought of that. Might not even be him, probably scammers looking for money." A small bubble in my breast deflates, and I realize how much I have hoped it is him, how badly I still want to meet him after all these years.

"I'm so excited for you."

"Am I inviting trouble home for dinner, though?" I want her to understand.

"No, not if it's him. A dad is important, even if he is coming to the table late." Charley never misses a visit with her dad at the prison in Joliet. He's coming up for parole next year, and his relationship with his daughter and her family has been integral in getting him a hearing.

Charley writes a letter a month to the dean at the prison, asking for a parole hearing.

"What will I say to him?"

"Start with 'Hi, Dad, I'm Alison.'" She cocks an eyebrow but doesn't say anything more. I stew, my stomach churning as if the meeting were imminent and not just something that may or may not happen in the future. I thought I had made peace with him not being in my life. I've made peace with my childhood and all my missing parts. I thought I had, but I may have just bandaged over the hole where they used to live.

Our booth has several people around it, and two different people are flipping through my photo albums. I look up, scanning the walkways, seeing streams of people as they work their way from the barns.

Dylan is standing on the other side of the aisle, his son beside him, holding his hand. He is watching me when my eyes finally land on his. His eyebrow twitches up, and they walk across the aisle. I have no idea how long they've been standing there, how long he has been watching me.

"These are good." He inspects *Tumult* for a moment, then turns to me. "Can I buy that?"

"No." I laugh.

"Well, you're not very good at the selling part." I put my fist against his chest and push lightly. I need to touch him, to feel the heat of him. He has no idea how *not goo*⁎ at selling I am.

"The original is not for sale, but I have prints," I explain and lead them over to the rack. "How are you, Daecus?"

"I'm good. Are you going to ride rides with us?"

"I am. Is that okay?"

Daecus nods, and Dylan lifts him onto his hip so that he can see down into the print stand. They flip through, stopping at one. "What do you think of this one?"

Daecus wrinkles his nose, and they continue flipping. I smile at his honesty and love that he didn't feel obligated to like it just because it's mine. "I like that one."

"I like that one, too," Dylan agrees. "Let's remember that one. There might be another one you like more." They continue flipping, and Daecus stops him.

"This is the one." He is confident, and Dylan nods.

I check the number on the print and pull a corresponding tube from one of the hampers I use to store them. I've already pulled *Tumult* and add the print *The Jenny Sue* to it.

"Of course, he picks a boat," Dylan says.

Daecus grins. "I like boats."

"Me, too," I say in a comradely fashion. Dylan is still looking through the prints, focused and intent.

"How about W-18?" Dylan asks, and I smile. The W series is from the woods that ran behind our houses when we were growing up, and 18 is looking from the woods to the pasture at Winthrop farm with the three horses.

"You like that one?"

"Looks like home." His voice is calm, unemotional, but when he looks at me, there is emotion marching across his face, and for the first time, I know Dylan has regrets. His eyes are soft, and even though he smiles at me, it is the saddest smile I have ever seen.

19

Later, when the afternoon spreads hot like fire, I leave the booth with Charley in charge. Her soaps have been a hit, and she is animated and happy, chatting up customers as they pause. She'll sell more of my work while I am gone for this hour than I've sold all day.

Daecus is halfway through a cone of cotton candy, and one sticky hand is in mine as we walk the trail between the rides. It's a county fair, and the smell of food mixes with the smell of trampled grass and the oil on the machines. The fair hawkers travel from town to town working the fair, and I remember a time when I thought it would be a glorious life to be free like that. Looking tired and dirty from their summer on the road, they call out to entice us to the games as we pass.

Dylan is counting our tickets, planning out which rides we will ride.

"They found her." I hear the words, a whisper on the wind, and turn, trying to find the source, but then the words are spreading through the crowd, jumping like embers to brush.

"They found her," another voice says. The rumor is spreading.

"They found her." Another voice from ahead of us in line at the bumper cars.

"It wasn't her." A voice behind.

I turn, pushing myself into the conversation. "Who?"

"Amy Kent." The girl nods at a faded poster hanging on one of the poles.

"They found her?" I ask, needing to hear it directly.

"No, they thought it was her, but it's some other chick, holed up in a dorm room in Champaign. Ran off with her boyfriend," the other girl says, rolling her eyes.

"It wasn't Amy?"

The girl shakes her head, looking at me like I'm intruding on her conversation—which, of course, I am.

I'm not convinced. Maybe it was Amy, and this girl doesn't know. I lift a finger, asking Dylan to give me a second. He nods, and I step out of line, pulling my phone and calling Detective Daniels, who had given me his direct line when I first came forward about Amy coming to the clinic, something I am sure he has grown to regret.

"Daniels here,"

"Hey, Detective. This is Alison. People are saying you found Amy?"

"No, Alison. That was a girl from Shelbyville, ran off with her boyfriend."

"So, nothing new?" I am too involved, too invested.

"Nothing solid. We have had some new light shed on Amy's case."

"What?" I am breathless.

"It's beginning to look like she is probably a runaway. We're still searching and have put out feelers to other departments, but chances are, if she doesn't want to be found, we won't find her."

"No. I don't think so, Detective."

"I understand that you feel particularly invested in this case, but it's really best if you let us do our job." Detective Daniels sounds weary, tired.

"But you are not doing your job, Detective. She's still missing," I say but without malice. "I wish I had seen who she was with."

"Yeah, me, too. We don't have much to go on, Alison."

"You can't just give up."

"Listen, I'm telling you this because you've been helpful in this case, and because I understand why you feel so strongly about it, but her family thinks she ran away. She took clothes; she packed."

"Oh." That does change everything. Would she have packed a bag if she had intended to come home? No. I feel like a dolt; I've been sucked into somebody's game. Why are they out there trying to get airtime, begging for her to come home if they just think she ran away? I apologize for calling, for disrupting his day, and disconnect the phone, stepping back in line. "Sorry," I say to Dylan.

"That's all right. Any news?"

"Wasn't her." He deflates, just the way I had, and I wonder if it makes him think of his lost brother. He drops his arm over my shoulders and squeezes. Daecus slips his hand into mine, and for a split second, he is not Daecus, Dylan's son; he is the little girl I lost so long ago. Tears spring from my eyes, streaming down my face before I even know they are coming. "They think she ran away. They aren't even really looking," I whisper, mouthing the words more than saying them, not wanting Daecus to hear.

Dylan folds around me in one deft motion, letting me bury my face in the heat of his chest.

"You okay?" he asks when I've begun to pull myself together.

I nod, hiccuping a small laugh. "I'm sorry." I wrinkle my nose at Daecus, who is looking up at me, worried. He shrugs, giving me a pass, taking my meltdown in stride. I wonder if he is used to seeing women cry. Is his mother prone to crying? Is she hysterical, the way I feel?

I pull myself upright and disengage. The line has shifted forward, and my blood thrums in my veins. What if they never find her? What if we never know what happened? How do I move on? I've been in limbo since she went missing, and she wasn't even somebody I knew. How does anybody go on? How can they just stop looking? Even if she is a runaway, she's only fourteen. She's not ready to be on her own.

But people are moving on. The news barely touches on her now, and she's not even been gone for a month. Maybe she did just run away, I think, trying to put a positive spin on it so I can move on, too. Perhaps she made a choice.

At fourteen? Running away doesn't ever turn out good. My mother's voice echoes from so long ago.

I catch snippets. "She told him she was pregnant. You know. Trying to hook him into marrying her." The low tone of derision in the speaker's voice makes me step away from Dylan and turn to the man speaking. They aren't talking about Amy; they are talking about this other girl. I bite my tongue to keep from reading them the riot act about how babies are made, how it takes two, but only the girl is ever blamed, left to deal with the consequences.

I'm grateful when the line shifts forward, and we finally make it to the steps leading up to the ride. The girl I had spoken with has moved away, deciding to ride something other than the bumper cars.

Dylan and Daecus have taken my tears in stride, and again Daecus stands with his sticky fingers in mine. Dylan stands slightly behind me, casting us in shadow, and when I look up at him, the sun melts around his face like a halo, an effect only somewhat diminished by his grin.

Daecus is a ferocious competitor. He is barely tall enough to ride on his own, and he manipulates the pedals and steering wheel of his go-cart with determination. He is uncompromising and hits every car that comes in range without prejudice.

"Are you practicing for Nascar?" I ask when we are climbing down the steps after the ride is over, and he grins.

We ride everything, the Tilt-O-Whirl, the Octopus, the Soul Train, and the Tom Twister, the last of which nearly steals my lunch. We head back toward the barns to relieve Charley.

"You're a little green," Dylan says, laughter in his voice.

"So are you," I say, although he isn't. He is gorgeous, the pink rising under his tan the way it does, the tips of his ears red from the heat and sun.

"No. That was nothing." He grins.

"I was fine till the floor fell out, ugh."

He laughs, his hand squeezing my shoulder as we come into the shade of the barns.

Our booth has a small group of people standing within, and we stay back, not wanting to interrupt Charley's routine. Every person leaves with a tube or soap, and I walk to the stall silently clapping my hands. "I told you she was amazing," I whisper to Dylan, loud enough for her to hear.

"P-shaw," Charley says, fluttering her hand. "Did you hear?" she asks, passing bottles of water to Dylan and Daecus from our cooler.

"About Amy?"

"Yeah, they found her. Up in Champaign."

"Wasn't her," I say, keeping my voice neutral, trying to keep myself in check this time.

"No, it was. This girl was pregnant."

"It wasn't her," I say, knowing for a fact.

"Sure sounded like her, ran off with her college boyfriend." Charley sneers. She doesn't have a very high estimation of the general population; she is jaded by the life she has lived.

"Well, somebody did, but it wasn't her. Some girl from Shelbyville." There was a time when I thought I could solve my problems by making a man take care of me. I glance at Dylan, blushing, remembering that it wasn't just any man I had wanted to care for me; it was Dylan.

"This has been fun," I say, shifting the conversation back. We've had a good afternoon. I don't want to end it with Amy.

"We're gonna head out," Dylan says, sliding his hand down the curve of my back, sending chills rocketing across my skin. He sees the gooseflesh rising. "I see I still have it," he whispers, close to my ear. I roll my eyes and shift away.

"Daecus, thanks for the whiplash," I say, kneeling down in front of him.

"You're welcome." His voice is cocky, confident, very suggestive of the teen he will be, but his arms wrap around my neck like he has known me all his life, just like a little boy.

When I stand up, Dylan folds around me before I can protest. There was no time for me to turn and redirect his attention. His body is hot and solid against mine, and I remember him, flashing in my mind. His hands inside my bathrobe, his lips on mine. I close my eyes and melt into him. I will take this moment, this one perfect minute.

His lips brush a kiss on my jaw as he pulls away, and I'm not sure if it was a kiss or just an accidental touch. My bones are liquid, my heart stammers in my chest, and the heat rising in my face is like a torch set to sear. When he releases me, I need support, something to keep me upright. I rest my hand on the table next to Charley's store of soap.

"Charley," Dylan says, tilting an imaginary cap. "It's always a pleasure."

"Indeed," she ruffles Daecus's hair, and then they walk away, glancing back only once as they reach the door heading back out into the sunshine, and I have not moved, watching them go. My breath has stalled in my throat.

When they are gone, eaten by the sun, I draw a stuttering breath, peeling my eyes from where they had been.

20

It's been upwards of two hours since Dylan and Daecus left the Art Walk, and Charley and I have had a steady stream of lookie-loos passing our stand. A single person made up the bulk of the afternoon's sales. She bought an assortment of Charlotte Suds and three prints from me. "I'm new to the area, just setting up a house," she had said, and after some conversation, none of which touched on her slightly foreign accent or where she had moved from, we understood that she was taking up a post at the university in the Economics department.

The prints she chose were some of my more placid offerings, done in subtle shades of blue and green, florals. She asks if I frame, and I agree, for an additional fee, to matte and frame the works and even deliver them to her home. "That would be just lovely." She smiles, and Charlotte and I both gush a little. She's the epitome of a well-mannered woman, well brought up, classy. She is exactly what Charley and I are not, and brushing up against her, having her tell us how "simply fabulous" we are, makes us both ache for want of a standard childhood.

Regardless of her elegant way, her affluent manner, we are both quietly relieved when she has moved on down the row. All of those niceties are exhausting. Exhilarating at first, but after a bit, it wears on us both. I'd wondered for a second which of us would curse first, to break the spell.

Charley looks at me when the woman is gone, and her little sense of otherworldliness has faded. We both let out a long breath as if it had taken us that long to again be able to breathe. Then we laugh, finally comfortable in the skin we live inside, as the people we truly are.

It is then that I see her, Amy, walking past the open doorway at the far end of the building. "Oh, God," I whisper, taking a step in the direction of the door.

"What is it?"

"I think I've seen Amy Kent." My first impulse is to phone Detective Daniels, but then I remember that I've already phoned him once today, and while he hasn't said as much, I know he wishes I would call less, intrude less, interfere less. I should be sure before I call. "I'll be back," I call out to Charley as I step into a jog, down the aisle, past the milling townsfolk.

It is as if the crowd has multiplied threefold since I was out earlier. I come up short, trying to catch a glimpse of the girl I had seen walking past the door. What was she wearing? I don't know; I don't know. Shorts, a t-shirt, probably, like every other person crowding the path between concessions and rides. I want to call out but imagine all the people turning to look at me, seeing me become visible, like a ghost dusted with flour. I don't call out but make my way through the crowd with as much haste as I can, trying to see into the rides as they spin.

There she is, up ahead, standing in line for the Hurricane. Her back is to me, but it's the same dark hair, the same build. She is on the ride before I can reach her, and I stand on the outside of the fence, looking like a crazy person, trying to catch sight of the girl as she spins past. She is laughing; her mouth open in the thrill of the ride, her lips painted a garish red, a color that is much too old for her. She is with friends, two others, squashed in the seat, laughing every time the ride jerks them back around again.

I'm uncertain, now that I see her, and I need the ride to end so I can see her without her head jerking. My phone is in my hand, waiting until I am sure, with my finger on the button that will dial Detective Daniels.

"I've found her," I imagine saying as the ride jerks and spins. I imagine the look on that horrible newswoman's face when she has to report that Amy has been discovered, safe and sound by the very same woman who failed to keep her safe in the first place. My thumb itches to press the button, but I wait. The ride is slowing down. Somebody pushes against me from the back, and my phone cracks against the fence, slipping from my fingers and falling inside the enclosure. I kneel down and retrieve it, and when I look up again, the girls are coming down off of the ride, and she is turning away.

"Amy," I call out when I think she is going to slip away again, and the girl turns, hearing the name and catches my eyes above the crowd.

It's not her. She is standing still, though, waiting for me, and I am moving in her direction. It's not her, but the features are very similar. Her friends stand behind her, waiting, and it is clear that this girl is the leader of the pack.

"I'm sorry. I thought you were someone else."

"Amy?"

"Yeah, the girl who is missing," I say, hoping that explains why I would follow, why a stranger would call out. "You look a lot like her."

"Yeah, she's my sister," she says, and I remember her now, with longer hair, standing between her mother and aunt on the news reports when Amy had only been gone a few days.

"Oh. I'm so sorry."

A light shifts in her eyes, and suddenly she recognizes me. "You're that woman from the clinic, aren't you?"

I don't quite understand her tone and am a little taken back, "I am. I wish I had kept her that night."

"Why did you tell the police that? Why did you make that shit up?"

"Excuse me?"

"No way Amy was pregnant. She didn't even have a boyfriend." She sneers. "Your life must be pretty pathetic to be saying something like that."

She turns away from me while I stand with my mouth gaping, feeling the way I did when I was young and didn't understand anything about why my life was the way it was. I feel like I've been slapped.

Beyond the insult, the suggestion that I made up the story about Amy coming to the clinic, which I didn't, the girl's insistence that Amy didn't have a boyfriend says that perhaps her family doesn't know her as well as they think. Is that why Detective Daniels has closed me out of the loop, told me they think she ran away? Do they think I'm some crazy person inserting myself into the situation? But she was there at the clinic. Mary was there; she'd remember. No . . . actually, she wouldn't. She was on a suicide call, had gone to the side room and closed the door by the time Amy Kent came in. She signed the roll but not with her real name. There is nothing but my word saying Amy was ever there.

My stomach drops, feeling all the pointed fingers, hearing whispers behind my back, hearing the word "dirty" from somewhere in my past. I stand for a long minute as the girls walk away from me, their hips swinging, and finally I close my mouth and turn to make my way back to the Art Walk. It takes me the entire walk through the fair to realize that the emotion I am feeling is shame, embarrassment, and I suddenly see the insane infatuation over the last weeks.

I tell Charley about the encounter, trying to infuse it with the dismay I feel. How could anybody think I would make something up like that?

"What a brat," Charley says.

"I don't care about that," I insist although the shame is still heavy inside of me. "The point is her sister doesn't think she had a boyfriend. Isn't that odd?"

"Maybe they aren't close."

"Maybe it wasn't a boyfriend." I remember that odd moment when Amy was in the clinic and I thought about how the men in my mother's life sometimes took advantage. I don't think about that often, and usually there is a trigger that transports me back to those times. It's from a different life, one that was only minimally about me.

"What are you saying?"

"You said her mother works with Carmi. Do you know anything about her?"

"No. She seems nice enough. I've only met her once."

"Where is Amy's dad?"

Charley shrugs, beginning the task of packaging her remaining soaps for the trip home, and I follow her lead, letting the conversation drop even as my mind swirls.

21

I arrive at the church in Sorento with minutes to spare and park in the lot next to Grandad's old truck. The lot is already about as full as it gets—ten vehicles, eleven with mine. The church is in town, so a good number of people walk. I don't come every Sunday; it's too far for that, but about once a month I try to get this way and spend the day with my grandparents. Uncle Steven meets me at the door, ushering guests to their seats. His hand rests on the small of my back as he guides me down the aisle.

"How are the boys?"

"They're good. Can't get Tyler to come, but his wife is here. Kids are downstairs."

I slide in next to Grandma and wave down the pew at Grandad and Tyler's wife, Heather, who reaches a hand out to touch my fingers. Tyler and I don't get on well, but his wife is a love. Tyler was a rising star when I came into the picture, and I think he always felt like I stole something from him. It's true that Grandma and Grandad are proud of me, maybe more than I deserve, and I know they enjoy me being around because it's a little like having a second chance with my mom. When I am in Sorento, I am golden, and that's the shade Tyler used to glow.

"I have so much to tell you," I whisper, and Grandma puts her hand into mine with a squeeze.

I never went to church before I started meeting them here, so while Grandma is frustrated by the introduction of guitars and drums into the music, I enjoy it. They don't get loud—it's not like a rock concert. It's just not what she grew up with, and nobody likes change, especially Grandma.

An hour later, we all file out of the church. Heather passes me the four-year-old while she catches one of the boys beelining toward the street. We walk together toward the parking lot, and Heather manages a stream of conversation, without requiring much from anybody else. She is bubbly and bright, and what she sees in my taciturn cousin I do not know.

One of the downsides to being a nurse is that everybody wants to tell me their ailments and ask my opinion. I spend the first thirty minutes hearing all their aches and pains and talking through ideas to combat Tyler's insomnia. Heather is grateful, and I know she looks forward to seeing me as much for medical advice as for the companionship.

"Why is he not sleeping?" I ask about Tyler.

"I don't know. He won't talk to me, but he's in such a funk."

"Did something happen at work?"

She shakes her head.

"Is he coming today?"

She shakes her head again, and Grandma picks up the thread of the conversation and says, "He needs to go see a doctor."

This surprises me. "What's going on?"

"I think he's got diabetes. You know his mother does."

"Really?" I hadn't known his mother. Diabetes is one of the worst diseases out there because it affects all the systems of the body. A diabetic person ages three times faster than a non-diabetic. It affects moods and brain function as sugar level fluctuates, and thinking back on my interactions with Tyler over the years, it makes perfect sense. "Has he been tested?"

"No. He won't go to a doctor. Says they just want to sell drugs," Heather says. "I'm worried about him. His feet have been tingling for weeks."

Diabetes affects the vascular system, especially in the extremities, so tingling feet is a symptom, although I wouldn't expect it to be an early indicator. "Does he have sores on his feet?"

"No. But he's so grumpy."

"Different than normal?" Grandma asks. Everybody knows Tyler is dissatisfied with life in a general way.

"No, not really."

"He needs to get checked. Diabetes isn't something you want to play around with," I insist, although I doubt anybody will be able to make Tyler do what he doesn't want to do.

"Maybe you can tell him that."

"Doubt he would listen to me." We're in the kitchen pulling lunch together, hearing the kids running out in the yard. Steven's wife, Maggie, comes in from outside, sweating in streams. Tamara is on her hip, whimpering about her scraped knee. Maggie and Heather leave to tend the scrape, and finally, I am alone with Grandma.

"So, hey, I have news."

"You met a fella?" she asks, her face lights up.

"No, Grandma. I didn't meet a fella." It's not a lie. I've known Dylan for always, and we're just friends.

"Someday. I want more grandbabies to spoil, and Tyler can't afford anymore, and I don't think James is ever going to get married." I'm proud of her that she can finally say that without crying. Two years ago James came out of the closet, and last Christmas he brought his friend Robert home to meet the family.

"Probably not," I agree. I let it sit for a minute, thinking she will ask about my news, but she traipses off down a different path in her mind. I finally say, "I had a visitor the other day." If I don't just jump in, she'll shift into a story about James and Robert, and I'll lose the opportunity to tell her about Stella Hayes.

"Who was that?"

"My stepmother. My dad wants to meet me."

She stops with the refrigerator open, cold air blowing into the room. I reach into my purse and hand her the letter.

She takes it and turns away from me, looking down at the envelope, her face set, cold and angry. Closing the refrigerator, I watch as she removes the letter and reads the words written there, waiting for her face to get soft again.

It doesn't. "What do you think?"

"He stole my daughter." Tears flood her eyes, and I suddenly understand the compression around her mouth, the cold anger in her eyes. Her reaction isn't about me; it is about Mom, and what Grandma lost. I should have known she would see it that way. I didn't think it through.

"I know. She had a hand in that, though."

She nods, but she doesn't want to accept it. She needs to have somebody to blame.

"I want to meet him."

"He's probably a drug addict," Grandma says, and it feels like a slap in the face. How can she see good in me if I came from a couple of addicts? How can she believe I am different?

"I don't think so."

"Why would you want to meet him? He never wanted anything to do with you."

"Maybe now he does."

Her brows knit together, and she shoves the letter back at me, crumpling it against my hands.

"Why are you angry?"

"I'm not angry," she says, her voice pitched high like I've accused her of something outrageous.

"You look angry." I keep my tone calm, the way I talk to patients.

She snorts and turns out of the kitchen, and I stand alone for a long minute, hearing her feet as she mounts the steps, hearing the closing of her bedroom door. At least I know where my mother learned to run away from uncomfortable things. I fold the letter, smoothing out the ridges my grandmother had put on the sheet when she shoved it back at me. I tuck it back into my purse before I finish carrying fixings to the table for lunch.

"Hey," I say, leaning out onto the front porch. "Lunch." I wait for Grandad as Steven calls to the kids. He puts his arm around my shoulder as we walk toward the dining room. "I made Grandma mad."

He chuckles. "What did you do?"

"I told her that my dad's people came looking for me. I told her I want to meet him."

"She's mad at you for that?" he asks, disengaging to wash his hands in the kitchen sink.

"Well, maybe not mad at me, but she's upset. She went up to her room."

"What are you going to do?"

"I don't know, give her a few minutes then go talk to her, I guess."

He shakes his head. "Not about her. She'll be fine. You know how she is. What are you going to do about your dad?"

"I think I want to meet him." I wait for him to get angry, to be annoyed, but he doesn't.

He drops his arm back over my shoulder and draws me in for a hug. "I think you should." He kisses the top of my head, and we go in for lunch.

That's all I needed to hear, and when Grandma comes back down the stairs and joins us in the dining room, she doesn't meet my eyes, but at least she no longer looks angry.

22

I understand something important about who my mother was as I am driving away from my grandparents' house. A couple of times over the years, Grandma has gone off to her room when presented with something unpleasant. The very first time I joined them for Thanksgiving, she interrupted the meal when I made some comment about my mom. Isn't that the same thing mom always did, but instead of running to her room, she walked into a bottle?

When Granddad said, "Not about her," something inside me clicked, and gears started shifting, and places that had been dark suddenly began to glow with light. My mother repeated the same mistakes her mother had. Mom was in danger when she was a child—wasn't that why her father finally left, because Grandma figured out what he was doing and made a stand? Would my mom have been a painful reminder of what Grandma had lost, how she had failed? Did they spend their lives together with a giant elephant in the room that nobody could ever discuss? How much of my mother's growing-up years were spent trying to make amends for upsetting Grandma?

It's the same way Mom had stopped looking at me after she made Eddie leave. I always thought it was because I had done something dirty, that I was terrible, but suddenly I see that she couldn't look at me because she felt guilty for what had happened to me. The same way Grandma can't look at me when she is displeased or faces a hard truth. No wonder my mom ran away. Then she got pregnant and never learned a single thing about herself; she never closed up any of her wounds. She just kept trying to pack them and numb them, hoping they'd stop aching. I am sad for my mother, seeing her life from this angle.

I feel light.

I'm not like that. I won't be like that. I did run away; I did get pregnant. But I've spent all these years since then trying to heal myself.

I stop for gas in Effingham, and after I've finished pumping, I move the car to a parking space so I won't be distracted while I make a phone call.

"'lo?" The first half of the word drops with a Southern drawl.

"Hello, um, is Stella there?"

"Yeah." The phone clicks—like it has been set on a counter or a table—and the man calls out a long bellow. "Stellaaaa," like Stanley in a *Streetcar Name▪ Desire*, and the belt of sound, the drawing up of a familiar and beloved play, helps relieve the tension building along my shoulder blades. "She'll be right here," he says, and the phone clunks down again. Is that my father, brusque, bordering on rude? Is this a mistake?

Should I hang up and drive away?

But I see Grandma, her mouth set in a thin line, rising from the table, running away from what is hard. I clear my throat while I wait.

Seconds feel like minutes.

"Hello?"

"Stella?"

"Yes?"

"This is Alison. You came to see me a couple of weeks ago."

I hear the intake of breath, the shift as she moves, maybe settling into a chair.

"Oh, thank God,"

I can't help but smile. That wasn't the reaction I expected.

"I'd like to come and meet everybody sometime, if you think that would still be okay?"

"Okay, darling? It's a dream come true."

"I don't know about that, but, um, when would be good?"

"Oh, honey, you come anytime. We'll come up your way if that would be better."

"I'll come to you. I'd like to meet everybody in their spaces, if you know what I mean." It's an echo of Grandma, not being able to visualize me when I was in California until I gave her pictures of the condo. Am I only a product of the gene pool?

No. I'm like Mitch, too, a hard worker willing to do what needs doing. I'm like Vaude, Dylan's mom, who thought everything through in such detail. I'm like Leslie, and I'm like Ina. I've made choices to be the person I am, and I'm proud of that.

We arrange to meet the following Saturday, and when she has told me how glad she is that I've called, I pull my seatbelt into place and feel weight shifting from my shoulders.

Neoga sits between Effingham and my exit for Charleston, and I drop off the interstate before I even know I've done it. Just like always, it is Dylan I want to see, Dylan with whom I want to share my life.

I call him as I drive. "Are you busy?"

"No. Just getting dinner on the table. Why?"

"I'm in town. Could I stop by?"

"For a little bit. I've got to get Daecus back to his mom's." He gives me his address, and I drive, singing along to the radio. I'm not even nervous, walking up to his front door.

"You look happy," he says when he opens the door.

"I am." I step through the door and into his house, and my euphoria peaks. Hanging above the fireplace is *Tumult*, framed and lit by a light above. "Wow! That looks great there."

"Yeah, I love it." We are interrupted by Daecus rushing down the stairs, having heard the knock.

"Hey, buddy," I call, and he launches into my arms. I hug him and set him again on his feet.

"Come upstairs. You have to see my room." He tugs my hand, and I smile back at Dylan as Daecus draws me forward. As I walk toward the stairs, I notice a collection of boxes in various stages of being filled and feel a small pang for the upheaval coming their way. "I just got mine back today," Daecus tells me. "I'm trying to decide where to hang it. I want to be a sailor when I grow up and go all around the world in a sailboat."

"You do? That would be a great adventure."

"I know. It would be so cool." We've reached his room, and I hear Dylan coming up behind us.

Daecus's bedroom is at the rear of the house, and his windows overlook the back yard, with a play set and what looks like the beginning of a treehouse, abandoned. His room is neat, the way rooms are when nobody lives in them most of the time.

The Jenny Sue hangs on the long wall above his bed; the colors match the blue of his spread. "Well, that looks great right where you have it."

"I know. I tried to talk Dad into letting me take it to Mom's, but he won't let me."

I glance at Dylan who has joined us in the room, and I see the small flash of pain that crosses his face. What must it be for his home to suddenly be part-time for his son? How does it feel that Daecus lives somewhere else where Dylan isn't welcome? I lean my shoulder against him, trying to convey that I get it, I understand.

"Well, that should probably stay at your dad's so you can enjoy it with him."

"Yeah, but I'm at mom's most of the time." I cringe, feeling the gut-punch for Dylan. Daecus doesn't know; he doesn't understand how hard this is for the grown-ups.

"Yeah, well, maybe I could put a word in with the artist, and she'll arrange for one to be at your mom's, too. How would that be?"

"That would be awesome!" he shouts. The doorbell chimes, *bong, bong, bong,* and Daecus runs from the room.

"Hey, hey, don't you open that door," Dylan calls, and we follow down the steps

"It's Mom!" he calls, and my stomach plummets. Daecus flings the door open, and there she stands, the woman Dylan married, dressed in a black pencil skirt, a gray silk top, and three-inch pumps. Her hair is cut short in a sharp, chin-length bob. She is freaking gorgeous, and I feel my khakis and polo as if they are dirty jeans and a t-shirt from years ago.

"Hey, Dakey. You ready?" She doesn't pass through the door, and I've stopped on the steps.

"Come on," Dylan says almost under his breath, placing his hand on the small of my back, moving me forward. "Might as well meet her now."

"Hey, Mandy," Dylan says, cool but polite.

"Look who's here," Daucus says, and she looks up, seeing me. Her eyes narrow at where Dylan's arm disappears behind my back, taking in the familiarity.

"Hmm," she says, giving a slow nod. "You must be Alison."

"I am. You must be Amanda." We don't exactly square off, but there is an awkward moment where we assess each other.

"I am."

I reach my hand out, and she looks at it for a long beat before accepting it. She still hasn't stepped inside. "It's good to meet you." I almost say, *"I've heard so much about you,"* but I bite my tongue. I haven't heard much of anything about her; it's just the next line in the meeting-people script.

"I've heard so much about you," she says, and a cold smirk transforms her face from beautiful to not so beautiful.

"Oh." I glance at Dylan, but he has stepped away, going to grab Daecus's backpack and overnight bag. I don't know how to respond, so I don't. We stand, awkwardly, waiting for Dylan to come back.

Daecus is unaware of the tension and says, "She's the one who painted my boat."

Amanda compresses her lips, letting her hand rest on Daecus's shoulder. "Yes, I was aware of that."

"She says she's going to send one to our house so I can have it there, too."

"How thoughtful." The tone of her voice is cold like ice, and I realize that she's not going to let him have a painting from me in her house. It's odd. She should have no grudge against me.

"I thought I was meeting you in Kankakee," Dylan says as he comes back from around the corner.

"I was down this way, so I thought I'd save you the drive." She has a deep, melodic, cultured voice.

"I wish you had called," he says, the tension between them arcing above Daecus's head.

"Oh, I'm sorry. I hope I didn't interrupt anything." The implication is like a cat scratch.

"No, but if you'd been any later, we would have been gone already, and then what would you have done?"

"I would have called and told you to come back." She speaks slowly, as if he may not be able to comprehend her words. She looks at him with such dislike, and Dylan's cheeks flush in those small points of color that appear when he is angry. What did Dylan see in her? Has she changed since college, into this cold professional?

"That's not the point," he says, and the undercurrent is a threat. I step away from them, needing not to be part of the family drama. I catch sight of Daecus's head lowering, his eyes studying the floor.

"Whatever. I'm here now. Would you like for me to leave so that you can drive up to Kankakee?"

"Of course not."

"Then what is the problem? I'm saving you effort. You should thank me." A long beat of silence follows before she speaks again. "Do you have everything?"

Daecus's response is almost inaudible.

"Good. Let's go."

It takes several minutes after they have left for Dylan to find me on the back deck.

"Well, she's terrifying," I say, not looking at him.

"Isn't she, though?"

"Yes. Very." We laugh, and the tension breaks. He leans against the railing, turning to look back at me.

"I'm sorry about that. She's abrasive." He stands to look out over the small yard, watching the swing shift back and forth. "Daecus wanted me to tell you goodbye."

"He's a sweet boy." The air around Dylan seems thick, and I wonder if I have seen too much for his comfort. I want to touch him, but his boundaries look fragile and thin, and I'm afraid he'll break apart if I offer anything.

"He really likes you," he says, a smile touches one corner of his mouth and leaves the other alone.

"I bet you miss him when he's not here."

His outlines are becoming more substantial, the air around him is thinning.

"Like a leg," he whispers, his voice sounding tight and brittle. As we look out over the yard, a breeze shifts the grass in lazy waves, and I finally hear Dylan expel a long, level breath. When I look back at him, he is his normal color again. "So what made you come by?"

"Oh," I say, excited to see him back on balance as much as at being reminded why I came to see him. "I've had an epiphany!" I tell him about Grandma, how she took my news about my Dad and turned it into a drama about herself. How it made me understand my mom a little better. I can see a bit better why she never went home; it wasn't just pride. She didn't go back because she had gone against Grandma, and Grandma holds a grudge. What would it have been like, growing up in a house with a mother who wouldn't look at you when you didn't do what she wanted, as if you were invisible?

"That's pretty cool."

"I've spent my whole life trying to not to be like my mom, and she spent her whole life trying not to be like Grandma." I understand now why she was always ready to fight, always ready to make her opinion known. She wasn't going to do what her mother did; she wasn't going to run away from confrontation. "I don't know why it matters, but it's just like something makes sense now." I'm not conveying it well, but he is nodding his head as if he understands.

"That is awesome." He lowers his eye and looks at our hands, turning my palm up, studying the lines. "You're never going to make the same mistakes she made."

"I know!" I am giddy and nearly jump.

"We all make our own." He laughs, low and guttural, and I hear the truth in it. He's made mistakes. I've made mistakes. No life is perfect.

"Isn't it strange . . . I've lived my whole life based on what I didn't want. Every choice I've made has been as much about my mother as it has been about me. That feels crazy all of a sudden."

"That is crazy," he agrees, but not unkindly.

"I am not going to do that anymore. You hear me?" The last I call out to the yard as if my mother is standing on the far edge and I want the message to carry.

"So what do you want to do?"

"I want to meet my dad," I say, turning to look at him, "and I want you to come with me." The last I've said entirely on impulse, but it's true. Dylan has always been the person I wanted at my side. He has always been the one who understood me better than anybody else.

"All right." He drops his arm over my shoulder, and I let my head rest against him, just like old times.

His fingertip traces a small line up my arm, and heat rises through my body. Just from that slight touch. I should push away, but I don't. I close my eyes and let the sensation take me.

"When will your divorce be final?" I finally ask, and I hear the way my voice has dropped, the way my words come out breathless.

"Beginning of August." His voice has the same quality, and I shift my body to face him, folding neatly into his arms. I slip my hand up the side of his neck, and he lets me draw his face down.

It's like a sigh when his lips touch mine, like a whisper, and every fiber in my body wants to draw him nearer. We've waited all our lives, and another month feels like too much.

The pressure of his arms closing tighter around my waist lifts me off my feet, and my legs draw up and clutch around his waist.

We reach his back door, and he turns to take us inside.

The back of my head collides with the door frame. "Ouch." I jerk my head, and my forehead crashes into his mouth.

"Damn!" he says behind his hand. I slip out of his arm and only manage to keep upright because he has had the good sense to keep one hand on me.

I'm rubbing the back of my head; he's touching his lip gingerly . . .

Suddenly, laughter explodes out of me, and I let myself sit down on the floor, looking up at his wounded face.

"Are you okay?" I ask when I can finally speak,

"Yeah." He slides down the wall beside me, pressing a paper towel against his busted lip. "I just can't get a break."

"You poor man."

Our hands nestle together, and I know we are both trying to decide how far we can take this. Out on the deck, we both just needed a horizontal surface, and maybe we still do, but I'm in the house he shared with his wife, a woman I just met, and somehow it feels wrong.

"Your head okay?"

"Yeah. I'm fine." He leans in and kisses me, and I'm careful not to press against his lip. When we separate, he leaves his forehead resting on mine, so he is foreshortened in my vision.

"Maybe we shouldn't do this here."

"Yeah, probably not," I agree, and I am equal parts relieved and disappointed. Sex has never been a simple thing—it's complicated and dangerous.

"I do love kissing you, though," he whispers, and I tilt my chin until our lips meet again. Kissing is something that I can do.

23

I get the notice on Thursday that the Charleston Historical Society has selected my cards for the holiday series and the calendar, and it feels like the turning of a tide. A month ago, everything felt unhinged like I was coming apart at the seams. Warren died, Amy Kent went missing, Dylan came back, and then Stella Hayes showed up. I had felt jarred, like everything I had worked for was preparing to fly out into the stratosphere.

Then I had watched Grandma receive the news that my Dad wanted to meet me. Her eyes turning to flint. Her lips tightening into a thin line. Her walking away from me, as if I meant nothing to her. Her telling me that he was probably a drug addict.

In the past, I would always rush after her, trying to make amends for whatever insult she had felt. I didn't this time. I just waited, with confidence from Grandad that it would all be okay. All the time she was upstairs, the gears were shifting, and my history was realigning on itself. When she came back down and she pretended that nothing had happened . . . when she couldn't, or wouldn't, look at me . . . my whole life seemed to click into focus.

I've done the same that my mother did, in my way. But I've also done what I did. I did repeat my mother's mistakes, not all of them, and unlike my mother, I tried to face up to them instead of putting them under the rug to trip me up later. Maybe I only made the mistakes that everybody makes because growing up is hard. My mother did what Grandma did. It's what we do; we repeat what we know with new information.

I'm going to meet my father. I've had two conversations with Stella Hayes, asking about food allergies and preferences. I've told her I am vegetarian but assured her that I'll eat anything else she fixes and be grateful. I'm taking a dessert, a pineapple upside-down cake. It's a recipe Leslie shared with me, and I have all the ingredients piled into my basket. I looked for Kelci when I came into Bancroft Market but only saw David, working in the meat department. I waved and walked on, my list flattened out in my hand.

I have never felt lighter. When I've looked in the mirror this week, I haven't seen Mom. I almost believe she had been tethered here with me until I could set her free. Now I only see me, and it feels like I've broken some barrier, and now that I have, she has gone. She was stuck until I figured something out. That sounds crazy, and I don't believe in ghosts. Except when I do.

Even more than that, Dylan fills my mind because, finally, we are going to wait for each other. Finally, we are going to find out about all this chemistry.

Turning down the dairy aisle for milk and eggs, I almost run into Amy Kent's mother and sister, the one I approached at the fair. I stop short, seeing her in profile, and for a split second, I think again that it is Amy—that she's back and I just hadn't heard yet. The girl looks at me, her brows drawing together, and she turns away. "Come on," she hisses. "I don't care what kind of yogurt you get."

"You're very rude. Please stop." Her mother says in a low voice, not wanting the world to hear, to know that she is not in control of her child . . . but the world already knows.

I walk past them, feeling my face flush at the memory of my conversation with the girl. Apparently, "rude" is just her way and not isolated to me. I imagine the strain the family is under, the pressure. How do you continue going to the grocery, how do you decide on what yogurt to get, when one of your children is missing, absent from your life? How do you live after that?

I did. My bones suddenly feel liquid, and I pause with a hand on the cooler handle, steadying myself until my head stops spinning. I continued going to the grocery; I continued choosing flavors of yogurt. Of course, it's different: Amy is lost, taken, in danger. Emily Ann was given, so she could have a better life. My head stops swirling, and when I look, the duo has moved out of the aisle, and I am alone in it. My heart is thudding, thud, thud, thudding in my ears.

I select a dozen unmarred eggs and continue down the aisle, feeling detached and disconnected from my body. Will my daughter ever want to find me? Will she ever want to know me? Will she give me a second chance, the way I am giving my father? Amy had reminded me of myself when she came into the clinic, and now all those memories won't be put away.

That's why finding her feels like such a mission. She showed me how far I've come. If only I had told her . . . What? What could I have said to Amy that would have made a difference in her life? It doesn't matter. She wouldn't have taken anything I had on offer, the same way I didn't listen to Faye when she'd tried.

I run my groceries through the checkout line and head to my car, feeling the thudding of my heart with less intensity. When I get home and lay everything out, I realize I forgot a cake pan. I stand to look at all the ingredients and dial Leslie, asking to borrow a pan. It's good that I forgot because right now, I need Leslie.

***

"I don't know; it was weird." I am frazzled, confused by my body's reaction at the store. I've told Leslie how I approached Amy's sister at the fair, and while she hasn't said as much, I can tell she thinks I shouldn't have.

"How did you think she should have responded?" Leslie asks, her voice determinedly calm.

"I don't know, but it was just odd. She told me that Amy didn't have a boyfriend. Is that true?"

"I never saw her with anybody." Leslie is an English teacher at the high school, and she's in charge of the yearbook. She knows everybody, and she knows who is dating whom.

"Then how did she end up pregnant?"

Leslie shrugs. "She must have been dating somebody outside of the school."

"Does her mother have a boyfriend?" Amy's father is not in the picture.

"Alison," Leslie says as if I've said something out of line.

"I'm serious. That girl was pregnant, and somebody brought her in to find out, and then she disappeared. They didn't want her telling anybody. So they got rid of her."

"Is that what the police are saying?" she asks, although if anybody knows what the police are saying, it would be Leslie. Dan McGill is in the fire department, and the police and fire are all tight.

"I don't know." I am exasperated. I feel like she is being intentionally difficult, not understanding what I am trying to say. "I just feel like nobody is even trying to find her."

"This isn't the first time Amy has run away."

"So, is that what the police are saying? Is that official?" I ask, throwing her words back at her. Detective Daniels had said as much to me when I called him from the fair. I don't care—it doesn't matter if she ran away. We still need to find her. "Even if she did run away, she is still only fourteen, and she was pregnant. Doesn't that matter to anybody?"

"Of course it matters, and I promise you, they are still looking for her. Nobody has given up."

"It feels like it."

"I know it does. Things take time."

I sit down beside Leslie, still feeling like my muscles are ready to tear through my skin.

"They think she ran away," I say, hoping it will encourage Leslie to share anything she may know.

"Yeah. They do. She packed a bag. Wherever she went, she knew she was going. They found her journal. The police think she was headed toward Chicago."

"Why do they think that?"

"Because it's what she wrote. The whole thing is full of pictures of Chicago."

"If she was going to Chicago, why would she have left that behind?"

"Alison, honey." The exasperation is like a thread weaving in her words. "I know that this has touched you, but you have to let it go. You've done everything you can for Amy."

"I don't think she ran away." The pleading tone in my voice makes Leslie put her arm around my shoulder and hold me.

"I promise you, the police know more than you do. I know she made you think of yourself when you were younger. I know that. But Amy's not you."

"Why would she run away, though? What was going on?" Finally, I hear it—the paranoia, the overzealous tone in my voice. I am that crazy woman. Leslie is looking at me with such sadness that I am embarrassed. How much of my conversations have been about Amy over the last month? "Okay," I consent. "All right. I'll let it go."

24

Saturday dawns with rain, a quiet, drizzling rain pattering on the windows. Dylan is waiting in his truck, and I feel like a teenager climbing in beside him. I slide across the seat and kiss him, and our lips linger, even though we've been cautious about letting anybody see us together. He's still married, and I never want anybody to tell Daecus that I had anything to do with his parents getting a divorce.

"You know I don't mind driving," I say.

"I know, but this is fine." He peels the lid from the cake pan and peeks inside.

"It's Leslie's recipe," I admit.

"Ooh. It looks good. Smells good."

I am so nervous about today that my muscles are twitching. I was awake all night, imagining what I'm going to find when I get to the address Stella gave me. Will he be living in squalor, in a trailer out in the woods? Is he a drunk? I have no reference points, beyond the fact that he was a man who got involved with my mother, and that Stella was clean. I don't know what to expect, and this morning, meeting him feels like a bad idea.

We head south out of town, and I inspect each car that we pass. Looking for the Camaro. It's a habit now. I look the same way that my mom and I used to look for Volkswagens when I was young. "Slug bug!" she would say and then reach out with a gentle fist. I think that's why I bought that little red Volkswagen from Don all those years ago. I had been looking for one all my life.

I tell Dylan what Leslie told me, how I need to let the whole situation go, how I have to trust the police to find Amy. He nods but doesn't offer an opinion. I talk in circles, justifying my interest, and Dylan lets me speak. When I have worn myself out, when there is nothing more to say, I finally fall silent. I've cycled the Amy conversation as long as I can, and now that it has expired, I have to face what I'm trying *not* to think about: the upcoming meeting.

The air around me is thick, like fog, and my shoulders are drawn forward making myself as small as possible. Dylan is working toward conversation, bless him, but I can't focus. My answers are coming short and clipped, and when I look down at my hands, they are trembling.

"I don't want to do this," I say, interrupting Dylan, not aware of what he was saying. I suddenly want to push open the door and jump out, even as we drive at sixty miles an hour. I'm claustrophobic, trapped, and I need to be free.

Dylan's hand falls on mine, and a stuttering breath shatters from my lips, sounding almost like a sob. "Hey," he says, lacing his fingers in mine.

"Can we go home?"

"Al. Look at me. This is going to be okay. You don't have to do it; if you want me to, we'll turn around and eat that cake all by ourselves. But it's okay. I'm with you, and as soon as you want to leave, we'll go."

"Pull over. I think I'm going to be sick." Heat flushes over my face, and my head swims as he downshifts and comes to a stop on the side of the road. "I can't breathe." I push out of the cab of his truck, gasping for air. Gooseflesh rises all down my arms, and suddenly I am chilled.

I flail my arms, snapping them to get the feeling back. They are numb. Am I having a heart attack? I can hear the hazard lights of Dylan's truck clicking behind me. Reaching the utility pole, I lean my forehead into the hard wood and close my eyes to keep the tunnel from narrowing any further. *Not a heart attack, a panic attack*—my clinical mind catalogs my symptoms, and in the cataloging my panic ebbs.

His hands land on my shoulders, and my first impulse is to pull away. I've never been very good at being touched. But this is Dylan, and I hold steady. He leans in, and his cheek brushes against mine, his breath minty and warm. A fingertip brushes along my cheek, moving a strand of hair away from my mouth.

"I'm here, Al. You're okay." He whispers the way I remember him doing with the horses when we were young and they were skittish.

I keep my eyes closed and listen to him, his voice so quiet it's lost on the breeze as often as it is not. The pounding of my heart slows and steadies, and my breath calms. When I open my eyes again, the tunnel has expanded and disappeared.

I drop my head forward, feeling strangely exhausted, as if I've run miles.

"Okay?" he asks, and I tilt my head enough that I can see him and nod. "We don't have to do this."

Now that the moment has passed, I'm not sure what I want. I nod, and he folds around me, encircling me with his familiar scents.

"You used to talk to the horses like that," I say, more of a whisper than words.

"Yeah. I did."

"I miss them."

"I do, too." Chessa died while I was in California, Adelaide wasn't long after, and Pride passed last year. Vaude had told me in the grocery store one day, and I had come home and sobbed like a baby. It felt like my childhood was genuinely lost at that point, that the past was irretrievable. It felt like Dylan was finally, at long last, unreachable. How many times over the years had I found my way to the Winthrop pasture, to stand and commune with Pride, the lone horse lingering? They had bought a goat so that Pride wouldn't be lonely. It was always a surprise to find the goat standing on the shed or the bunkhouse, or sleeping on the seat of the tractor.

"What happens if you don't go?" he asks.

I sigh and push away from him. "I don't know. I wake up tomorrow and feel like a runner."

He follows me back toward the truck, and I wonder if he understands what that means, or if it's too cryptic for someone who hasn't been in my life for all of it. We reach the truck, and he says, "So I guess we continue."

I smile back at him; he gets it. He has been enough in my life to understand. "Onward."

***

Stella and Tom Hayes live in amongst the Shawnee National Forest, and Dylan makes a wrong turn that leads us to a dirt road and a dead end. By the time we get back to the main street, I call Stella to confirm directions. A paved road leads to a rocked lane, which leads to a dirt path that finally opens into a drive. The yard is wide with a small pond shimmering to the right of the drive, and a wraparound porch shields the house in shadows.

"Ready?" Dylan asks, and I nod, although I am afraid that my legs won't carry me out of the truck. "When you are ready to leave just say it, and we'll go."

He waits for me as I come around the truck, and the screen door pushes open. Stella comes out, and behind her is a tall, handsome man, looking every bit as terrified as I feel. I am so grateful that Dylan is here. I would have never made it without him.

25

We are sitting on the shaded front porch, our stomachs full, our fingers still holding the sweet fragrance of the roasted corn from lunch. They all had barbecue, which still smells like heaven, even if I don't eat meat. Stella knew that I'm vegetarian, and while she didn't cut meat from the menu, she certainly made sure there was plenty enough of everything else for me to be satisfied. She is thoughtful, and after that first phone call, she's felt like someone I've known for years. She's that kind of woman.

Tom Hayes is not at all what I expected. Sitting here on his front porch is peaceful. He is quiet, not in a timid way, but in an "I don't have a lot of breath to waste with useless chatter" kind of way. The pink elephant is standing over by the pond, and at some point, the conversation of my mother is going to come up, but for now, it is peaceful. We are digesting.

My father is lean with dark hair that curls in the heat. He reminds me of Mitch, the way his hands are stained with oil from working on machines. I have always thought I looked just like my mother, except for my smile, but looking at him from the corner of my eye, studying the shape of his face to find similarities between the two of us, I can see that the shape of his brow is familiar, and the fullness of his lips. I expected this meeting to be discordant, and maybe when that pink elephant comes up, it will be. So far, we've talked about art and cars, and we've even talked about the ocean, which he has never seen. We are establishing our boundaries, man and grown daughter, and we are both cautious not to overstep.

"How long have you had your shop?" I ask, rocking forward, feeling the breeze coming up from the yard. Chickens are pecking in the grass, and I could watch them all afternoon and never have to say another word.

"Oh, about twenty years, I reckon. I worked there growing up. When the old man retired, he offered it up for sale, and me and Curt Peters went in to buy it. Curt sold out to me about five years ago, moved out to Arizona to start a dude ranch."

The conversation bends, and the pink elephant turns and drinks from the pond, one gimlet eye on me, one lazy ear flapping.

I am having the hardest time reconciling this man with my mother. He isn't a drinking man; he hasn't even offered a beer or cocktail, and when I looked in their refrigerator there wasn't a beverage beyond milk and orange juice. But even more than that . . . he is so quiet. What did they see in each other?

When the conversation warps back from Curt Peters and the dude ranch in Arizona, the pink elephant finally steps up, and I can't keep myself from asking. "I'm having such a hard time imagining you with my mom. I mean, you seem like a nice guy."

Guilt washes through me, the implication of what I've just said, what it implies about my mother. Then I remember her as she was when I was little, before everything that happened with Eddie, before she fell into the bottle, the way people loved her.

"That didn't come out right," I mumble and feel tears stinging at the back of my eyes. How could I betray her like that, to someone I don't even know?

Tom Hayes does the only thing he can probably do to make it right. "I thought Al was the most amazing person I ever met," and I hear the lump in his throat as he says it. When I look at Stella, she is nodding as if this is some great truth. I almost expect her to call out "Amen" or "Hallelujah," the way the older women in the church do when the preacher says what they know is right.

"You called her Al?" I glance at Dylan who holds my eyes for that split second, giving me the courage to go forward.

"Yeah. She wasn't much of an 'Alice.' She had too much fire for such an old name."

"That's a truth. She had a lot of fire," I agree, but in my mind, I'm still seeing her as she was before—holding my hand, telling me stories, singing songs to put me to bed. Hugging me as if she would never let me go.

"We were so young."

"I know she was young when I was born." I let the implication hang, that she was a child and he was grown, because that's how I always believed it.

"We both were. I dropped out of school when we knew you were coming. My parents helped us out. I started working full-time at the shop." He sniffs.

"You mean you dropped out of college?"

"No." He chuckles. "Neither one of us finished high school. I never went back for my senior year. I got the GED. We both did."

I remember the photograph, the one I've brought with me, of the two of them on the motorcycle. Had my mom told me he was older, or did I assume? He certainly looked older than seventeen in the photograph.

"I have a picture of the two of you. I thought you were a lot older than her."

"That mustache." He chuckles and rubs his fingers down along phantom facial hair. I gaze out across the yard, my mind churning. This new information changes everything I thought about him. He wasn't like Warren, a grown man when I was still a kid. He was like Dylan, growing up just a step ahead. "I'd love to see that picture."

Stella smiles and puts her hand on his arm. "I would, too."

I left my purse in the truck, so I walk across the sunlit front yard, past the chickens, to get the picture. When I look back, I see Dylan nodding his head, a wide smile splitting his face and Stella laughing. I slow my pace, trying to etch the scene into my mind. I never want to forget this moment.

I give the picture to Tom, and I'm surprised by the wave of sadness that washes over his features. His emotion is so heavy that I feel it from the steps.

"Oh, I remember her," Stella says, leaning over Tom's shoulder, misty-eyed and nostalgic. "Do you remember when we set the chicken house on fire?"

Just like that, all the sadness is wiped away with stories of that first year, when they were all friends and just a step outside of trouble. This is not at all what I expected.

"Why did she leave?" I ask when the stories stop and Stella hands the picture back to me.

"Hm, well . . ." Tom pushes his hand up through his hair, and it stands in spikes. I brace myself for the tale. "We were young. We were both just pretending at being grownups. I didn't know anything except what I'd seen from my own father, and she had nobody she could look to. She had broken with her family before you were even in the picture. Neither of us was ready to be married. We did it 'cause we were expecting you, and she needed it, I reckon. We weren't good to each other when we were married. We both felt a little trapped maybe, and then you were born. It was just a tough year."

A pang pulls in my stomach—that's how they felt about me, that I made it a tough year. They had done everything wrong, but *I* made it a tough year. Dylan's arm has been stretched across the back of my chair, and now his hand rests on my shoulder, helping to keep me in place. I imagine myself standing up and storming down the steps, leaving with anger and fury that I, who never asked to be born of them, holds any blame in the wreck that was their life together. But I force myself to stay still, to hold my face steady and calm, to not betray the rage welling.

"You were a really sweet baby, almost never cried, and Al just was something else with you." His voice has dropped, and when I look at him, his eyes are far away, looking out across some memory playing in his mind. "She had so many stories, and when you'd wake up in the night, she'd hold you, telling you stories about fairies and goblins. You were just a baby; you didn't understand anything she was saying, but she'd talk until you finally would fall back to sleep."

Whatever was warring in my chest flutters and spills over, and I reach a hand up to touch Dylan's fingertips. I don't want to cry, but imagining her like that feels like sadness, like a loss, like everything that should have been that never was.

"It was my fault she left." He sniffs, and his lips pucker out then draw back between his teeth in a sucking sound. "I thought I was a man, you know, and my father always cheated on my mother. I thought it was just the way. Well, Al wasn't a woman to be cheated on, and when she found out, she met me at the front door with a gun in one hand and you in the other. 'If I ever see you again, I'll kill you,' she said, and I believed her. We were both pretty hot-headed back then. We liked a good knockdown, but when she said that with that revolver cocked, I knew she wasn't playing. So I let her go. I thought she'd cool off and come back. It wasn't the first time we'd been on the split. You were just beginning to walk and into everything . . . you know how kids can be at that age. I remember you watching me as she carried you away. You didn't make a sound, just looked at me like you had the measure of me. You already knew I was no kind of man."

"She never came back?" I ask, but I know the answer.

He shakes his head. "I went to the police, but they weren't any help, said it was probably best if I let her go. It was a small town; everybody knew how we were. My dad had a heart attack and died that next year and I took over here, helping my mom. Al filed divorce papers on me, and I went to find her, to try to talk her into coming back. I missed her. I missed you. But she had a new man, and she wouldn't even let me see you. We kinda got into it. I broke that new man's nose for good measure. The next week I was served with a restraining order. I don't know. I could have fought for custody I reckon, but back then, kids belonged to their mamas. Fathers didn't get a say. I was busy at the shop, trying to keep up with all the work, and it was just easier to let you go."

I hear the thread of shame weaving in his voice, peeking between the excuses, and I let it sit.

"Did you know the man she was with?"

"Yeah, he was fella from down this way. I knew him growing up. I guess I wasn't the only one who'd maybe fooled around."

"What was his name?"

"Ed Carmichael, do you remember him?"

I nod, slowly, I remember Daddy Eddie and bumps rise on my arms. "Whatever happened to him?"

Tom Hayes shrugs.

We sit quietly, for a long minute, the ice melting in our glasses, the silence peopled with those who are not here.

I always knew there was somebody before Daddy Eddie, and even though I don't remember Tom Hayes in any real way, I can imagine him, waiting for me at the end of a first walk. I draw a long breath coming back out of the past, and when I look at Dylan he is watching me, I lean into him, feeling the tackiness of his skin against mine.

"Well, I'd sure love to see your shop."

***

Tom Hayes's shop has a simple sign hanging over the front of the building. It is old and worn with spots of rust. I wonder if it has been here as long as the building. It reads "Auto Body and Paint." The shop looks small from the front, and we pull into to a white-rocked parking lot.

"It's nothing fancy," Tom says, and although it isn't an apology, it feels something akin to one.

"I think it's great!" I say, proud of him for not being a drunk, not being a wasted soul. "Can we go inside?"

"Sure."

He unlocks the door and allows Dylan and me to enter first. Inside it smells like paint and oil and old cars. It's not neat. Parts catalogs are stacked on the counter next to the register, and a coat rack looks like a man standing, it is so full. It's precisely what I would have expected. Past the front lobby, with its three metal-framed chairs, a door leads into the long, open space that is the body shop. Several cars sit under tarps; others are only partial, missing a front end or a fender. One at the far end is a dull color that blends into the surrounding gloom.

I take it all in, noticing that several of the cars are classics, and as we pass one, a Mustang from somewhere in the 1960s, I stop and study the ornate pin-striping on the hood. At first, I think it is white tape, the lines are so precise, but when I lean down and the fluorescent lights overhead stop flickering and settle on a hue, I see that the lines are painted,

"Did you do this?"

I look up at him and see his hand trailing the line of the roof, pride glowing from his face.

"Yeah, this one's mine. My dad had one when I was growing up, and I always loved it. I came across this one in a junkyard about three years ago. It was quite a project."

"It's beautiful. Does it run?"

"Oh, yeah."

Is this where I got my love of art?

The fluorescent glow doesn't reach into the far corners of the room, and when we move in that direction, I catch sight of a car that makes me stop in my tracks. It's not the car that stops me—I don't even know what kind it is. It is the color that catches my eye. It's the same dull color of the Camaro that dropped Amy Kent at the clinic. The Camaro had paused just out of the glow of the street light, flat and unreflective.

"What color is this car?" I ask when we've reached the car at the far end of the shop.

"That's not a color. That's primer brown."

"What's that mean?"

"It's like a base coat."

"Of course. That makes sense." I nod, squeezing Dylan's hand in mine as we turn back toward the front of the shop.

Tom is talking, telling me small details about this car, and something about that car, and we make our way, enjoying listening to him.

This is his space. This is where he is at home, where he has something to say.

"It was so nice to meet you," I say, when we are again outside the shop, surprised at how much I mean it. I lean in to give him a hug that doesn't feel awkward at all. Dylan and I will be leaving from here rather than returning to the house in the woods. It's been a long day of visiting and getting to know each other, and while I would enjoy staying for dinner, I have to work tonight.

"We hope you'll come see us again," Stella says, squeezing me, and for the smallest moment, it's like a hug from my mom.

26

When I call Detective Daniels as I drive out to the hospital for my shift, my call goes straight to his voicemail, and I have a clear vision of him choosing not to take my call.

Part Three: Fall

27

The Springfield Arts Festival takes place over Labor Day weekend. It is by far the largest one Charley and I attend. It's expensive to get a booth, and if it were just her or me, we probably wouldn't go. It's been an eventful summer, and the last month has included several trips south to visit with Tom and Stella Hayes and my two half-brothers, Sam and Rob. Sam is a preacher at the little church in Elizabethtown and un-married. Rob is finishing college and studying agriculture. Neither of them is married, and both of them seem familiar with me in a way I am not familiar with them. It wasn't until the third time I visited that I noticed one of the framed pictures on a small end table—it was of my mother and me. In the picture, I am maybe a year old, my wispy hair sticking up with moisture. My smile is broad, and even though the im-age is in black-and-white, I can see the color in my cheeks. I am holding my mother's finger, bobbing, and I imagine I have just learned to stand. I am learning to walk. It's the way my mother is looking at the person behind the camera, though, that catches my breath. She is in love. She is shining and beautiful, and there is so much love and happiness glowing from her face that I almost can't reconcile her as the woman I knew.

"Wow," I had said, picking up the frame and holding the picture with reverence.

Sam had come to the table to see what I had found.

"We always knew you were out there somewhere," he said, his voice quiet, Southern.

"I wish I had known."

"Dad always made sure we included you."

"How did you do that?"

"We had birthday cake on your birthday every year."

I bark a laugh. "I didn't even do that." I'm a little jealous of all that birthday cake.

"I'm sorry."

"No. It's fine," I said, and my voice broke on the last word as I placed the photograph back on the table. Sam had put his arm around my shoulder, and we had strolled from the living room and out onto the porch, where we could see Stella coming up from the barn carrying a box. We made our way to her and discovered kittens.

"You found them?" Sam asked.

"I knew where they were; I just couldn't get to them."

"Where's the mother?" I asked.

"That's Miss Titty, won't let anybody near her. This is her second litter. She left the first set, so when I heard these babies, I been keeping an eye."

"Miss Titty?"

"She's just always pregnant, but she don't take care of the kits. Can't catch her to get her fixed."

"So what are you going to do?"

"I'm gonna raise them. It's always good to have a mouser." And we had spent the rest of the afternoon feeding kittens with cloth dipped in milk. None of us spoke, it seemed. We just held the babies and let them mewl until they were all fed and fat. It was the most peaceful afternoon.

It felt like even more of my pieces had started to fall into place that afternoon, with a brother and a stepmother and a bunch of kittens. It had felt like a beginning an▸ an ending as evening began to fall over the farm earlier than the last time I visited.

This morning, as Charley and I load the last of my canvases into the back of her van, it definitely feels like fall. A damp chill fills the air, and although I won't need it later in the day, I'm glad that I grabbed a jacket.

My eye catches the remains of one of Amy Kent's flyers as I settle into the passenger seat, and my mood shifts. She has fallen entirely out of the news cycle, and I feel guilty that she has even dropped out of my thoughts sometimes over the last month. I thought it would be quick once they knew the color of the car, but it seems they aren't making any progress. The posters, like the one I just saw, that coated the town a month ago are faded and wilted, and most are gone. Detective Daniels's assurance that "My men are looking into it, Alison" didn't seem like enough at all. I know what he meant was "You need to let me handle this," because I've been a nuisance. They aren't handling it, though. They are just being lazy and not doing anything to find her.

Even Charley is tired of hearing about Amy Kent. The consensus is that she ran away, but I don't believe it. Even if she did, they should still want to find her; she's just a kid, a pregnant kid. She needs help. She needs to be with people who care about her. I know maybe better than anybody how hard it is to go through a pregnancy without support. I calculate how far along she is, and I hope she'd be almost through the morning sickness as the first trimester ticks past, although I know that some women struggle with it throughout and some never have it at all. I wonder if she is showing yet. Every night when I am at work, I expect her to come into the ER, beaten and torn, but she doesn't. Others do, but not Amy Kent. I look through parking lots, everywhere, especially at night, trying to find the primer-brown Camaro.

It is not yet daylight as Charley and I pull out from the curb. She is not a morning person and is still quiet. I'm just off my shift at the hospital, so I'm wide awake. The van is aromatic with her soaps and stout coffee, which she thought to bring for me as well. When we are finished loading, I climb into the passenger seat, and we pull out from the curb. We are sitting at the stoplight to turn onto Lincoln when an old truck rattles by, its flat paint barely catching any light from the glow of the lamp.

How strange that now I see that clay color everywhere. Sometimes I see it just on a fender. Other times, it's a whole car, like the Camaro, like the truck. My stomach churns, and my fingers itch to call Detective Daniels to ask if they've found anything. It's been a week since I last called. Why hasn't he called me in to look at photos again? Has he not found any Camaros waiting for paint? Has he looked?

From the corner of my eye, I can see Charley in profile, not looking at me, focused on the road ahead, and I bite my lips to hold back the words. Everybody thinks I am obsessed. Charley believes it's about the baby I gave away. She says I'm projecting. I can't say she isn't right. I just keep thinking that if Emily Ann were missing, I would stop at nothing to find her. What is wrong with her mother? Why isn't she still out on the news? Why isn't she putting up new flyers? There haven't been updates in weeks, and it's like everybody has just forgotten her. It makes me want to scream.

"You okay?" Charley asks, finally feeling the vibrations from my side of the van.

"That's the color of the car," I say, not answering her question. I've told her, but I wonder if she knows how primer brown looks. Her eyes follow my hand, and she nods, her jaw tight and flexed, biting her tongue. "I just don't understand why Detective Daniels hasn't called me in to look at cars. Are they even looking for her?"

To her credit, she doesn't actually roll her eyes, but she does let out a long breath before speaking. "I'm sure they are still looking for her."

"It doesn't seem like it." I snap my lips together, hearing the broken record quality of my voice.

"You've done everything you can do."

"I don't think so," I insist. I am a pit bull with a rope, hanging on and spinning.

She nods but offers nothing. I keep talking, filling the air, about how it will narrow the search. They've been looking for finished cars, cars on the street and in parking lots. What they needed to look for were cars in auto shops and junkyards. "I just need to call Detective Daniels and see where they are." I pull out my phone and start to dial, but before I can, Charley's hand reaches out and takes the phone. It's slow motion, surreal, my phone slipping from my fingers and crossing the divide to rest on her leg. The silence in the car echoes with the absence of my rampaging voice.

"She isn't Emily." Charley's voice is barely a whisper.

"What?" We never say her name. She is "the baby." She is never named in conversation and hearing her name now, when all my senses are tensed and spring-loaded, makes something in my mind snap, and a high, resonating tone fills my ears, thudding as the blood rushes through my veins.

"You have to stop this. Everybody says she ran away. It's not the first time, and she always comes back. They're just waiting for her now. I think they may have even heard from her."

"They heard from her?"

"No, I don't know . . . I'm just saying that you are obsessed with this girl, Al. I saw that painting." One of the new additions to my collection is edgy with bold colors, painted from the photo they used on the TV and in the posters. I painted it in an hour one night when I didn't have work and couldn't sleep. Frenetic words fill the background, the foreground, mixed in her hair, "find me, find me, find me, find me."

"Somebody should still be looking!" I explode. How can this town just let her go? The way they let me go, the way they moved in to fill up the hole where I had been and forgot that I was ever there.

"They are still looking. It's in police hands. They'll find her if she wants to be found."

My jaw clenches and flexes, and I turn to look out the window, away from her. They didn't look for me. Nobody ever looked for me. But I did run away, and I left notes telling them I was going. I can't be angry. I was emancipated, free to do what I wanted. "She's only fourteen. She doesn't know what she wants."

"This isn't even about Amy Kent, and we both know it."

I feel slapped; tears sting the back of my eyes. I bite my lips all the way to Springfield. This is about Amy Kent! I shouldn't have let her go.

I shouldn't have let her go. I shouldn't have let her go.

In my mind, I see the baby girl as I remember her best, tucked close with a fist in the curtain my hair. I should never have let her go.

Maybe it isn't all about Amy Kent.

29

We find a balance, Charley and me, as we are carrying our tent and tables from the van and into the street. She's wrong, but not entirely wrong, and I know I have been stuck in this groove all summer. Even Detective Daniels, who still sometimes takes my calls, sounds weary of me when I call from the stall of the bathroom. "We're looking into it, Alison. I'll let you know if anything comes up."

I've done what I can. I take a deep breath as I leave the restroom, my phone stored in my hip pocket, my hands still slightly wet from washing them, but instantly dry as I step into the sunlight. The sun rose above the building while I was in the bathroom making my clandestine call, and now the full force of the heat of the residual summer in Illinois is rebounding from the sidewalks. I pull free of my jacket and fold it over my arm as I walk back toward our booth. We are set up on the lawn, as most are, and Charley is sitting in the comfortable shade of our tent as I come across the grass. I smile and wave and nod at other artists as I pass their booths. Charley is ready, her soaps displayed in their trays.

"I'm gonna do a tour, okay?"

"Sure." I smile, trying to put aside the qualms from the ride up. When she has walked away, I set to work on finishing my displays. The last piece I place is *The Baby*, on an easel, to show as people walk from the entrance. I open the books to display some of the portraits, some of the other baby work. Last year, I earned almost as much from commissions on baby work from this one show than all the other festivals we did combined. That's why Charley always pushes me to put *The Baby* out; she knows it's a hook. All those new mothers trying to capture the essence of their little creation before it transforms and the sweetness melts into its human form. When Charley presses, I insist that it's successful in Springfield because people have more money here than at the county fairs. I've never quite admitted to her, although I've come close, how putting *The Baby* up tears at my heart. She should know. She should understand, but still she always asks. We've talked about doing the Chicago round, where all the real Illinois money is, and I'd probably book a lot of work. *The Baby* would be a draw there, but we're both intimidated by the traffic. Maybe we'll try it next year.

They come with their bellies rounded and their hands stretched protectively over the fabric of their shirts, their rings catching and flashing in the sun. I pass out cards. Charley sells soap. We talk to the other artists in the booths nearby when there are breaks in the flow. Prints leave the barrel, and I begin to worry that I've not brought enough stock. The festival is heavily attended, and all through the afternoon, I watch the supplies on *Tumult* as it diminishes.

The aroma from the food trucks fills the air, and I clean the smeared fingerprints from the plastic page coverings in my display books over and over. Music drifts from one of the booths, and when I make my way out to explore, I discover the source, a DJ, available for parties and weddings. There are potters and weavers and so many painters offering portraiture that I'm surprised I've received any interest in my work. I stop and talk with acquaintances from years before, admiring their work, celebrating their new awards. I don't know if other communities are like this, but it's my favorite thing about being an artist. Yes, I love the painting, I love the work, but mostly I love the people. They are generous with praise and happy for your successes. We are all competitors, in a way, trying to capture the patron's dollar, but that's a side. I don't know how many times today I've had a fellow booth holder stop to praise my work, to celebrate Charley's fragrances. I love artists; they are the truest of people. I breathe best amongst them.

I am standing in line at one of the food trucks, studying the selections. Ahead of me is a group of three girls, talking to and above each other, and I catch snippets coming back to me. They are probably Amy Kent's age, but so different from her. They have the look of affluent girls, with artfully torn jeans and layers of tanks under off-the-shoulder t-shirts. This is the Kelci Bancroft crowd, I think, and I smile when I consider how much more I would have fit in now. I had torn jeans; I could do t-shirts.

The girl in the middle is tall with dark hair cut short in a bob, and her neck looks a mile long. She is the leader, the star of the crowd, although her flanking friends shine almost as bright. They make their order, and the one on the right turns and looks straight at me, nodding then looking past me into the crowd.

My heart stammers in my chest. She has the most beautiful storm-cloud-blue eyes fringed by black lashes, and copper hair cut in jagged edges at her shoulders.

My mouth is suddenly dry.

"Where is she?" she says, almost under her breath.

"Who are you looking for?" the tall girl asks, turning to look out across the crowd with her.

"My mom. She was supposed to meet me with money, but she probably got stuck talking to somebody." She smiles, and my heart stops altogether.

"Don't worry about it. I'll get it," her friend says, handing over the money. "You can pay me back."

"Well, thanks." She turns forward again, and I shift to the side, studying her profile. They accept their food through the window and turn out of the line, a small bubble of laughter trailing them at something one of them said. I watch them go.

I'm right here.

"Ma'am, what can I get you?" The tone is abrupt, irritated, and I realize she's already said it twice; I hear it now echoing in my ear canal.

"Oh. Oh. I'll have to come back. I think I left my wallet at my booth."

I step out of the line. It has to be her. She's got Warren's eyes and my hair. My nose. Warren's mouth. My jaw? Maybe Warren's jaw.

I follow them, trailing well back through the crowd, keeping them in sight, my heart hammering when they pass my booth.

"Charley!" I hiss, pausing, but keeping the girls in sight. The booth is in a lull, and Charley is restocking her soaps when I grab her hands.

"Are you okay?"

My skin is rippling with gooseflesh in the heat, and it's true that I feel swimmy-headed, but I am better than I have ever been.

"I thought you were getting lunch." There is an edge in her voice, a sharp line of irritation.

She has a firm set in her lips, her irritation from this morning still present, and I shutter my soul. "I got distracted. I forgot," I whisper.

I turn to find her again, but she is gone.

29

I never knew where the people who adopted Emily Ann lived. I assumed they were somewhere in the Midwest, since they came to Missouri to get her. He was a college professor, and she was an art teacher. It isn't impossible that the mom would be at the same art festival as me. It isn't impossible that she would bring her daughter and friends to help. Tom and Meredith, who owned a motorhome and traveled for six weeks through the summer. Would that be where they traveled? To art shows to sell her work?

I am remembering Meredith kissing my forehead before they took the baby from the room. Every cell in my body is pulling me to run through the festival in search of the girl, but there is the memory of that gentle touch that keeps me standing in my own booth. I still watch, hoping to catch sight of her again, but I stay put. Charley, half-annoyed, heads to the food truck herself, since I am unreliable.

Does she know about me? Does she know she was adopted? Does she ever wonder about me? I try to imagine finding Meredith, walking up to her and saying, "Hi, do you remember me?" I want to! I feel like my bones are going to come free of my skin with the need of it.

I force myself to converse, to hold semi-intelligent conversations, even to accept a family-portrait commission. Charley comes back with food, and my mind worries at ways to get away from the booth, excuses, but in the end, I do the right thing, like I always do. I promised Meredith and Tom that I would not come looking for her. I swore I would not disrupt their family. I promised it when they promised to give her a good home and puppies. They have done their part. It's up to Emily Ann to decide if she is going to meet me, and that is still years in the future. I'm in the database.

Two hours have passed, three, and down the row, a few of the booths are coming down. My stock is substantially diminished, as is Charley's, but we both planned well, made a good guess, and the only thing I've run out of is one of the ocean prints that people like for living rooms.

I have pushed the girls I saw down and out of my mind. The way I used to put things in a box inside my head to deal with later.

30

The days after the Springfield Art Festival, I make a list of all the junkyards and body shops in a sixty-mile radius. If the police aren't going to do it, then I will. I try to work out the logistics of how I will get into the back of the body shops to see the cars. I ask Tom about his shop, about where all the cars come from, and he explains: they belong to other people, and he is working on them. If I were a stranger and came to him and asked to see the cars in his shop, there is no way he would let me. I am frustrated for days while I try to work an angle, but I finally have to give up on getting into the body shops. I'll have to focus on junkyards and leave the body shops to the cops. At least it feels like forward motion. It's better than standing still. The days pass, and I make lists, scouring the Internet for businesses in a sixty-mile radius.

I am hesitant to do it on my own. I want Dylan to go with me, but he, like everybody else, thinks I need to leave it in the hands of the police. I print off my list of junkyards and body shops and take it to the police department for Detective Daniels, who doesn't invite me to his office. "Please make sure he gets it," I say to the dispatcher as I slide the sheet of paper through the slit beneath the bulletproof glass.

Days slip past, Amy is still lost, slipping from the town's consciousness more every day. She has been gone a whole summer, and now it is almost fall and she is still gone. Nobody is doing anything, and I feel like my hands are tied.

Saturday morning dawns with frost on the ground, and I make my way to Dylan's house in Neoga. He's rented a truck and has two kids from the football team coming to help load his belongings. They are already there, carrying a dresser down the stairs when I arrive.

"Hey," I call when Dylan comes out of the truck. He is tanned, and the streaks of blond in his hair are shining.

"Hey." He leaps from the truck and wraps his arms around me.

God, I love him. He kisses me, and neither of us breathes as the world stops rotating for the moment we are touching. When he draws his lips from mine, I know that he has felt it, too, that stopping of the world, and we sigh, as if breathing from the same lung.

"Thanks for being here."

"I wouldn't miss it. Is Daecus here?"

"No. Mandy has him for the day."

I'm disappointed, but it wouldn't have made sense for him to be here today. "So how can I help?"

"You already have." He leans down, putting his forehead to mine, inhaling a long breath. "Just help carry boxes. Everything is packed."

He takes my hand, and we make our way into the house, and I see that he isn't kidding. The house is staged for the move. The dining room, directly off the entrance, is stacked and lined with boxes. The walls are entirely bare; even *Tumult* is down from its place over the fireplace. It makes me incredibly sad, although I have been waiting for this day since Dylan showed up again in my life. This was supposed to be the last step to him being an unmarried man. It turns out not to be, since the divorce is still pending. They are fighting over the custody agreement. Mandy got a promotion, and Dylan insists that Daecus is going to spend more time with daycare workers than family. I don't ask about it; he has enough on his plate today. I heft a box and follow Dylan, who is carrying another box, past the boys as they come back into the house.

When did he have time to get everything packed? The last time I was here, it still looked mostly like a home, but now everything is down. He must have been up nights working on it because his days have been full of football camp and me. A small pang of guilt that I haven't offered to help more hits my chest, and I see a little more clearly the shape of the man he has become. He doesn't ask for help. He does what has to be done and doesn't complain about it. I see the past three weeks with a different perspective, realizing how tired he has been when I've seen him in the evenings, as if he's been running all the scrimmages with the boys. I understand now that when I went to work at night, he went home to pack. There is no other way this could have happened.

***

It is well past dusk when we finally finish unloading the truck for the second time. Dylan sends the boys home with a hundred dollars each from his wallet. Neither of them is comfortable accepting the money. "No, Coach Winthrop. We're happy to help," they say, but Dylan insists, and again I see the man he has become. I stand to watch the exchange from the open door. When the boys are gone, Dylan turns to come inside.

The small house on Foxglove is full to bursting with boxes, and I take his hand and lead him through the clutter until I reach what will be his bedroom. All afternoon I've been planning the seduction. While he was helping with the last load, I pulled the mattress from where the boys had propped it on the wall and made the bed with fresh sheets. I'd brought the sheets, freshly purchased and laundered, with this very seduction in mind. We were going to wait until the divorce was final, but we've waited long enough.

"What's this?" He grins, taking in the mattress on the floor, the candle flickering on the plastic-wrapped dresser.

"A little housewarming gift." I wrap my arms around his waist and stand on my toes to kiss him.

"Hmm," he says against my lips as if I taste like honey.

I pull him with me, back toward the mattress, and when my heels hit it, I step up, making us equal in height. Fire flickers from the candle, and when he drops his head onto my breasts, I hold him, feeling his breath against my skin.

He drops to his knees, his fingers trailing under the hem of my shirt. Chills erupt across my skin as he draws the fabric up and off, over my head. His lips brush over my bra. My nipples are erect and tingling, and when his hand unfastens the clasp at the back, I gasp, desire taking my breath away.

He nudges me back, and I lie down on the mattress, drawing him with me. We are too hungry, we've been too long on this fast, and where I had planned a slow seduction, I only want to feel his flesh against mine.

If words are spoken, I don't know them, but the moment he slides inside me, I freeze, suddenly aware of where we are and what is happening. Sex has always been so complicated that I'm confused when it doesn't feel complicated at all. It's the most natural thing to want him inside me. He holds my eyes with his, not moving. He must see the transition across my face. Our eyes are locked as much as our bodies. He doesn't move, or speak, or breathe until my hips shift, drawing him deeper inside me, and he breathes a long breath.

He is holding himself up, still timid of me, his lips parted, and I wrap my legs around his hips, and he finally thrusts fully inside. He lowers his face and kisses my lips, my throat, as his body moves in rhythm.

We rock together, and for the first time in my life, I fully understand what all the fuss is about. When we breathe again, when collapse is all that is left, I kiss the small hairs along his jawline, tasting the salt of his sweat, remembering the ocean, and we both finally sleep, tangled in sheets and each other.

31

I love the little house on Foxglove. I love the way the light falls across the bed in the morning. I love the way Dylan has asked my opinion as he has placed the dresser, as he has hung *Tumult*, as he has arranged Daecus's room. It feels like I belong here with him. It feels like home.

It isn't my home, though, and Dylan isn't my husband. I remember that fact on the morning I've decided to finally go on my Camaro hunt. I park in the drive and make my way up to the porch. I don't want to go alone and know that we will take any excuse to be together.

It is a bright and shining morning, not yet hot, but the promise is in the air. I am deep in my thoughts, plotting which lots we will hit first, thinking that if we hit the ones in Charleston and Mattoon, we could have lunch at Neimurg's in Effingham before checking that lot out. I ring the bell and listen as it sings through the house. I brush my shorts, pushing out a wrinkle on my t-shirt. The door opens, and my muscles jerk. I am looking down at painted toenails and a slim ankle and calf. I jerk up and stand facing Dylan's wife, Mandy.

"Oh," I say, suddenly unsure of what to say.

"What do you want?"

Why is she here? This isn't her house. She doesn't belong here. My stomach flips.

"Is Dylan here?"

"I think he's in the bedroom." *The* bedroom. Not *his* bedroom. The bedroom. What is she doing here? Why would she be here?

"Oh. Okay." I back off down the steps.

"Do you want me to let him know you stopped by?" A small quirk spreads her lips, and I know that she knows she is killing me. She knows and she doesn't care. She knows and she likes it.

I put my hand up, waving the question away. Have they gotten back together? Have I been a fool? Was it not the custody agreement that was holding the divorce up but an uncertainty of moving forward? She shrugs and turns back into the house, closing the door, as if it is her home and I am a solicitor. I am down to the end of Foxglove, turning onto Division, and I shout in the cage of my car, the sound echoing back to me. I am my mother's screaming ghost, turmoil and chaos raging inside of me. This is why I don't date! Stupid, stupid me.

My phone rings. Dylan's face blooms across the screen, and I decline the call. It rings again, and again, and again until I am finally on Lincoln heading toward the first lot.

"What?" I ask, finally answering, finally angry and agitated enough to be a bitch.

"Why did you leave?" he asks, and his voice is so low and quiet that I imagine him sitting in the closed pantry, hiding his conversation.

"Your wife was home."

He chuckles. "Come on back. She's leaving. She came to bring Daecus."

"Where was her car?" I ask, feeling that I've caught him. It wasn't in the driveway, so it had to be in the garage. Who parks a car in a garage when dropping off a kid? Who takes off their shoes and settles in when dropping off a kid?

"It was on the street. You drove right past it."

I hadn't noticed a car. Wouldn't I have noticed? Is he lying to me? I blow out a small laugh.

"What's going on, Al?"

"I don't know, Dylan. I don't like her being there."

"I know. I'm sorry. I wish you'd come back. I have news." He is happy; I hear it in his voice.

"What's the news?" I ask, pulling myself together, trying to sound normal.

"She signed the custody agreement. I get to keep Dake."

"Oh." A small pearl of happiness for him blooms, but it is overwhelmed by an immeasurable sadness for me. Tears are flooding my eyes, and I have to blink to see the road.

"Come back. Dake and I will fix you breakfast. Right, buddy?" I realize then that Daecus is with him, probably wondering why I won't just come back.

"I can't."

"Al, what's wrong?"

How can I tell him that I'm crying because he gets to keep his son and I didn't get to keep my daughter? What's wrong with me that I would even feel like that? Of course I want Daecus to be with him—of course I do. I finally say, "I just didn't expect her to answer your door."

"I'm sorry about that, but I don't understand why you're so upset."

"It's just like you're still together."

He laughs a hollow, weary sound. "We are not together. Didn't you hear me? It's final. She signed everything. We'll file it with the court on Monday."

"She'll always be a part of your life," I say, feeling sad because he has never been able to just be mine, and it's all I've ever wanted.

"Yeah, Al, she'll always be a part of my life. But she's not my wife anymore. Why are you so upset?"

Why am I so upset? Because she's beautiful. Because she is the mother of his son and that was supposed to be me. I heave out a long breath, hearing how ridiculous I am in the voice inside of my head.

"I'll come by later. I have something I have to do," I whisper. He wouldn't be able to go with me today anyway, not with Dake.

"Do what?"

"Just something." I don't want to tell him; I don't want to hear him tell me I shouldn't go at all, let alone by myself.

"Come on, Al. Come back."

I am tempted, but I'm embarrassed. I'm frustrated. I am precisely the person I was the night he took Kelci Bancroft to the spring dance. I'm still jealous and insecure and stubborn.

In the moment it takes for me to answer, I promise myself two things. One, I will finish this search through the junkyards that are on my list and be done. Two, I will tell Dylan everything about why I am the way I am when I get back.

If I don't find the Camaro today, I will drop it. If Amy Kent is to be found, she will have to be discovered by somebody other than me. My obsession, my inability to let it go looks insane. Of course, Charley is right. Of course, my fixation is about Emily Ann and not Amy Kent. Even worse, it's about me. Amy Kent took me back in time to when my life was out of control and I felt hopeless. She reminded me of myself, and I have somehow thought that if I could find her, then I could fix myself. There is no way to fix my past, and the only way to fix my future is to come clean with Dylan and let him decide if I am someone he wants in his life. I should have already told him, and it feels like lying that I haven't. He thinks I am one person and he loves that person. Will he still love me when he knows my truth? I don't know, and that's what has kept me quiet all this time.

"I can't. I have to finish this, then I'll come back, okay?"

"I wish you hadn't left."

"I'm sorry. I just wasn't prepared to see her there." I wipe a tear from my face. "I'm sorry." There are so many ways I could have prevented the last half hour. I could have called to tell him I was coming. I could have waited for Mandy to get Dylan and acted like a big girl. I could turn around and set the search aside and go back and fix everything that will make my life right.

"It's okay. Come for dinner?"

I hear Daecus in the background, calling, "Tacos, tacos, tacos!"

Dylan laughs, and I'm ashamed again, because Daecus, who has just been dropped off at a new house as his parents divorce from each other, is more grown up than I am. "That sounds good, Dakey," Dylan says, then to me, "What do you think?"

"That sounds great. Six?" I ask, and he agrees.

"We can't wait to see you." His voice is solemn, and I hear his longing. I wish I hadn't left.

"Love you," I whisper.

"Me, too," he says. I understand that he can't say it in front of Daecus, not yet, not so soon.

We disconnect, and I press the gas pedal, accelerating until I fly past the car that had been in front of me, anxious to start and then be done.

32

I pull over to the side of the road when I reach the first shop and pull my features into place, planning my approach, rehearsing my roughly constructed story. When I get out of my car and cross the street, I put a bounce in my steps.

"Howdy, ma'am. Can I help you?" says a man who sees me coming across the lot.

"Yeah, I'm on the hunt for a muscle car, like an old Camaro maybe, that my boyfriend could rebuild. He likes to tinker, and it'd be a perfect gift." I try to pitch my voice in conspiratorial tones as if the imaginary boyfriend might just come up behind me at any moment. This first lot, like the next two, run pretty much with the same script. They all offer a look around, suggesting the old Trans Am at one and a Mustang at another, but none have the clay-colored Camaro. When I leave the only lot in Neoga, it's past noon, and my stomach rumbles.

I send him a text: *Can't wait for tacos. One more stop.* It feels like a first step.

I've been spiraling for days, ever since I saw the redheaded girl at the Springfield Art Festival. My nerves are frayed, and with the little bit of distance between this morning and now, I see how I overreacted about Mandy. She was just so pretty, standing there in his house as if she belonged. I understand that it's complicated, and I wish I hadn't run off like that, that I had been polite and mature and not acted like a child. I keep replaying it, try to see myself as less foolish, but every time I think through it, I look more ridiculous than the time before.

My phone vibrates as soon as the text has flown, and I answer his call.

"Hey," I say by way of greeting.

"Skip the last stop. Come now." I can't help but smile. Just hearing his voice changes my body's chemistry—my body liquifies, my heart flutters against the cage of my ribs, a bird taking flight.

"I'm almost done. One last stop."

"Where?"

"Effingham. Then I'll head back."

He groans as if it's too long a time to be away from me, and my stomach pulls with desire. God, I hope he still wants me after he knows about the baby. It's what has been swirling—the fact that I haven't told him the truth is why I exploded when I saw Mandy. He's been honest, and I'm still hiding my secrets. How can we build a relationship if he doesn't know who I am?

"What are you doing?" he asks, and I can almost see him stepping out onto his front porch.

I have reached the only junkyard I have on my list in Effingham. I'm tempted to tell him, but know that he'll respond the same way Charley had, the same way Leslie had, the same way everybody does when I bring up Amy Kent. I'll tell him when I get back; then I'll keep no more secrets.

"I'll tell you when I get home."

"You just said home." The smile in his voice feels like a kiss.

"You know what I mean." A quick look across the street tells me this shouldn't be a long stop. The gate is locked, so it's just going to be a looking-through-the-chain-link excursion. "It shouldn't take long."

"All right. See you soon."

"Yep, soon." I disconnect, pull the key from the ignition, and leave my car. The junkyard is vast. I try the gates, even though the lock is clearly engaged. A sign is posted on the fencing: *Call for appointment 217-536-6161.* I contemplate calling the number, but then I'd have to wait for them to come, and I just want to be done so I can go home.

Home.

The search has worn thin, and I feel weary. Why am I doing this when nobody else seems interested? I want to be done so I can go and see Dylan and lay my life bare.

I make my way down the perimeter of the fence, climbing links when my view is blocked by the cars, sometimes stacked two high. By climbing up, I can see above the cars that line the outer rim of the lot.

The sky has grown darker as I've driven from Charleston, and the heat that the morning promised has blown away. The clouds are dense, and my hair whips around my head. Street lights begin to flicker on, and in the gloom, and I recognize the curve of the back fender.

I climb another six inches to see more clearly the back end of the Camaro parked behind the building, mud-colored, muted. From my angle, I cannot see if it is a complete vehicle.

"What are you doing?" a voice calls out, and I drop down off the fence, my heart ratcheting against my ribs. Beyond him, I can see that the gate is now open, and I understand that he was inside and came out to see what I was doing out here. I should have called the number; now I look guilty.

"Oh! You startled me. Do you work here?" I ask, and he nods, snorts, and spits a wad of tobacco into the brush. I force myself not to recoil, not to show my disgust. I steady my breathing, composing my face, trotting out the fabricated story about my search for a car for my boyfriend to rebuild.

"I don't know that I got anything that would be a good rebuild. Most of the cars on this lot are parts." His tongue works his teeth, and he spits again. There is something in his speech patterns that feels off, as if he is putting on the accent, twanging, dropping consonants and vowels in a procession. He's not a bad-looking guy, but I'm so repulsed that I take an involuntary step away from him. He's just a country boy; it's not that. It's the tobacco. It's the spitting. It's his overactive tongue.

"What about that one? The Camaro. Is it whole?" I point toward the corner of the building, and my heart skips a beat and stutters on the next. It suddenly feels hazardous to be on this search.

He turns and looks, taking in the back end of the Camaro before turning back to look at me. His eyes narrow. "Naw, that's not for sale. That's my brother's car."

"It's exactly what I'm looking for. I'm sure we could agree on a price." I give him my best smile and look up at him from under my lashes, pulling out flirtations that I had long since forgotten I knew. "Can't I at least come in and look at it?"

"You'll have to call for an appointment. Gates are closed. I was heading out."

He turns away and walks back toward the gate. I follow. "But you're here; I'm here. Can't I just look? I won't take much of your time." He doesn't respond but replaces the lock and closes it with a solid click. "Does it run?"

He shrugs, an elaborate raising and rolling of shoulders. "You can make an appointment with Grady, but he ain't going to sell it."

"All right," I say, agreeing. "I'll call for an appointment. Thanks for your time." I turn and trot across the road, back to my car, and wave at him as I close my door, sheltered.

He nods and waves back, the way you'd shoo a fly. He turns to walk off down the block. I start my car and pull out into traffic, merging, passing the young man, feeling him watching me as I go. I drive the length of the block and double back, parking farther down the street, away from the gate. I think about calling Detective Daniels, but I can't call him without something substantial. I've made a pest of myself, and I'm embarrassed by the memory of his tone the last time I'd tried to talk to him. I am going to look at that car if it's the last thing I ever do. I have to know if it is whole. I have to know if it has the crunched front fender, or Detective Daniels will think I am wasting his time, interfering in his investigation.

The clouds are so thick that it looks like dusk, and I'm glad for it because, in the gloom, nobody will notice me climbing the fence. I choose a spot between two "no trespassing" signs. It's a bad idea, with all the notices and warnings, but I have no other choice. I think the car just on the other side of the fence looks like it is almost tall enough for me to drop down upon without making any noise. That's the plan anyway. Scaling the diagonal links is easy, but maneuvering to cross the barbed wire on top proves tricky. The wide leg of my shorts catches as I go over, and the jolt, as my downward plunge halts, jars all the organs of my body. For a moment I hang, suspended, unable to retreat or continue. I'm a scant foot above the car below, but I am a fly caught on the sticky strip. A duck in an oil slick.

The seam of my shorts gives way as I am considering the possibility of squirming free of them. Lightning flashes, and the first pelt of rain hits my head. I crash to the hood of the car and bounce to the ground in a tangle of legs and arms. It is a miracle that the only thing broken is the stitch in my shorts. I lay flat for a moment, as fat drops of rain splatter around me. When my breathing is steady, when I am beginning to feel like a drowned cat, I scuttle to my feet and crouch. Thunder rolls.

It was a bad plan. I didn't even think about how I would get back out of the fence, but looking up at the angle of the barbed wire convinces me that I will not be able to get out the same way I got in. I crouch in the shelter of one of the ruined cars and listen. I thought I'd heard a sound inside the building, before that last peel of thunder. A sound like a voice, or the closing of a door. Now I am not confident what I heard, if anything. I should not have assumed that because one person left, there were no other persons around. I'm not thinking! Frustration rides the ridge of my back, and I contemplate my next move.

I listen. Nothing, except the rain falling in fat drops on the crumpled and rusted metal and traffic moving down the street, horns honking farther away. I begin to relax when no sounds of doors, no feet rushing in the grass come to me. I pull my phone from my hip pocket, sheltering it beneath me, making sure I didn't break it when I fell.

I will check out the Camaro; then I will call Detective Daniels and wait for him to arrive. I'll have to see the driver's-side fender to know for sure. I'll have to pass under the security light, which is no longer flickering but is now steadily on. Detective Daniels won't let them arrest me, surely, if I help them find the answers to Amy Kent's disappearance.

When the only sound around me is the whoosh of a car passing down the street and the rain, my heart finds its steady pace and stops reverberating in my ears. Another flash of lightning and another roll of thunder passes. The storm is beginning in earnest now, and the wind picks up to a howl. I draw myself from my shelter and walk, hunched and small, toward the back of the building, wishing I had thought to wear something that would blend in, feeling like my t-shirt is a glowing beacon.

I half expect the car to be just a back end with a mangled front, but when I pass through the glow of the security light, I see that it is complete and intact. I come to it, and walking along the edge of light, I see clearly that the tires are not rotted. Weeds are rising around the wheels but in a rolled-over fashion and not a one-with-nature fashion. This car has not been parked for millennia. It has not been left to rot and decay. The tires are thick with tread, knobby even. There is no plate on the car which makes me wonder if I am mistaken. They couldn't take this car out on the street without plates.

Then I remember that dealers sometimes drive cars from the lot, and they have dealer plates that they can exchange as need be. Do junkyards have dealer plates? This one might. The place is named Milton's Parts and Sales.

I step into the glow of the light and look through the window into the pristine interior of the Camaro, a car being restored with love. Such a surge of certainty rushes through my veins that I pull my phone and open it to call Detective Daniels. I know this is the car that dropped Amy off at the clinic. I can see the slight rise in the opposing fender, even from this side, and remember very clearly the bow in it. I know in that split second that I have found something extraordinary. I dial and the phone rings, but before the call is connected, I hear movement behind me, and as I turn, something crashes into the side of my head.

33

I am not dead. I know I am not dead because my heart is thudding inside my head with such force that I wish it would just explode and release me from the pain. I try to pull my hands up, but they are tied behind my back. I'm lying on my side, my shoulder aching from the awkward position.

I don't know where I am or how I got here.

The floor is cement with dark stains in irregular circular patterns. My back is against a wall, an interior wall. My body shivers, cold and wet.

"We need to get rid of her." A woman's voice slips through the wall, and I'm relieved that there is another woman here. Maybe she will help me.

"Said she was looking for a rebuild. Wanted to look at Grady's car." I recognize the voice of the man I'd met on the street.

"Is that why she'd be calling the police? Idiot." It's a different male voice.

"Doesn't look like the call connected. Have you ever seen her before?" It's the woman again.

"No, but she was looking for something. What did she say to you?"

"She was just looking at your car, Grady. Said she wanted a rebuild, for a boyfriend, or something."

"Well, it's damn well not for sale."

"Well, yeah. Of course. I told her that."

"She wasn't just looking at the car, boys. She was looking for something." The woman paces, her heels click on the concrete floor.

"I'll get rid of her." The older male voice, Grady, says, and I hear resignation, something akin to defeat in his tones. "I'll take care of it."

"I'd like to know what she was looking for. Who is Detective Daniels? She was onto something, calling a detective, 217 area code."

"That doesn't have to mean anything," Grady says, but even above the throbbing in my head, I can hear that he is rattled. "That could be from damn near anywhere." The area code stretches a vast span from Springfield to Rantoul to Champaign and even farther south than Charleston and Mattoon. There is a long pointed pause, and I imagine her looking through the phone, back over the call history. "This is about that Kent girl. Damnit, Grady," the woman hisses. "Your mess, you're gonna fix it." She has gone through my texts, she has seen my last conversation with Charley. I shudder.

Their conversation drops until I can hear only the tone of the voices, hers and then his, and hers again, but no words make their way to me.

What have I done? I have to convince them I don't know anything. I try to remember all the acting techniques I learned in California, but my head is too thick and my mind is too slow.

"You awake?"

I make no sound. I make no move.

A boot nudges against my shin, shifting my body, and I groan with the pain in my head.

"Get up." The door falls closed. He kneels in front of me. When I can't pretend any longer, I open my eyes.

His hand closes around my upper arm, tugging me as I struggle to sit.

"Thank you," I mumble, before I even know the words are in my mouth.

He chuckles, a puff of air passing through his nostrils, like a horse. "You're welcome. Come on. The lady wants to talk to you." It's not the boy I met at the gate. This must be the brother, Grady, who has promised to "take care of it." The same way he promised to take care of Amy? I should never have let her go! I knew she was in trouble and now *I'm* in trouble. Serious trouble. He is older than the boy I met at the gate, but with the same angular features, the same small, penetrating eyes.

I nod, feeling my head thrumming on my shoulders, a drum pounding.

"Why am I here?"

"You tell me."

"I can't. I don't know how I got here. Do I know you?" Do I sound confused, addled? I look up at him with wide eyes, trying to look young and trusting.

He laughs, and my head pounds. He isn't buying it. The gray fog recedes for just a moment, but then rushes back to fill all the space in my mind. He pushes me ahead of him through the doorway. My right shoulder is shoved up by his hand, which is still firmly on my upper arm. I try not to stumble. The bright light assaults my eyes.

My head throbs.

The woman is tall with dark hair hanging loosely around her shoulders. Her lips are full and red. Her brows arch above eyes that are wide open. She looks stretched, with all the skin pulled taut over her features. She could be fifty or seventy. It is hard to imagine the number of times her face has been stretched. She is beautiful in a plastic-doll way, with high cheekbones and a strong, but not-*too*-strong chin. I am not confident what I see until she speaks. Then I know I am looking at the boss.

"What were you doing here?"

"I don't know."

"Who did you call?" She glances at me then at the tall man who brought me from the other room. He reaches out to point to the phone lying on the table in front of the woman. Is that my phone? I try to make my face vacuous, empty of comprehension. *Do I even have a phone?* Of course it is my phone, and we all know it.

"Did I call someone?" I shake my head, then stop when it makes the world swim. "I don't remember calling anybody." I have a concussion; the knowledge is just there in my mind, like knowing that I am in serious trouble here.

"Hmm." She walks in a slow circle around me. "Trespassing is a serious thing around here. I can just kill you. Nobody would ask questions. You intruded on my place of business after you were told to leave. I can kill you now. Be done with it."

"I didn't mean any harm." The effort of speaking makes me feel nauseous. "I was just looking for a project for my boyfriend."

"'You gotta let this Amy thing go,'" she hisses, reading from my phone, and I remember the text thread. She goes on, "'I can't. We'll find her when we find that Camaro.'"

I cringe. No doubt in anybody's mind why I am here. She has set the phone on a metal table and walked a distance away into the shadows, and when she comes back, she is carrying a hammer. I think she is going to smash my head in. I think, with her unmoving plastic face, she is going to kill me.

She lifts the hammer and brings it down with a crash, and my head throbs. The phone shatters, and she continues to smash it until shards fly in every direction.

My vision tunnels to a pinprick and then blinks out entirely.

34

When I wake, it feels like hours have passed, days. I am in a tight space, jostling, the rumble of an engine reverberating on my cheek. The arm beneath me is awkward and numb. The fumes of exhaust are chokingly thick. It isn't dark; the space is lit red by the glow of the taillights into the trunk. My mind isn't clear, but I understand I am in the trunk of a car, even if I can't remember how exactly I got here. It's my car—I know because I can see the small tool kit that Don Robinson gave me when I bought the car. A dip in the road jostles me painfully, and I cry out, trying to rearrange my body to release the pressure on my shoulder, but my hands are tied behind me, and I'm unable to free them. I shift, pushing my hips back, angling them through the crook of my hands, desperate to have my hands in front of me, if for no other reason than to release the pressure on my shoulder.

I lay gasping when my hands are finally in front of me. Rolling onto my back, I shift my body into a defensive position for when they open the trunk. I'm ready when the car engine dies. I'm prepared to kick and fight and scream as soon as the trunk opens.

I wait.

I wait.

Muffled voices come from outside the trunk, and I wait. I can't make out words but realize that the car is moving again but with the engine off, as if they've left it in neutral on a hill. I shift my body back until my head presses against the backside of the seat, and I remember that the rear seat folds down from the trunk. I raise my arms and push against

209

the seat, ignoring the sharp pain in my shoulder. The car is picking up speed, bumping down a slope.

It stops abruptly with a great splash, and the force of the stoppage shoves me against the back seat, which finally gives way and pops loose, jarring my body.

It is full night, and the storm from earlier has passed, leaving a clear sky with a fat moon glowing. The light glistens on the surface of the water beyond the windows, and I scramble from the trunk into the back seat, knowing that it only takes minutes for a car to submerge. A light flashes through the rear window, and when I look behind me, I see the nose of a pickup truck backing up and beginning to turn.

What do I know about submerged cars? Nothing. There is something about equalizing the pressure before you can open the doors, but I don't know what I remember about it.

I don't think I'll be able to open a door once it goes under, and I'm too scared to open it now because it might be enough movement for the men to see. The truck has not left the bank, and I imagine them watching to be sure the car submerges. The window. The window. I begin to roll the window down, hoping it will go unnoticed, grateful that my car is old and that it still has cranks, thankful that I managed to get my hands in front of me, although it feels like I may have torn a muscle in my right shoulder.

Water is rising over the hood, and steam is rising above the surface as the engine block submerges. I look again behind me, seeing the tail-lights of the truck glowing but not moving. "Go," I hiss, needing to see the pickup pulling away. It doesn't. It sits, its lights flooding the bank. They are watching to be sure the car goes down, making sure I am "taken care of."

Terror washes through me. If I get out of the car, would I be able to reach the far bank, away from the men? Not with my hands tied. *Shit.* Not with my shoulder throbbing, radiating pain.

I wait unable to decide what I should do next. Water begins to flow over the front console and in through the window. My head is pounding. As the water starts pouring through the window, the car tilts. I hastily roll the other rear window down so I can get out either side. It takes forever, it seems, for the car to slip deeper into the water, while the men sit in their truck on the bank. It's a lifetime as the water rises over the front seat and fills the back, although I know it is just seconds. I bite my tongue, and when the water rises to my chin, I tilt my head up, drawing in long deep breaths in preparation for the moment the water takes the car beneath the surface.

I expect that moment to be calm, a simple slide, but it isn't. The water buffets me, shifting and pushing as the body of the car groans under its pressure. I am knocked back against the door as the car slips deeper, and the water is roiling around me. I grasp the frame of the window with my hands, still bound, and begin to pull myself free of the flooded interior. I want to wait until the car settles so the two men watching from the bank will think I'm trapped in the trunk, but as soon as I feel the pressure in my chest, I know that my heart is pounding too fast for me to hold my breath long enough to pull off the feat. I am free through the window, pushing against the draw of the downward pull of the car, already feeling my lungs burning for want of air.

I kick off of the roof and erupt through the surface of the water with a gasp. I push myself onto my back drawing breath and spitting the brackish water from my mouth. I look toward the bank and am confused when I see no sign of the truck. I hear shouts, though. Then I see that several cars have stopped on the road; people are leaning over the railing, calling out.

My head is pounding. My legs are exhausted from kicking. My vision tunnels as I try to stay above the water. When I try to call out, my head bobs below the surface, and I sputter, drawing water into my mouth, choking my shouts. I kick, erupting again from the surface, and a hand reaches out, wrapping in my hair and pulling me away from the spot where the car was only moments before. Arms close under my arms, and my head falls into the curve of a neck. I don't know if it's the men who put me in the trunk or one of the people from the road, but either way, I let him take me. When he drags me from the water, I cough until I think my head will rupture and finally lay still, pressed close beside the man who pulled me out. He is talking, keeping up a monologue of "you're okay" and "the police are coming" and something about an ambulance that I don't quite catch. The people from the road make their way down to the bank to gather around us. My head throbs, and I let my eyes close, exhausted by life.

35

Sirens explode in the distance, and I wait, regaining my breath, shuddering as shock settles in my blood and my teeth clack together. Somebody is running toward me, a blanket flapping as she comes, and she folds down around me, wrapping the blanket around my shoulders. It smells of dog, but it is warm, comforting with its animal scent.

"Oh my God!" the woman shouts, drawing my hand up from where they rest on my lap. "You're tied. Oh my God. Oh my God." She scrabbles at the rope that binds my hands.

"Stop. The police need to see that. Stop." He pushes her fingers away and folds his own hand protectively over mine. I glance up, and she is spinning, her eyes scanning.

Conversations float above me, and some of it I catch, but most of it I miss in the chatter of my teeth.

"A car cut me off pulling back on the road from down here. That's why I stopped. Damn near hit me."

"It was a truck," somebody else says.

"That's when I saw the car in the water," the man behind me, cradling me, says. "Do you know who did this to you?" He's the one who pulled me out of the water.

"Milton's," I say, but the screech of sirens drowns my words. The crowd makes way for the police and paramedics as they arrive. Chaos erupts as all the people around me speak at once, telling the police what they saw—the car . . . no, the truck pulling back up on the road, the car submerging, then me erupting from the surface of the water.

The dog blanket is replaced by a warm blue thermal when the paramedics lead me up and away from the bank to the waiting ambulance. The police had photographed my bound hands and then cut the restraints. Rope burns encircle my wrists, and I stare down at the angry flesh. I hadn't even noticed that it hurt until the cords were cut away. The paramedic flashes a light in my eye, checking for reaction, and probes the contusion on the side of my head for fractures in the skull. I lean to the side, sick.

"Concussion," I say when I can, remembering the night Derrick Jessop brought his small daughter to the emergency room, how she had been sick from the injury.

"Can you tell me your name?"

"Alison. I'm Alison Hayes."

"Can you tell me how many fingers I am holding up?'

"Three . . . no, four." I have to squint, but I think I'm right. It's just that the world is spinning too quickly on its axis, and my body can't find the right momentum to rejoin it.

"Good."

They wash my wounded wrists and apply bandages, then they clean the laceration on my head, cutting away swaths of hair to get to it. One of the tufts of hair falls by my hand, and I hold it between my fingers until it breaks apart and the individual hairs fall to the floor of the ambulance. They wrap my head in bandages and encourage me to lie down on the gurney. Two police officers come to the back of the ambulance, and one climbs in, sitting across from me on the bench.

"Can you tell me what happened?'

"I was looking for Amy Kent," I say, shuddering and rolling to my side so I can see him without moving my head.

"Amy Kent?"

"A girl from Charleston. Went missing early in the summer."

"Oh, yes. Fourteen-year-old?"

"Yeah. Call Detective Daniels in Charleston. He'll know me." I tell him the barest skeleton of the story, how she had come in for a pregnancy test and disappeared. Even I can hear how my words aren't lining up through my chattering teeth.

"You're a bit away from Charleston. Why here?"

"I was one of the last people to see her," I say because that should explain everything. It doesn't; I know by the expression on his face. "I didn't see the guy who brought her to the clinic, but I saw his car. The primer-brown Camaro. At Milton's."

"The junkyard?"

I nod. The world spins.

"Grady Milton did this to you?"

"Yes," I say, not daring to nod again.

Another officer, who has been listening as he stands off to the side, reaches up to his radio and speaks into it, his voice low, lost to me.

I'm getting tired. The paramedic gave me something for nausea, and I try to remember the name of the medicine as my eyelids become more weighted with each passing second. The officer is there when my eyes open briefly and gone the next time. I feel the ambulance rocking beneath me, and let myself finally drift.

36

I am at work. I can smell the antiseptic scent of the hospital, clean and sterile. I must be working a double and catching a catnap between shifts.

I want to open my eyes, to get up and get back to work, but they are so thick and heavy that I let them be. I'll sleep for another five minutes, just five.

37

"She's waking up." His voice is thick and husky, close above me. I raise my hand, and my fingertips feel a stubbled cheek, the curve of his lips.

"Dylan." My voice is a whisper.

"Hey, Al," he says, and there is such a kid-glove tone to his words that my chin instantly puckers and tears sting the back of my eyelids. Finally, after all these years, Dylan understands that I am shattered.

He folds his arms around me, and even that is done without any pressure, as if he is scared to touch me. It destroys me. The threat of tears become an assault; he holds me closer. Against my will, I call out when the emotion inside me becomes too much to contain. He lessens his hold but does not back away. Instead, he lowers his face toward my shoulder, the same way his horse used to when I was young.

He smells like horses, such an odd, unusual smell for him to have after all these years, now that his horses are gone. But I smell hay and the faint hint of oats and the vague aroma of horse sweat mingling on his skin. Maybe it's just him. Perhaps he doesn't smell like any of those things, and I just associate those things to him. I am transported, with the quiet closeness of his face, his chin resting on the backside of my shoulder blade, and when I close my eyes, I can feel myself standing in the pasture all those years ago.

"You're awake." The voice startles me, but Dylan still doesn't release me, his face pressed into my neck, holding me closer until I feel he may absorb my liquid, blubbering self into his flesh. *You are flesh of my flesh, bone of my bone.* The words roll through my head, and I can't place them. Some archaic wedding vow, some pledge? Something from a book I once read?

When the doctor has stood patiently for some minutes, breathing into the room, not interrupting, Dylan finally begins to draw away. I clutch him, stopping him. His pale eyes hover, and the fleck in the one holds my attention. For a second, I think he is going to kiss me; I desperately want him to kiss me. He doesn't, but he keeps my eyes for a long second, as if searching for someone he once knew but is afraid may have been lost.

"Please don't leave." I'm not even sure I have said it, but he drops a kiss on my forehead, lowers my head gently onto the pillow, and straightens.

"I'm right here." He stands beside the bed, our hands linked in the air, fingers twined together—the way teenagers do when they can't get enough of each other, when there isn't enough skin to touch. Our hands are a bird in flight. My hand has wings.

We face the doctor; she is lovely with luxurious black hair falling loosely around her angular face. I see all of that, the way I would paint her with a brush, but what is emanating from her is kindness, like a glow. She is not looking at me with that horrible expression of sorrow that so many people carry. She is looking at me with hope.

Something in my chest releases, and the tension in my frame slackens.

"I'm Dr. Barr, a psychiatrist. I want to make myself available to you." She has the smallest hint of an accent, something foreign but subtle, as if she has worked very hard to eradicate the un-American quality of her speech.

"What happened?" I ask, unable to remember anything past the point of climbing the fence into the junkyard.

"What do you think happened?"

"I climbed over a fence. I must have fallen." I push the button under my hand to raise the head of the bed. "Did I fall?" I reach up to feel my head because the shift in position has made my mind swim. I feel the wrapped bandage.

"You don't remember?" Dylan asks and looks to Dr. Barr. "Is that normal?"

"Not unusual."

The memory begins to unlock. I was looking in the car. I found the Camaro! I was looking in the window, and somebody came up behind me and hit me. The next memory is of the water rushing through the window into the car.

"I was looking for Amy." My voice is a whisper.

"Yeah, that's right."

"Did I find her?"

"No, but you moved the investigation several steps closer."

"How do you mean?"

"Let's let the police talk to you about that, okay?" Dr. Barr says, her voice low and calm, and I wonder what it would be like to talk with her. Do I need a psychiatrist? It has taken several seconds for the reality of all that has happened to filter through my mind. No, I don't need to talk to anybody. I just need to close the door and go back to my life. I haven't yet had time to reframe my existence to include what happened at the junkyard and later at the lake. It's just a movie I once saw, not an experience I lived through.

Does she see it, the closing of my eyes, the defenses drawing into place, the bricks being laid one layer higher? She must, because she smiles, and there it is again. Hope.

Chills chase down my body. I look up at Dylan. "Did they catch them?"

"Yes. They did," Dr. Barr answers, and the smile that spreads her lips is not happy but is maybe relieved.

"What about Amy?" I ask. Dylan squeezes my hand

"They're searching. They are dredging the lake," he says.

Does that mean the people told them they killed her? Did the man, Grady, get rid of her the way he tried to get rid of me? Is that how he took care of her when she came up with an inconvenient pregnancy?

"Oh." Tears sting my eyes. I don't want to think about Amy being in the lake. I look up at Dylan and see his emotions shining in his eyes. Is he remembering his lost brother, lost in the lake?

Terror at my own near-drowning dawns.

"I just wanted to introduce myself," Dr. Barr says when another doctor comes from the hall. "I'll let you rest."

There is something about her that I like, something that made me feel calmer before she left than I do once she is gone. I almost want to call her back, to schedule my first appointment while I still remember how I felt with her present, but I don't.

"How are you feeling?" the doctor asks as Dr. Barr makes her way out the door.

I shrug, not sure how I feel. My throat hurts. My head feels heavy and swims. I put my hand up, touching the bandage. "Concussion?"

"Yes. Can I ask you some questions?" I nod, and he runs through a series of routine questions. What year is it? Where do I work? And so on, until he asks me about my highest level of education. I answer that it is a "GED," even though I have an associate's in nursing. I correct myself, and he makes a note on his clipboard. "You're a lucky girl."

"Yeah." I don't feel lucky, though. I feel like I almost had her, but I was too late.

Part Four: Winter

38

Don Robinson, Warren's brother, the one who runs the Ford dealership in Mattoon sent a loaner car. A young man delivered it, handing me the keys and a note. It felt like charity, but I accepted the loan because I still needed to get to work and wasn't ready to consider buying anything. It's new, and when I get in it, I feel like somebody else. I've never had a new car. I've never even had a car from the same decade. I need to talk to somebody, but I'm not ready to talk to a psychiatrist. Last night was the first night since I got out of the hospital that I stayed in my apartment. I spent the first two nights with the McGills and finally came home yesterday. Everybody is treating me like a hero. I feel like a fraud. I didn't save anybody but myself. I drive to Charley's without even calling first.

Cheyenne, Charley's oldest daughter, answers the door and leads me to the kitchen where Charley is standing at the island, the shells of avocados and the skin of onion on the counter in front of her. Tears are running down her face.

"Hey." She smiles, swiping at her eyes.

"You don't have to cry about it," I say, leaning close to give her a hug. She laughs when my eyes water from the onion.

"Tell me about it." She slides the skin of the onion into the trash, turning into the pantry for tomato. "You okay?"

"Yeah. You know they found her?"

"I heard. What a tragedy."

Detective Daniels came by my apartment last night to give me the news. They'd had divers in Lake Sara at Effingham for the past three days, and yesterday afternoon, they discovered Amy Kent's body, badly decomposed and tied to an engine block from a Chevy. Dental records confirmed it was her. I had thanked him, closed the door behind him, taken a shower and gone to bed. I slept like the dead and dreamt of nothing at all.

I nod, unable to speak. How I wish I had kept her. How I wish I had not let her go.

"How's your head?"

I flip my hair on one side where the hair was shaved for the stitches, and she cringes.

"I think I want to cut it all off," I say, holding a hank of my hair up.

"Why?"

"I don't know. I just feel like I need a change."

"We could match." I hear it now in her voice, the strain, the pressure she is under not to let me dwell on what has come before.

"We could. How would I look?"

"You'd be beautiful." She scoops tomato into the bowl and mashes the avocado. My stomach churns. I look away, seeing Amy, seeing her fingernails falling free of her hands, seeing her hair floating in the water. "I'll cut it for you."

"Okay." I nod because I desperately need something, and this feels like a start, a new beginning. I'm quiet as she clears the counter, and she doesn't offer any conversation. It's one of the best things about Charley; she can be silent when she needs to be.

***

My hand rubs the bare skin of my neck when Charley finally stops cutting and steps back.

"It's a bit of a shock. Isn't it?" I ask when we've walked together to the mirror in the entryway and look at our reflections. It's almost the cut Cici had when I met her, without the spikes. It makes me look younger and older at the same time. It makes me look less like my mother.

"You're beautiful." She holds my shoulders and squeezes, putting her face next to mine. I smile through tears.

"Thank you," I say, but not for the haircut. It's for the friendship, the sisterhood, the understanding, and Charley knows that. "I'm telling Dylan about the baby."

"Good," she says and kisses my cheek.

39

The storm that had blown through Milton's junkyard brought the shift of the seasons. The sun hid behind clouds for the weeks following, and while I could remember starting to school with temperatures well into the nineties, the kids were wearing jackets when I saw the first buses running. Rain spit in angry bursts for days, and when the sun finally did reappear, it was weak and unable to penetrate the gloom that had settled over the farmland of Illinois. The farmers stood together outside the Rural King and discussed the strange weather as an omen. It would be a severe winter, with it turning so early. We had been touched by tragedy, as a community, and it seemed that Mother Nature felt it as well. Parents kept their children closer to home; they talked a little more about the dangers of modern life.

Amy Kent's story had a brief resurrection in the news cycle, and although I requested anonymity in the reporting, word got around about my involvement. If I hadn't done what I had done, it would have been a cold case. People left small offerings outside my apartment—a single rose, a stuffed animal—in recognition that I had searched harder than anybody else and nearly lost my life for it. I did not go to her funeral, although after they placed her stone, I went to the cemetery between cloudbursts and told Amy how sorry I was for letting her go, and for once, it was of only Amy I was thinking. The date on the stone was the date we found her, although we all knew she had been dead the night she left the Crisis Clinic in the Camaro. The cause of death was ruled homicide by blunt-force trauma, and they discovered blood in the trunk of the Camaro. I prayed that she had died quickly, that she never understood what he had really meant when he said he'd take care of her.

For all the weeks of September, Dylan and I struggled to find time together. I couldn't find the right moment to tell him about the baby. School had started the week after they found Amy, and Dylan's days were full. When he was finishing his day, I was heading to work. I saw more of Daecus than Dylan, since I had volunteered to pick him up after school and take him out to the farm. Jake and Vaude fixed him dinner and helped with his homework until Dylan came to get him. Sometimes I stayed for dinner, and it felt like a gift to stand in Vaude's kitchen and help with the meal. Tonight, I am in the kitchen with her, and the smells filling the air are of basil and tomato sauce and the lasagna is a promise.

"I really love what you've done with your hair," she says. I reach up to touch my bare neck. I still feel naked.

"Thanks." I smile, and she sets down the knife and tosses the cucumber into a bowl.

When I look up, she is staring at me, and I give a small laugh. I have spent ten years trying to be invisible, and her looking at me feels like being seen. "What?"

"I'm just so impressed with the woman you've become."

"Oh, I'm nothing special."

She had wounded me all those years ago. She was as much a cause for the way I am as anybody else. I had thought she cared for me, but that long-ago night when I came to Dylan out of the rain, I had overheard her saying that I was going to be just like my mother. Not in so many words, but it was what she meant. It was why she had cautioned Dylan away from me. I have wanted to confront her every time I have seen her since then, but I never felt like I had proof that I had not become my mother. I'm not angry at her, not after so long, but it still hurts that I thought she cared about me and, really, she was only being polite.

"Dylan told me you met your dad." I nod. She lifts the knife again and starts cutting a tomato. "What was that like?"

"He's a nice man. He has two sons, one of 'em is a preacher. My step-mom, Stella, she kinda makes me think of my mom, but in a good way. Ya know?"

"Such a shame that he was never part of your life."

"Yep. I probably wouldn't be who I am if he had been."

"That could be true," she agrees after some time.

"I don't think I'm much like my mom," I say with just a touch of caution, feeling how it edges on the conversation I've needed to have for years.

"No, not a lot."

I finish lining the pan with layers of cheese and pasta. Then I say it. "Do you remember the night you told Dylan I would be like her?"

She looks up at me, and I can see that she does not remember anything like that.

"It was the night you and Jake came home and I was here because she had thrown me out. I heard you talking about it."

Her memory stretches, and I see when it finally comes to her.

"That's not what I meant." Her hand shoots across the island. "I didn't mean I thought you'd be . . ." She stops, clearly not comfortable insulting my mom. "Well, clearly I was wrong."

"I hope so. I've tried really hard to make you wrong." I hold her eyes for a split second and then smile.

"I'm sorry. I didn't mean it to sound the way it must have."

"It sounded like good advice." The tension in the room deflates, and she tells me that I was always a special part of their family and how glad she is that I am here.

"It's nice to be here."

"That was such a horrible time for you. I'm so sorry if I added to it." There is real remorse in her voice, sadness in her eyes.

"It's okay. You were right. I mean, I didn't know it at the time, but looking back, I was doing just what my mother had done, looking for somebody to fix me."

"How about now?"

"I think I'm mostly fixed." I hold her eyes for a long second and offer it as a promise that I am not going to hurt her son. I look away, "You know my mom was my age when she died."

"She was so young."

"I'm scared that I don't know how to live without her to gauge myself against."

"You seem to know who you are pretty well. I think you will figure it out." She smiles.

"Maybe," I agree, because I do feel like I know who I am after all these years, and I'm proud that I talked to Vaude about that day. I'm glad that I wasn't like my Grandma, walking away from what may be uncomfortable, and I wasn't like my mom, trying not to feel. The silence between us stretches, each of us processing the conversation we've come through, feeling the clean of the air.

"I saw a flier promoting the calendar up at Bancroft's. Dylan told me you had some work in that?"

I smile. It has been surreal seeing the fliers going up in storefronts promoting the Historical Society's calendar and cards. The bookstore below my apartment has them available for preorder and has an entire rack of the Historic Homes of Charleston cards on display. I was one of three artists they chose. Several people, many I don't even know, have stopped me at the store to tell me they've ordered their calendar. I've become known in town, and finally, it is for something good.

40

I've just left the farm, leaving Daecus with Jake and Vaude for the night. Dylan is with the football team at an away game in Taylorville. I'll be at the house on Foxglove when he comes home. He'll be late, but the anticipation of him coming back to me, of being able to sleep with him, of not having to leave, of making love and staying through the night is exquisite. It's that which has me preoccupied, as I drive down past the lot where my mother and I once lived. I'm almost past it before I realize the frame of a building is standing on the formerly vacant lot. I'd gotten used to seeing it bare, with just the grass and the few trees, I had almost reached the point that I could drive past without noticing the land, without remembering our life there.

Almost.

But not quite. My car slows nearly to a halt before I press my foot on the brake to bring it to a full stop. Rain is falling, again, a steady patter on the roof of the car.

I can't even remember the last time I drove past the lot. Clearly, it has been weeks, if not months. There are two roads that come into Bushton, one that goes past the lot and the other which is a more direct route to the farm. I usually take the other one, which is more convenient, but tonight I wasn't thinking and drove down the road by course of long-forgotten habit.

Now there is a foundation erupting from the ground. Framed walls and a green tin roof. I feel gut-punched. The lot is my place. Nobody is allowed to build here. It's sacred and cursed, but it is mine. I never knew who owned it after my mother died, and just assumed the county had taken it over for nonpayment of taxes. I always thought that some-day I would buy it back, my blood land, paid by Eddie to my mother, the price of my innocence. I never thought about anybody ever wanting the lot, let alone building a house on it. Who would do that? I cannot imagine who it might be, but somebody did, because here stands the stick-and-stone house my mother and I had planned all those years ago.

The rain patters on the roof of my car, and I reach across the seat searching for the umbrella that I keep but can't find it. Then I remem-ber, the umbrella was in my car. This is the loaner Don Robinson sent. Actually, it's not a loaner anymore; I went by to thank him and ended up signing papers for it. Don gave me very generous terms, and with the money from the insurance claim, it was like buying used.

The realization that I am not in my old car, but this new one brings all the vivid recollections of the night at Lake Sara into sharp focus, and I gasp, sucking for air, feeling blown apart. Days go by, and sometimes I forget Amy, I fail to remember the terrible moments in the car as it was slipping under the surface of Lake Sara. I forget because of Dylan. I am preoccupied because I am happy. Being in love with him is so much more than I ever thought possible. Being in love goes a long way to-ward helping me forget.

My conversations with Dr. Barr are sparsely worded, and even though I feel like I am wasting her time, I keep going every week, and sometimes we only talk about the weather, the strange, ominous weather, end-of-days weather, apocalypse weather.

I scramble out of the car, needing to be free. I need to breathe air from the world even in the rain. Once I am there, scuttling across the street, I realize that it is so much worse, being in the rain, because it makes me feel like I am drowning. The water on my face feels like the water from the lake. Even though it is not the same and I know it is not the same, it still has me gasping for breath by the time I reach the house. My panic has risen, my chest hammering with my heart trying to escape my body. I clamber over the braces and onto what will be a front porch, passing through the doorless entry. Stopping to catch my breath, swiping water from my face.

The exterior is deceptively small. The front room spreads lengthwise, and I make my way from one wall to the next, feeling my mother walking with me, remembering the house we had staked out and dreamed of when we had only been in the trailer a year. Was this the home she would have built if anything had ever gone our way?

Water is pooling on the floor in the farthest back room, which stretches the whole width of the building. A rectangular hole is cut through the rise in the roof where a skylight has not yet been installed. The back wall is lined by holes for windows, and I imagine waking up in this room, looking out across the back yard. This is exactly where my room was in the trailer.

It is raining outsi♦e, an♦ I am home alone. The words form in my mind, and I say them aloud. It's a fully formed memory conjuring, a day when I had come home to find soggy Fruit Loops still on the table from a breakfast that somebody else didn't eat. I'd found her at the end of the trailer, drunk and passed out. I never did find out how she had gotten home, because she had not driven her car back to the trailer after she'd been fired. Had somebody given her a ride? Had Mitch picked her up before heading back to his job?

It was the beginning of the end for us. That day. That moment in time when I gave up on her and knew that she was never going to stop drinking. Tears are rolling slowly down my cheeks, and I put my hand out to feel the water falling through the hole in the roof. I miss her.

How can I miss her when I just wanted to be free of her?

I failed her every bit as much as she failed me.

I wish I had asked why she was unhappy.

I draw in a long breath and let it out, pulling myself together.

A wish in one hand, spit in the other.

I sit on the cold floor, the air damp around me, and watch the raindrops falling through the hole in the roof. Remembering my life, feeling the boxes in my head overturning and spilling out with the rain. It's just life. All those moments, they are just life. Everything that I stuffed in those boxes because I couldn't cope was just life. Did I have a hard childhood? Sure. Did everybody? Of course. Growing up is hard. Even Kelci Bancroft had bad days. What would it have been like to have had to live up to the perfection presented by Mrs. Bancroft? Would that have been an easier road?

It's an unlocking in my mind, and suddenly I see everything from a million different angles. Kelci felt inferior, Dylan felt lonely, and they were the two people I had thought had the perfect life. Why did I think that? Because they looked right; they had the nice clothes and the trappings provided by their parents. But those trappings weren't even about Dylan or Kelci. Trey knew that, the way he always reminded me that his parents' achievements were not his own. Charley struggled, I know, but she's now the most resilient and happiest person I know. How does that happen?

It happened because she doesn't live in the past.

A flash of lightning flares, and I step away from the open hole in the roof.

I totally live in the past.

That's why I'm stuck. I'm not living for today. I'm living for stuff that happened seventeen years ago. My mother didn't know what she was doing, but she tried until the alcohol took a true and honest hold. Not every day was hard. Some days we talked and even laughed. How did I let the bad moments overwhelm and define me? Us? Why?

She did the best she could. That's all. She could have done things better, but it's not like she suddenly understood what she should do just because she got pregnant. I certainly didn't. At least I knew I wasn't ready.

But she was married. She had somebody she thought she could count on, but neither of them was ready. Neither of them was a grownup. Tom admitted that. Who is to say that at the end of her life, when she was thirty-two and calling it a day, who is to say that she wasn't still trying to understand the things that had happened to her? She hadn't had an easy road, and it would have been very confusing to love your abuser, the way grandma said she did. At least I know that my abuser was selfish and serving only his needs with the things he did to me. He was sick but not evil. He was broken. It wasn't even about me, and if it hadn't been me, it would have been somebody else.

The release in my mind is like an unflinching, and all the boxes in my head, my neatly organized trauma, holds less power. I forgive my mother for not being perfect. God knows I'm not. I forgive her for being weak and unable to cope with her life, and I set her free of me. I ask her to forgive me, for holding her up to a standard she couldn't achieve. I make amends with her after all these years. We walk the ninth, and I can breathe easier when we have done. All the petty insecurities I've carried on my back begin to drop away. I don't have to own the life my mother lived, only she could do that. But I do have to own the one I have lived.

I don't know how long I sit, listening to my breath entering and exiting my body. The rain begins to slacken, and my mind finally stops churning. I find myself just looking out the back window feeling the strangest sense of peace. The first place I ever remember living was here.

"Hello?" A voice finds me, and I turn back toward the front.

"Hey." I try to find a smile, but it falters. It's probably the owner, and I pull myself up to meet them.

"Who's here?"

Then I recognize his voice, and I find my smile.

"Mitch!" After I've hugged him in the front room, I say, "Well, look at this!" It seems right somehow, to have him here in this space with me. He would probably understand better than anybody the emotions that seeing a house standing here has caused.

"Yeah, what do you think?" he asks, grinning.

I knew that Mitch had been working with Hague Construction for the last several years, and I saw him most often on a roof, replacing asphalt shingles.

"Is this yours?" Of course, it would make sense that Mitch would have bought the land after mom died. He had always liked living out here. A pang pulls at the thought of Theresa living here, but I push it aside. I don't have anything against Theresa anymore, and I'm glad she and Mitch are happy.

"No. I've been working on it, but it's not mine." A smile plays around his lips. "I just brought some plastic to cover that skylight."

"Well, who bought it?"

He cuts his eyes at me then shrugs, that smile still on his lips. "Your mom used to talk about building a house out here."

"I know. I was just thinking about that."

"She loved this piece of land." He hefts the roll of plastic up over his shoulder, and I follow him back to the room with the skylight.

I nod but my throat is constricted, and I can't speak for a second. Mitch walks away, and when he comes back, he is carrying a ladder that must have been in one of the rooms I hadn't yet explored. He stretches it and props it up into the hole, and I hand up the plastic to him.

"How you doing?" he asks.

"I'm all right. Lucky to be here, I guess."

"Ah. We're lucky to have you. Theresa will be glad to know I saw you. She was pretty worried for you when all that went down."

"Tell her I said hi."

He nods, and I ask about his sons.

"They're both playing football."

"Yeah, Dylan says they're fast."

He smiles down at me, proud. "He's a good coach. The boys all have a lot of respect for him. He's tough, but he's fair."

"I'll tell him you said that," I say, remembering how humble Dylan had been when I'd first met him again, how he had only hoped he was good at his job.

When he has finished putting up the plastic and the water has stopped dripping onto the floor, he says, "So these here . . . these are gonna be arched to give the best view of the back. They sent us the wrong windows, or they'd already be up. Should come in on Monday, I reckon."

"That'll be nice."

"Come on. Let me show you around." I follow him through the house. "Would you ever consider living out here again?"

I shrug, not meeting his eyes. "It's got bad water. I hope they know that."

"Naw, the water's fine."

"Not unless they got a new well. Don't you remember how rusty the water was?" I finally catch his eye, surprised that he wouldn't remember how we had to take all the whites to do at the laundry.

"No, they piped it three years ago," he says.

"What's that mean?"

"It's got city water now."

"Oh." It changes everything that it has clean water. I see a vision of myself coming from the living room and down the hall, making eye contact with myself, nodding, walking past. It takes everything within me not to turn to see if I really have gone by.

"It's gonna be nice when it's done," Mitch says without missing a beat, without also seeing that other me. We've come back to the front room. "You gotta see it from the front." He clears his throat. "This here," he says, "is the living room, but down here at this end will be an office or a library." I follow him, and we reach another room, "This is the kitchen." When he says it, I can see the framing for the refrigerator, the stove, an island.

Then he shows me a bathroom, a bedroom, and another bedroom. His enthusiasm carries us forward. When we reach the room in the back, with the open space for the skylight and the empty frames for windows, he turns and splays his arms. Vanna White, turning a vowel, "This is . . ." He looks at me, a small smile playing on his lips, and shrugs. "Well, I'm not sure what this is. Probably the master."

"I like it. It feels peaceful."

"It does, doesn't it?"

We stand for a long second, letting the calm of the back yard fill us, before I say, "Well, I probably need to be getting back to town."

"Yeah, me, too. I'm just gonna push that water out,"

"All right." I give him a hug and tell him how good it was to see him and make my way back across the street to my waiting car.

41

The winter is brutal. By Thanksgiving, we've had three layers of snowfall plowed up alongside the road, and Thanksgiving morning dawns with gray clouds and whistling winds. I moved to the day shift in October, finally ready to be part of the world and not out of it. It was really about Dylan. I needed to be able to see him, to not have to rush off just as he and Daecus were finishing up dinner. I got scheduled for the holiday. I'll get Christmas off, so it's a trade.

Halfway through my shift, ice is spitting from the sky. I worry about even getting home, let alone out to the farm to share a late Thanksgiving with the Winthrops. I send Dylan a text an hour before my shift is set to end, telling him I'm afraid I won't make it.

The ice is coating the sidewalk when I make my way into the lot. The evening staff mentioned that they've closed 130 heading toward Tuscola. There was a six-car pile-up on the other side of Mattoon. I won't be driving out to the farm, and I'm sad that I will miss everybody. The maintenance crew is making another round with the salt and sand as I pick my way across the parking lot. It is already dark.

I'm so intent on my progress that I don't even register the pickup next to my car until the horn honks, and I look up, startled, nearly losing my footing. Dylan waves from inside the cab. I scuttle in beside him, leaving my ice-crusted car in the lot.

I still haven't told him about the baby, although I promise myself every day that I will, as soon as I have the opportunity. Every day slips by filled with other conversation. I'm ready, but the timing hasn't been right. I've been ready since the day I stood with Mitch in the house. Springs are uncoiling inside of me, and what was once forbidden seems suddenly speakable. My weekly conversations with Dr. Barr have been full to bursting once I figured out how to talk. I've told her about the baby but seem unable to broach the subject with Dylan. I've even talked about that with Dr. Barr, how I don't know if it is that I had a baby with someone else or that I let her go that keeps me quiet. My last session was full of my angst over divulging my secret, and in her customary fashion, she never told me what I should do, but nodded when I came to it myself. "I have to tell him." Even that felt like a spring uncoiling.

We are alone; it's the perfect moment to have that conversation. It's the right time because he can have time to process it before we go out to the farm. It's the right time because Daecus is with Mandy. I'll tell him when we get to my apartment, not while we are driving on the treacherous, ice-covered roads.

"You know I love you?" I ask when we have almost reached the square, where we'll stop at my apartment for me to change my clothes before we head out to the farm.

"Yes, I do, and you know I love you?" We've gotten comfortable saying it, hearing it.

"Yes." I laugh.

"I'm glad we got that settled."

"Took us long enough." I reach out and put my hand in his. "I want to show you something when we get to the apartment." It feels like jumping in with both feet.

He cocks his eyebrow, and my resolve flutters, but I nod.

I lead him through the apartment and past the bedroom to my painting room.

"I've meant to talk to you about this for a long time, but I didn't know how to do it, and it just seemed that the time was never right." I bump into him as we walk. "You know me, I can always find an excuse not to talk about stuff, but I feel like I'm lying to you if you don't know all the pieces."

"Okay." I see the shade draw over his eyes, the protective coating.

I push through framed paintings leaning against the wall until I reach *The Baby*. I pull it and flip it, tipping it on the wall. She is fully visible.

"Do you remember when I ran away?" I don't mention Warren, although Dylan clearly remembers that I ran away with another man.

"I do."

"Well, this is Emily Ann. She was born three weeks before I turned eighteen."

"What?" I don't know from the tone of his voice, how he feels.

"I gave her up for adoption because I was alone and didn't think I'd be a good mother." My voice puckers and warps.

"Oh, Al." He steps closer, pulling me into his arms, and my soul begins to repair itself.

The words begin to fall, and soon I have told him everything about how Warren left and then I figured out I was pregnant. I explain how Lola, from the dry-cleaners, helped me arrange for a room at Life House in Kansas City. I tell him how I had let the baby go to a woman I thought would do it better. Through it all, he doesn't say anything. Just sits beside me on the floor and looks from me to the painting.

"I'm sorry," he finally says when I've run out of words. "I'm sorry you had to go through that alone."

"I'm sorry I didn't tell you before. I hope you don't feel like I lied to you."

"No. Not at all." He squeezes my shoulders. "That had to be so hard."

I breathe a sigh; it's not what I expected, although now I can't imagine him responding in any other way.

"She'd be fourteen now."

"She is fourteen," I say, telling him about seeing her at the Springfield Art Festival.

"Did you say anything to her?"

I shake my head, telling him about the adoption database, and how she'll be able to find me when she's older.

"How did you not say something to her?"

"It may not have been her. But I just kept thinking about how her parents would feel if I showed up. I don't even know if she knows she was adopted."

He leans toward me and kisses me. "You are an incredible person, Alison Hayes."

I laugh, not feeling incredible but feeling warm at his touch.

"I think you will be an amazing mother." He kisses my forehead and sits back. "Any other secrets you want to tell me?"

"I tried to kill myself once."

His eyebrows crumple together as he looks down at my hands. He reaches for one and rolls it until my wrist is facing up, running his thumb over the white scar, which unlike the small cuts I had made on my feet, have never faded. "I know . . . not much else those could be." He pulls his lower lip between his teeth and draws my wrist to his mouth. "When was that?"

"When I was in California, not long after I saw you last."

"Was it my fault?"

"No. No. God. No." I pull my hand free and press my palm against his face. "No. It wasn't because of you. I was pretending to be somebody else, and one night my past and my present collided. I couldn't cope."

He looks completely shattered. I wish I could pull the words back.

"Thank God you didn't succeed." His phone rings, and he shuffles it from his pocket. "Hey," he says into the receiver, his voice thick with emotion, his eyes holding mine. "I don't think we're gonna make it out . . . Yeah, the side roads are awful . . . No everything is fine; we just got to Alison's apartment. The roads that way were getting bad when I left. I don't think we should risk it . . . All right . . . Yeah. I'll tell her. Love you, too."

He pockets his phone, and his eye lands on the painting of my mother standing on the back steps, her shirt fluttering in the breeze. He blows a breath through his nose. "That looks familiar."

"Yeah. That was the day you told me about your brother."

He nods. "I know a little something about secrets." His eyes scan the room, taking in the painting of him on Pride leading into the woods, seeing Cici with her black wings erupting. When he looks back at me, his eyes are wet as if he has seen the shape of my life without blinders for the first time.

It's not that life I want him to know. I want him to see the present, where we are today, because we have finally found each other and nothing else matters. I stand and take his hand, leading him to the bedroom. It's the only way I know to bring him back from the past. We make love in my bed, with all our secrets out in the open. I have nothing to hide. I have no more secrets. We have no place to be and no way to get there if we did. We take our time, and every curve of my body knows a bend of his.

When morning comes, I wake with his body curled behind me and his hand cupping my breast. I close my eyes and let myself sleep again.

42

The house is beautiful, a splash of color against a desolate landscape. It has the same coloration as the Winthrop house, white with a green roof. It doesn't offer orange shutters like the farm. It's a different style of home, more modern somehow, with cleaner lines. Dylan is out of the truck and coming to my side before I even have the belt unbuckled. I wrap my scarf around my neck, protecting my bare skin from the freezing air as I climb out of the truck to join him on the street. We've stopped in front of the house on the lot that was my mother's.

I've made a point to drive past it when I come to town. I've seen it as the siding went on, watched as blinds went up behind the windows. I've looked for people who own it but have only seen workers.

I don't understand why Dylan has stopped here in front of the house. Why he has turned off the truck and gotten out to come to my side. He holds my door open with a flourish.

"What's going on?" I ask, but give him my hand and slide down from the cab.

The front door opens, and Daecus and Vaude come through, waving to us.

He grins, leading me up the stairs to the porch. I lean into Daecus for a hug, and he squeezes tighter than usual. "We'll be down the road," he whispers, and he and Vaude leave us on the porch.

"We'll be there in a minute," Dylan says, and I watch him as they get in Vaude's car to drive away.

"What's going on?"

"This is my secret," he whispers, putting his hand on my elbow and opening the door to allow me entry.

Tumult graces a wall in the living room, visible from the door. The bulb above it glows, making the painted horses shimmer. It looks like a gallery-quality piece. On the desk in the library is a picture of the three of us, me and Dylan and Daecus that Jake took one day when we were out at the farm.

"What is this?"

"When your mom died, Mr. Billups bought this land from the county when it went on auction. I bought it from him about five years ago."

"Oh."

His hands are sweating, although it isn't hot. "You told me once about the house you wanted to build out here. Remember, you even had it staked out?"

"Yeah. I remember."

"Well, I don't know how you feel about this, and I don't know if you could see yourself living here . . ." He stammers and pushes his hand up through his hair, making it stand on end.

We've made our way through the house, and I see portrait lights above bare walls throughout.

"What are you saying?" I think I know, but I need him to say it.

We've reached the door to the room that had the hole for the skylight, the place that overlooks the back yard.

He opens the door, and the sunlight is bouncing up off the snow and through the domed windows.

"I didn't buy you a ring. I don't know what you would want, but," he drops to a knee, holding my hands, "I want you to marry me,"

It's the craziest thing, him kneeling before me like something out of some old movie, and I tug him upward, laughing.

"You know I'm a mess."

"Doesn't bother me."

"I'm not a good cook."

"Me neither. We can learn."

His arms wrap around my waist, and my hands rest on his chest, feeling the rhythm of his heart.

"Are you sure?" my voice wavers, and some piece of me is terrified that he will realize this is a mistake and say, *"Oh, no, maybe not."*

"I love you. I've always loved you. Marry me."

"You're insane. What does Daecus think?"

"He's already planning our family-moon."

I laugh. "What does that even mean?"

"I'm afraid he's coming on the honeymoon."

I laugh and wrap around him, my feet off the floor.

"You still haven't answered me." His voice is a whisper in my ear, and it sounds very much like "I love you."

"God. Of course I will. Yes. Yes. Crazy man."

He whoops, and we spin in the room that will someday be my studio.

Epilogue

We have a spring wedding in the back yard of our house. Mr. Billups stands with me, even though we've removed the language about giving the bride away. I'm a grown woman and nobody's to give away. Dan McGill, Mitch, and Tom Hayes sit on the bride's side. If anybody doesn't like Mr. Billups walking me down the aisle, they do not say anything. It was only Dylan's opinion that mattered, and he loved it.

During that worst year, when I was so ready to give it up, Mr. Billups had believed in me more than anybody else ever had, and all the years since then, he has been steadfast with his advice and his support. He is an old man now, having seen his wife and his only daughter laid in their graves in the last ten years. When his wife died, six months after his daughter, I had sat beside him as his family. It feels like a gift, a small thing I can give him, to have him stand with me this day. Charley is my matron of honor, and Daecus is his father's best man. He did finally buy me a ring, a simple gold band that suits me just fine. Our rings are a matched set, just like the two of us.

My entire life, I had felt like I was in a fast-moving stream and only felt grounded when I was alone. It's why I was so scared to date; I was always afraid of getting caught up in the current. What Dylan did was pluck me from the middle of the river and place my feet on solid ground. I have no delusions about what marriage will mean. I know it's not a fairy tale and that we won't always be clicking-our-heels happy. But I've chosen the person I tolerate the best, and I hope he has done the same.

245

It took us long enough to come to it.

Enjoy this Sneak Peek of the
Angie's first psychological thriller.

OFF THE DARK LEDGE

Angie Gallion

PART ONE

SUMMER:
NEARLY THIRTY YEARS AGO

Off the Dark Ledge

1

He's leaving me! I jolt up inside the cage just as his face disappears through the window. No. No. No. He can't leave me. I scramble out, my legs weak and wobbly from the hours or days we've spent in lock-up. She's gonna be so mad!

I scramble to get to the box he has pushed up under the window, banging my shin against the corner. I bite my lip to stay quiet. He's leaving me!

I pull up, and I see him running across the yard. I want to call out, but then she may hear, and we'd both be in trouble. So I don't.

I pull up and push my shoulders out through the open window. I'm falling, and I hit the ground with a thud. All the air whooshes out of me, and I gasp like a fish out of water. When I can breathe again, I get up and start to run across the back yard, tucking tight into myself so I am small, and if Mama or Dr. Curtis look out, they maybe won't see me. Dr. Curtis lives in the house next door, and I'm even more scared that he will see me. He doesn't like me; he only likes Slim. We were in the cage because of something Slim did to Dr. Curtis, but he wouldn't tell me what. He is a long way ahead of me, not looking back. His long legs stretch out in front of him and behind him, and he is barely touching the ground. He is almost to the trees. Then I will lose him. Fear rises, and I stumble but keep running.

I want to call out, but I don't because she might hear me, and then we would be in trouble—because we are outside and we're not supposed to be outside during the day. I pump my legs as fast as I can, trying to find flight the way he does. I have to catch him, but my legs feel weak, and I can't run as fast as he can.

He is passing into the trees, eaten by the shadows. I can't see him anymore, and I don't know what to do. I am scared to go into the woods alone, and how will I know which way he has gone? Should I go back to the trailer and get back into my cage? She's gonna be so mad! Dr. Curtis will kick us out if he knows we've been outside. He's only letting us stay because Mama promised we'd stay out of sight. Dr. Curtis doesn't like children, Mama says. That why she's training Slim to be a man.

I stop just at the edge of the trees, looking into the dark shadows. My feet prance ... Where is he?

I call out in a loud whisper, "Slim!" He used to have another name, but we haven't used it in so long that I don't remember what it was. It's just like everybody calls me Baby, but I think my name is really Shiloh. Slim doesn't answer, and I spin in a circle, glancing back at the trailer, seeing the window high up on the side. There is no way I could get back up and through it. My legs buckle at the thought of going to the front door and interrupting Mama. A man is in the house, and Mama doesn't like it when the men see us—it's one of the rules. Only Dr. Curtis can know we are here. I sprawl on the ground, trying to flatten myself, so I will only look like a pile of dirt if she looks out and sees me.

I sob, but no tears flood past my crusty lashes.

I am going to die.

Hands lift me around my waist, and I ball myself inward, expecting the smack that I know is coming. She has seen.

It's Slim. He hasn't left me; he has come back for me. I spring up and wrap my legs around his waist, like a monkey. I bury my face in his neck.

We are out of the yard and into the shadows of the trees. I know because all the warmth is gone. He carries me, stepping through bushes. The brambles scrape against my bare legs and make them bleed.

He stops when we are well into the shadow. "You have to walk." He pushes against my hips, and I release my hold on him and slide down the length of his body, careful not to touch the long painful-looking welt going down his arm, until I am on my own feet. "You shouldn't have come. You're gonna slow me down, and then we'll get caught."

He turns and walks away from me, and I don't say anything, just run to keep up with him. I don't want him to leave me behind here; then the wolves would eat me. Mama says there are bears out here, too . . . and tigers. Panic rises, and I glance at the trees around me, looking for glowing eyes. I scrape my bare foot against a rock and hop on the other one, unwilling to stop. I run. Keeping my eyes on his back, I climb over a fallen tree that he only had to step over.

We finally stop, when Slim thinks we have gone far enough that they won't find us. He drops to his knees and cups his hand in the stream, drinking the water in great gulps.

I do the same, squatting beside him. It is only then that I know how thirsty I am, how empty my stomach is. I drink, and when I feel my stomach stretching against the water, I splash some on my face, washing away the crust from my lashes.

"Where are we going?"

"I don't know," he says, finally looking at me squatting beside him. "I wish you hadn't come."

I shrug my shoulders and look away from him. I am used to never doing the right thing.

Dirt and blood crust my feet. An angry red scratch weeps a thin stream.

We are on the move again, and I have to keep up or he will leave me behind. He is angry, and I'm scared, because sometimes when he is angry, he hits me. Sometimes he does other stuff, even if he says it's training.

But I won't go back. She will be so lonely without us. Guilt climbs from my ankles to my chest, and my heart squeezes. I make some sound, and his head ratchets around, scanning the woods, but then he jerks forward again, saying something under his breath. He is very angry.

I run behind him keeping my mouth quiet, because, otherwise, he'll stop and push me down and run on without me, and then the wolves or bears or tigers will eat me. We run, and we run.

My stomach is churning, angry as the water sloshes. It rumbles, and when I can't run anymore, I stop, putting my hands on my knees, bending over, trying to catch my breath. All the water I drank at the stream comes rushing from my mouth, splattering on the leaves and dirt, making a slurry of mud.

A chill runs through my body, and my legs feel heavy. I'm afraid I won't be able to lift them again. It's cold, but only because we're not inside anymore and I don't have my blanket. I forgot my blanket. What am I gonna do without my blanket?

When I look up, I can't see him; he is gone.

"Come on!" I hear him hissing ahead of me. "I'll kill you if you get me caught," he says, mumbling under his breath, and I stumble forward, my arms outstretched in the dark.

I finally find him in a ditch between the woods and the empty road. "We made it," I whisper.

My brother nods, and I can tell he is trying to figure out what we should do next.

Lights flare in the distance, and we watch as a lone car travels toward us and then past. I'm happy to be squatting beside him, not to be moving. I am so tired from the run through the woods.

We wait, our breath slowing, becoming lighter and less strained.

Another car comes from the other direction, and we watch it pass.

"What are we going to do?" I whisper.

"We're going to catch one of those cars and make them take us away."

I nod.

Minutes pass before we see another car, and when it gets close enough, Slim stands up from the ditch and starts waving his arms.

My heart jolts in my chest as the car slows.

"No!" I call because the light is bright in his eyes. He cannot see the car.

He glances back to me. The car comes to a stop and the passenger-side door opens.

"I reckon you got your sister hidden back there somewhere?"

Slim's shoulders slump and he turns to run. Dr. Curtis is out of the car and takes three long steps toward my brother, catching him by the length of his hair, drawing him back and to his knees. Slim is crying.

"Baby," she calls from inside the car. "Come on, Baby. It is time to go home." She is so pretty, sitting in the glow of the car. The car looks so safe and quiet.

I stand up from where I am crouched in the ditch, pulled by an invisible thread.

About the Author

Angie Gallion grew up in East Central Illinois and now resides with her husband and their children outside of Atlanta, Georgia. Angie's writings often deal with personal growth through tragedy or trauma. She enjoys exploring complex relationships, often set against the backdrop of addiction or mental illness. Her debut novel, Intoxic, received the Bronze Medal from Readers' Favorite in the General Fiction category. Intoxic was well received by audiences, and reader response inspired Gallion to continue the Alison Hayes Journey, a coming-of-age series, which now include four novels: Intoxic: Alison Unseen, Purgus: Alison Lost, Icara: Alison Falling, and Emergent: Alison Rising.

Angie's first psychological thriller, Off the Dark Ledge, is about Stacy Linde, a wife and mother who discovers dark secrets about her origin story and must reconcile her past or risk losing everything. Two new projects are expected in 2021 and 2022.

Follow Angie at www.angiegallion.com and connect with her on social media.

Books by Angie Gallion

Intoxic: Alison Unseen, Book 1
Purgus: Alison Lost, Book 2
Icara: Alison Falling, Book 3
Emergent: Alison Rising, Book 4
Off the Dark Ledge, a Psychological Thriller